"Look, I'm sorry if you were worried, but there was no reason...."

Jones slapped the door beside her head. "There was every reason," he disputed, shoving his face close to hers. "Do you have any idea what can happen to a woman on her own in a place like this?"

His second hand joined the first against the door on the other side of her head, effectively caging her. And she couldn't be sure whether the wild pumping of her pulse was due more to his words or to his nearness.

"You're right, of course. But believe it or not, I do take precautions. I don't take chances, and I am not without self-defense training."

"Prove it." The note of mockery in his voice was at odds with the dangerous light still burning in his eyes. "You've got a man cornering you, wanting more than you care to give. Stop me."

Dear Reader,

A new year has begun, so why not celebrate with six exciting new titles from Silhouette Intimate Moments? *What a Man's Gotta Do* is the newest from Karen Templeton, reuniting the one-time good girl, now a single mom, with the former bad boy who always made her heart pound, even though he never once sent a smile her way. Until now.

Kylie Brant introduces THE TREMAINE TRADITION with *Alias Smith and Jones,* an exciting novel about two people hiding everything about themselves—except the way they feel about each other. There's still TROUBLE IN EDEN in Virginia Kantra's *All a Man Can Ask,* in which an undercover assignment leads (predictably) to danger and (*un*predictably) to love. By now you know that the WINGMEN WARRIORS flash means you're about to experience top-notch military romance, courtesy of Catherine Mann. *Under Siege,* a marriage-of-inconvenience tale, won't disappoint. Who wouldn't like *A Kiss in the Dark* from a handsome hero? So run—don't walk—to pick up the book of the same name by rising star Jenna Mills. Finally, enjoy the winter chill—and the cozy cuddling that drives it away—in *Northern Exposure,* by Debra Lee Brown, who sends her heroine to Alaska to find love.

And, of course, we'll be back next month with six more of the best and most exciting romances around, so be sure not to miss a single one.

Enjoy!

Leslie J. Wainger
Executive Senior Editor

Please address questions and book requests to:
Silhouette Reader Service
U.S.: 3010 Walden Ave., P.O. Box 1325, Buffalo, NY 14269
Canadian: P.O. Box 609, Fort Erie, Ont. L2A 5X3

Alias Smith
and Jones
KYLIE BRANT

Silhouette®

INTIMATE MOMENTS™

Published by Silhouette Books

America's Publisher of Contemporary Romance

SILHOUETTE BOOKS

ISBN 0-373-27266-9

ALIAS SMITH AND JONES

Visit Silhouette at www.eHarlequin.com

Printed in U.S.A.

Books by Kylie Brant

Silhouette Intimate Moments

McLain's Law #528
Rancher's Choice #552
An Irresistible Man #622
Guarding Raine #693
Bringing Benjy Home #735
Friday's Child #862
*Undercover Lover #882
*Heartbreak Ranch #910
**Falling Hard and Fast* #959
Undercover Bride #1022
†*Hard To Handle* #1108
Born in Secret #1112
†*Hard To Resist* #1119
†*Hard To Tame* #1125
***Alias Smith and Jones* #1196

*The Sullivan Brothers
†Charmed and Dangerous
**The Tremaine Tradition

KYLIE BRANT

lives with her husband and five children in Iowa. She works full-time as a teacher of learning disabled students. Much of her free time is spent in her role as professional spectator at her kids' sporting events.

An avid reader, Kylie enjoys stories of love, mystery and suspense—and she insists on happy endings! When her youngest children, a set of twins, turned four, she decided to try her hand at writing. Now most weekends and all summer she can be found at the computer, spinning her own tales of romance and happily-ever-afters.

Kylie invites readers to write to her at P.O. Box 231, Charles City, IA 50616. Or you can visit her Web site at www.kyliebrant.com.

For Aunt Bonnie and Uncle Wilbur, with love

Chapter 1

Analiese Tremaine didn't go around seducing men. If asked, the available men in Tangipohoa Parish could attest that even thinking of Analiese in a sexual way would be tantamount to signing a death warrant. Her three older brothers were as protective of her as a pack of wild dogs, and since the Tremaines owned just about everything round those parts, a fella could be dead and buried and no one would dare question the disappearance. The talk hadn't hurt Analiese's brothers' reputations a whit, but neither had it done anything interesting for her social life.

She'd never had more reason to regret her dearth of experience. The man she'd traveled a thousand miles to hire was scowling down at her. His face, which might have been handsome without the day's growth of beard, was a mask of impatience. At a time like this a woman could use a bit more exposure to the art of flirtation and seduction. As it was, she could only chalk up one more grievance against her brothers and hope that the smile she aimed at the man looked more confident than desperate.

"Listen, Mr.—"

"Jones. No 'mister.' Just Jones."

The fact that he gave no first name made her pause. There'd been no mention of one in her brother's files, either. Just Jones, and a private number she'd traced, with no little difficulty, to this island. To this half-naked man.

He either hadn't bothered with a shirt that day or had dispensed with it as the temperature soared. His brown hair was clubbed back into a short ponytail, and the sun had streaked it tawny. His lashes, absurdly long for a man, were tipped with the same color. But there was nothing warm about his expression. Most people would have quailed beneath the menacing look in his narrowed gray gaze, but Analiese considered herself something of an expert in dealing with short-tempered males.

"I'll double your normal fee."

"I said no, lady. I meant it."

He turned and began striding down the dock. Hurrying after him, she divided her attention between her words and her footing. Huge cords of rope lay in jumbles on the dock, a treacherous obstacle course for the unwary. "Do you really think that's wise? You're turning down quite a bit of money. A man who makes his living as you do can't afford to be picky, can he?"

Her remark brought him around, but because her gaze was on her feet, she rammed into him with enough force to jolt her teeth together. Two hard hands clamped around her forearms and set her away, but not before she'd felt for herself the steely muscles beneath that burnished skin. Smelled the mingled scents of sun, sea, sweat. Scents that shouldn't have been so appealing.

"What the hell's that supposed to mean?"

Analiese preferred to blame her breathlessness on the force of the recent impact rather than her proximity to his rock hard body. "I'm...um..." Since the sight of his tanned muscled torso seemed to have stricken her dumb, she averted her gaze from the distraction in question and gathered her scattered thoughts. "I meant your occupation, of course. It's dependent on tourists and weather, isn't it?"

When she chanced another look at him, his expression had eased infinitesimally, but was no more welcoming. "Listen, lady..."

"Smith." Raising her Ray Bans with one hand, Analiese offered him the other, along with the phony name on her passport. "Ann Smith."

He ignored both her hand and the introduction. "Like I said, I've got a three-day fishing party to take out at dawn tomorrow. Try one of the other charter services I told you about. I'm booked."

"Are they as good as you are?"

"No one's as good as I am." His well-formed mouth didn't even quiver with a hint of humor. It was a simple statement of fact from a man who lacked an ounce of humility. "But I'm not available." He turned around again, clearly believing the matter closed.

She trotted after him. "Your party could be sent to one of the other services. They wouldn't have to be inconvenienced at all."

"They won't be. Because they've already got me."

"I'll give you two and a half times your regular fee." Desperation sounded in Ana's voice, and she made a conscious effort to smooth it. It wouldn't do to let this man suspect how badly she needed him. Or why.

"Nope." Nimbly he leaped from the dock to the deck of the gleaming white ship with *Nefarious* emblazoned on its bow.

She took a moment to wonder if the ship had been named when he'd bought it or if he'd christened it himself. And if he had, what the name symbolized. But frustration edged out curiosity. "Would you mind telling me why?"

He sent a glance her way, then bent forward to more tightly secure the ship's mooring. "No, I don't mind." His sudden verbosity should have warned her. He'd been maddeningly reticent up to now. "Number one—I gave the other party my word. That might not mean much to folks like you, but it does to me. And two..." He looked at her then, really looked at her. An insolently thorough once-over that left her flesh tingling as though he'd stroked her skin with one callused palm. "...you look like trouble. I don't like trouble."

There was a definite glimmer of satisfaction in his pale gray eyes as he took in her gaping jaw, before he turned his back on her.

When she found her tongue again, she managed, "Trouble? What kind of trouble could I possibly cause?"

"You're a woman, aren't you?"

Her answer, if she'd been able to form one, would have fallen on deaf ears. He'd gone below deck and left her, jaw hanging open and temper on the rise, to bake in the tropical sunshine.

Well, damn. Crossing her arms over her less-than-ample chest, Analiese snapped her mouth shut and fumed. Of all the possible scenarios she'd imagined, somehow this one had failed to occur. Belatedly aware of the interested stares from people on ships docked nearby, she turned, raised her chin and stalked away. The man was being a bit more recalcitrant than she'd anticipated, so she'd have to go back to the motel. Regroup. Form a new strategy. She had until dawn tomorrow to do so.

Because none of the other charter services would do, of course. It had to be Jones. Just Jones.

A cool shower and a complimentary rum punch in the hotel bar did wonders for Ana's optimism, and she got down to the Machiavellian task of changing Jones's mind. Staring blindly at the useless paper parasol adorning her drink, she gave the matter careful consideration. Thwarting bullheaded men was an area in which she *did* have a great deal of experience—again, thanks to her three older brothers, who, without frequent reminders, were apt to treat her as though she were a rather dim house pet. But Jones had already proved immune to her famed perseverance. Which meant that the situation called for a bit more creativity.

Idly she watched the area fill up with people, as many locals as tourists. The tiny South Pacific island country of Bontilla was, according to the travel agent, a little-known gem of a tropical paradise with a budding tourism trade. This hotel was the only decent one on the island. Staring through the open-air walls toward the shattering blue of the ocean beyond, Ana couldn't help but think it would be a shame to see its beauty marred in a few years with hordes of stressed-out stockbrokers and their discontented wives.

A loud burst of laughter interrupted her thoughts, and she looked up at the group of half a dozen men sitting nearby. No one would mistake them for locals. Each sported painfully sunburned faces and loose shirts with loud prints. Their conversation centered on their drinking prowess and fishing. Wrinkling her nose, Ana turned away.

She brought the glass to her lips and considered moving to another table as another loud bout of laughter assailed her.

"Wanna lay a little bet on that, Stevo?"

She barely noted the words. There was a small table for

two open near the railing, so she started to rise, intent on changing places.

"We'll see who's the master fisherman tomorrow when we board *Nefarious*. You'll be begging me to share my secrets then."

Ana stopped and turned back to eye the men speculatively. One of them noted her interest and nudged the one nearest him, and their words tapered off as each turned to look at her. She had only a split second to plan before she smiled brilliantly, moved toward them. "You fellas aren't planning on going out with Jones tomorrow, are you?" At their agreement, she reached for a chair and pulled it up to their table. "Mind if I join you for a few moments?"

With six beers under his belt and a hot, willing woman on his lap, Jones's mood was still on the surly side. Losing a three-grand charter fee was enough to sour the most affable of temperaments, something he couldn't claim at the best of times. Business, which had already been slow, had recently gotten slower. Steve Fisher, the spokesman of the group, had been vague about the details, but the message had been clear enough. They'd canceled the fishing trip they'd booked with him.

Lexie, the bar's full-time waitress and his part-time bed partner, whispered a suggestive remark in his ear. Ordinarily it would have earned her a laugh and a lusty hug, but only garnered a half smile. The beer had done little to soothe his resentment. Some checking had shown that Fisher and the others had chosen to forfeit their deposit in order to go with Ranachek, another service on the island. And although he knew there was little that Emil Ranachek wouldn't do for a fee, Jones still couldn't figure out what he could have promised the men to convince them to make the switch.

Lexie leaned over him, providing him a view of her impressive bosom. "Maybe I can help chase that mood of yours away," she whispered suggestively. Her fingers stroked over the jaw he hadn't bothered to shave that day. "I get off in an hour. And I can get *you* off about fifteen minutes after that."

"In an hour I plan to be drunk."

Her laugh was low and sultry. "Lover, that's never stopped us before."

As if he needed a reminder, she planted a long wet kiss on him, one that caused definite signs of interest to stir in his groin, despite his mood. Since it seemed a shame not to show his appreciation, he cupped her breast and nipped at her neck. "See you in an hour."

With visible reluctance Lexie got up, smoothed her short skirt and gave a toss of her long, dark hair. With one last, smoldering look, she swayed back in the direction of the bar, leaving Jones to his beer, his temper and what must certainly be an alcohol-induced hallucination.

He lowered the bottle, squinted across the smoke-hazed space. If he hadn't been the wrong side of sober he'd have sworn the woman sitting near the entrance was the same one who'd spent the better part of an hour today pestering him about a charter. Which was ridiculous, of course. Because there was no way a lady like that belonged in a place like this.

The tavern he occupied didn't even have a name. It was little more than an open-air shanty with a couple of beer signs flickering on the walls. It damn sure wasn't frequented by tourists, which was one of the reasons he preferred it. After hours or days onboard with paying customers, he liked to spend his free time as far away from their type as possible.

He watched the woman toy with the straw in her drink,

while she looked around interestedly. Damned if it *wasn't*
the woman from this afternoon. What had her name been?
Something ordinary. Johnson. Smith. Yeah, that was it. He
ran his thumbnail under the label of his bottle, his attention
riveted on the female several yards away. Ann Smith, with
the wispy blond hair that was shorter than his own by several inches, and the big innocent blue eyes.

His mouth curled derisively. It had been a long time
since he'd believed in innocence, especially when it came
to women. So it must be sheer stupidity that had led her
here, far enough off the beaten path to spell risk for a single
woman on her own.

Ignoring the smile she aimed in his direction, he lifted
the bottle to his lips. Whatever her reasons, it was none of
his business. He wasn't the type to play white knight, and
any chivalrous instincts he'd ever possessed had been
ground out of him years ago.

But the woman couldn't have looked more out of place
in the seedy tavern if she'd worn feathers and a top hat.
Her white dress had straps instead of sleeves with a row of
black buttons marching down its front. Giving a quick look
around at his neighbors, Jones was certain that he wasn't
the only one wondering what he'd find beneath if he un-
fastened them one by one. Which is why, when she left her
table and came to stand before his, he kept his attention
trained on the bottle in his hand.

"I just wanted to tell you that my offer still stands, if
you should change your mind."

Her words abruptly yanked him back to the reason for
his presence here tonight, and the memory still had a bite.
Deliberately he let out a long, satisfying belch and
scratched his jaw. "And what offer might that be?"

Her expression left no doubt about her reaction to his
behavior. That dainty little nose of hers wrinkled up, and

she looked at him as if he'd just crawled out from beneath a rock. "The charter."

He blinked for a moment, a thought forming, too nebulous to register immediately. And then it bloomed, fertilized by distrust. "It was you, wasn't it?" That innocent look on her face only cemented his suspicion. "You screwed up tomorrow's charter for me."

Her chin angled, and she met him glare for glare. "I don't know what you're talking about."

Alcohol hadn't totally fogged his senses. He was on to something, and he knew it. Straightening in his chair, an act that seemed to require more agility than usual, he fixed her with a jaundiced eye. "My fishing party canceled tonight. Went with someone else. And then you just happened to show up here, after being quite persistent earlier today, and offer again to hire me. Kind of a coincidence, wouldn't you say? I've never cared much for coincidences."

"Well, let me just make a note of that." With a dramatic flourish she pulled a small black leather notebook from her purse, dug for a pen and opened the pad to a blank page. "Not only does Mr. Jones not…like…trouble—" she spoke the words as she jotted them down "—he doesn't…care… for coincidences." When she caught the tip of her tongue between her perfectly even teeth, she gave the impression of a woman diligently documenting research for future use.

She also gave a damn good impression of a smart-ass. He scowled. "I told you before…"

Without glancing up, she completed his sentence for him. "Not 'mister.' Just Jones. Gotcha. And while I'm at it, I'm just gonna make a note of that, too."

Because it seemed more judicious than strangling her, he lifted his beer to his lips and drained it.

With an audible click, she replaced the cap on her pen and gave him a careless smile. "I can't guess why your group canceled—" she gave his empty bottle a meaningful glance "—but since you still aren't interested I'll ask around tomorrow for another service."

He let her get about four feet away before financial reality took precedence over gut instinct. "I didn't say I wasn't interested."

She looked over her shoulder, and he definitely didn't trust that glint in her eye. "You've changed your mind?"

Not really. Not at all. He wasn't convinced she'd had nothing to do with him losing that fishing group, but try as he might, he couldn't figure a reason for her scuttling his schedule. Maybe the alcohol was fogging his normal common sense, but what was clear in his mind was the looming payment due on his ship. "Exactly what is it that you have planned? I can't see you as the deep-sea fishing type."

"Actually, I was just looking for a relaxing way to spend a few days traveling around the local islands, soaking up some sun. I've been under a lot of stress lately, and I thought a little island hopping might be a great way to unwind."

He rolled his eyes, uncaring that she would see the gesture. Yeah, she looked like she knew a lot about stress, all right. The kind that came from not finding the right shade of fingernail polish or maybe not getting a date with the captain of the football team. He'd bet a dollar she'd been a cheerleader. There was just something so damn...perky about her.

The last inner warning voice was silenced. The woman was probably just a flit-headed college girl with easy access to her daddy's money. And with the notable exception of her very excellent ass, she was exactly like dozens of other women who found their way down here looking for a cure to their boredom.

His decision made, he said, "There are tons of islands around here, most too small to be inhabited, but if you're looking for little-known beaches, I can show you a few really great ones that haven't been discovered yet."

"That sounds like exactly what I have in mind." She shot him a dazzling smile. "I'm supposed to meet a couple friends the day after tomorrow on Laconos. We can go there first."

"Laconos?" He looked toward the bar, noticed the dark look Lexie was regarding him with. As long as he had the woman's attention, he lifted his empty bottle toward her in a silent request for another, before shifting his attention back to his potential client. "I'm not sure that's such a great idea. The government hasn't been exactly stable there."

She waved away his concern. "That trouble six months ago? They've got a new government in place now, don't they? As a matter of fact, I heard it's jockeying for position in the Global Trade Organization. Sounds pretty stable to me."

Her knowledge of the island's recent history surprised him. Maybe she wasn't as empty-headed as he'd thought. With a mental shrug, he dropped the argument. The ports were open at Laconos, and their beaches were remarkable enough to impress Ms. Smith. No doubt, once she'd roamed them for a day or so her attention would shift elsewhere. "Just how long a trip did you have in mind?"

Her voice was vague. "Oh, I don't know. Four or five days. Can we leave it open-ended?"

Open-ended. Sweet Jesus. Jones picked up the beer that Lexie slammed down in front of him, ran a discreet hand along her bare thigh and squeezed lightly. The waitress's expression lightened a bit, fortunately. Despite their casual relationship, she had a jealous streak that required careful handling.

Wrapping her arms around his neck from behind him, she leaned so her breasts pressed against his nape and murmured in his ear, "Thirty minutes, lover." Then she swayed back to the bar.

At the fascinated expression on Ms. Smith's face, Jones felt an unfamiliar thread of embarrassment. Lexie wasn't exactly the subtle type. He cleared his throat. "So. About the length of the trip… I'm gonna need a firm commitment on the minimum number of days, paid in advance. Then if you decide to extend it, the rest can be payable upon return."

"Fair enough. I'll have to wait until tomorrow morning to have the money wired. I assume you have an account here on the island?"

There was the barest gap discernible between the top two buttons on her dress, giving him a glimpse of a lacy pink bra, sheer enough to reveal the creamy skin it encased. With effort he pulled his gaze away from the sight and focused on her face. "You don't have to wire the money. I'll take a personal check, verified by a phone call to your bank."

"I prefer to have it wired. I didn't bring a checkbook, in case my purse got snatched."

He shrugged. As long as the money reached his account, he wasn't particularly fussy about how it got there. "Now, about payment…"

"I read it on the sign posted by your ship. A thousand dollars a day, right? Let's say a minimum of four days with a possibility of longer."

Reaching for the fresh beer, he tipped the bottle to his lips. When he placed it back on the table, he said, "I seem to recall you offering me two and a half times my normal fee."

Although he'd thought to rattle her, she only gave him a cool look. "That was this afternoon, when you had another charter scheduled. And you turned me down, remember? There's no competition now, so why would I pay more?"

"Oh, I get it." He snorted. "You're one of *those* kind of women."

She tilted her chin upwards. "What kind of woman is that?"

"The kind that make promises they have no intention of delivering on."

"I deliver on my promises!"

When he only looked at her, she flushed but went on. "And besides, it wasn't a promise, it was a business offer. You can blame your own bad judgment for not taking me up on it when I laid it on the table."

"Yeah, right."

She was getting mad now, and temper turned her sky-blue eyes stormy. He wondered why he was deliberately provoking her. He should count himself fortunate that he had a replacement for the charter that had canceled. But something about the woman got under his skin, and he remained unconvinced that she hadn't had something to do with the cancellation. "Don't worry about it. Sure, you were in a yank to hire me this afternoon when I was booked, but now I'm free. You're not the first person to take advantage of a situation like this."

"I'm not taking advantage." When he only raised his brows and reached for his bottle again, she ground her teeth together. "Surely you can see that the situation this evening is completely different from the one this afternoon."

"Two and a half times different."

"I honestly don't know what the big deal is. You lost a

charter, I'm offering one to replace it. Mine will be worth more money anyway because it's going to be longer.''

"Yeah, you're right. That's fair. It's not your fault the other group pulled out, is it?" He folded his arms on the table and leaned toward her. "You can't help the fact that the fishing group decided at the last minute to book with someone else. And there's really no reason why that should concern you. But me, I'm still kinda wondering. So while we're waiting for the wire transfer to go through tomorrow, I think I'll mosey over to Ranachek's and see if one of the group wants to be a little more forthcoming.''

Either she was a world-class actress or she really hadn't had anything to do with the canceled charter. There was only a flicker in her eye—there and gone so quickly he couldn't be sure he'd seen it at all. "Suit yourself. But I think your time would be better spent getting your ship ready for the charter you *do* have. And since it seems to mean so much to you, I'll agree to one and a half times your normal fee, for the first three days only. That's how long the other charter would have lasted. I have to warn you, though. I'm going to expect exemplary service, and if you fall short in any way at all, I'll be deducting a suitable amount from what's owed you at the end.''

"Honey, my service is always exemplary." Satisfied, he reached over and caught her hand in one of his, unmindful when her eyes widened and she would have pulled away. Solemnly he shook it, cementing their bargain, certain that she knew more than she was saying about the canceled fishing outing, or she'd never have offered him more money.

And he was equally sure that despite the inflated fee she'd agreed to pay him, he was still the one who'd gotten hosed on the deal.

* * *

Analiese paced her motel room, the specially made phone to her ear. It looked like a normal cell phone, except that a regular one would have been useless on an island without even one transmitter tower. This unit relied on waves from a government satellite to transmit signals to a totally secure line in a location that was kept secret even from her.

"C'mon, c'mon, pick up," she muttered with each stride she took, and then stopped, relieved when the familiar fussy voice answered. "Sterling? Did I wake you?"

There was silence, then a long-suffering sigh. "Analiese. I trust this is urgent." It didn't escape her attention that he hadn't answered her question, nor was she surprised. He was too well trained to give away even that much about his whereabouts.

All she knew of the man was the sound of his voice, which had helped paint the mental picture she had of him. From his proper British accent she had an image of a slender man in his midfifties with impeccable tailoring and a David Niven mustache. The reality was likely to be just the opposite. For all she knew, the accent was affected only for his phone conversations as a way to maintain his cover. "Have you had any word from Sam yet?"

His hesitation was its own answer, and desolation swirled in the pit of her stomach. "As I said before, I'll contact you when—"

"You still don't know where he is," she said flatly. Her nerves churned and clashed like grating gears. And despite Sterling's effort at an impassive tone, she knew he was as worried about her brother as she was. Or else he would never have called her at home several days ago to inquire, oh so discreetly, about the last time she'd spoken to him.

"I know the waiting is difficult, but I have no doubt that Sam will work himself free of any sticky situation he might have encountered." *If he's able.* Although the words remained unspoken, they eddied between them. "The best thing you can do is remain at home and wait for—"

"I'm on Bontilla right now."

His sharply inhaled breath was evidence of more emotion than she'd ever heard from him. "Analiese, listen to me carefully. I want you to go home immediately."

"I was able to hack into Sam's computer files and trace him this far," she said recklessly, stopping before the window to stare out at the waves with a sightless gaze. She didn't bother to tell him that she'd been chipping away at her brother's computer security for over two years now. While a great deal of it remained maddeningly encrypted, she'd pieced together enough to have a good suspicion that his cover as an international lawyer hid a career much more dangerous, much more covert. And that Sterling knew every detail about it. "I've set up a charter to go to Laconos tomorrow." She thought, but couldn't be sure, she heard a low groan coming from the other end of the connection.

"I don't think that would be prudent."

She whirled from the window, concern suddenly turning to anger. "I don't give a damn about *prudent,* Sterling. My brother has been missing two weeks, and you don't have the faintest idea where he is. Now, unless you're about to tell me that you've got a search-and-rescue plan lined up, you'd better get used to the fact that I'm going in."

"And just what is it you think you can accomplish there?" Sterling's voice was harder than she'd ever heard it. "Sam has years of experience handling difficult matters while you...you've done only occasional courier work, which, I might add, would be totally against your brother's wishes if he were to find out."

"I'll let you worry about that, since you're the one who enlisted my services on those occasions."

"A fact I've often regretted."

If she weren't so anxious about Sam she would have been offended. As it was she pressed her hand to her stomach in an effort to calm the nerves there. "You aren't sending anyone in after him, are you?"

"I had some inquiries out a few days ago," he admitted. "I learned nothing."

She winced at the news, but if anything it made her more determined. "Then it's not going to hurt for me to poke around a bit."

Silence stretched, so long that she began to wonder if they'd been disconnected. When Sterling spoke again, there was a note of resignation in his voice. "It has to be done discreetly, or you could jeopardize his position if he's still on the island."

Analiese clutched the phone more tightly, aware that she'd just received as clear a go-ahead as she was going to get. "I can do discreet."

Had she been talking to anyone else she would have sworn she heard a snort in the man's voice. As it was, she attributed the sound to a cough. "Quite so. Listen carefully, then. You are not to swerve one iota from my directions...."

It was more than twenty minutes later before she pressed the button to end the conversation. Twenty minutes of directives, dire warnings and commands. She was on a fact-finding mission only, Sterling had repeated again and again. And the scope of her investigation centered solely on the whereabouts of her brother.

When the man wasn't issuing orders, he was filling her in on a bit of history that might or might not affect her brother's case. She'd listened because she thought it wiser not to mention what she'd discerned from Sam's files. She had a pretty good idea of what her brother's mission had been and, despite Sterling's silence on the subject, an even better idea of the reason behind it.

She tucked the phone back into her purse and noted, a bit distantly, the unsteadiness of her hand. Among the details she'd failed to share with Sterling was the fact that Jones's name had figured in her brother's files for the past several years. And that she had reason to believe that Sam had used the man's charter service to cross to Laconos. It was clear from his notes that the two had some sort of relationship, and she was concluding that her brother trusted Jones on some level.

What she didn't know was the exact nature of their relationship. Or just how far *she* could trust Jones.

Chapter 2

Analiese went to the island's largest bank the next morning and arranged to transfer money from her newly established account in the States—the one in Ann Smith's name. As she completed the transaction she regretted more than once her agreement to a higher fee. Jones had been taking advantage of the situation, but she was no pushover. No, it had been her own guilty conscience that had led her to pay the inflated price.

It really hadn't taken that much effort to convince the men in the fishing charter that Jones's drinking habits made him an unreliable captain, and that they'd be better off with another service. And once she'd seen Jones at the tavern last night, there had seemed to be more truth in the story than she could have imagined.

The dock was within walking distance of the bank, so she strolled toward it, enjoying the sight of the brilliant white ships rocking gently in the water. She'd arranged to have the hotel send her bags over, so she took her time, loitering at the market and dickering with a local merchant over a necklace made of tiny shells. Minutes later, the necklace around her neck, she headed toward the docks at a brisker pace. She didn't want to be late and give Jones something to snipe at her about. She had a feeling he'd already been regretting their venture before she'd left the bar last night.

Or maybe, she thought with a slight sneer as she headed in the direction of the *Nefarious,* he'd regretted only the necessity that had kept them talking long enough to have his skimpily clad girlfriend throwing glares his way every few minutes. The woman hadn't looked like the type to suffer competition gladly, although she certainly hadn't had any in Analiese. When she was interested in a man, she tended to pick ones who shaved on a regular basis and didn't drink themselves stupid on their time off. Of course, that interest, if returned initially, usually died a sudden violent death as soon as the male in question found out who she was. Or rather who her brothers were.

Thoughts of her brothers brought a stab of guilt. She couldn't blame them for their cautious attitude toward her safety. It had been forged by events two decades earlier. But understanding that didn't change her feelings. As much as she loved them, she often felt like she was slowly suffocating under their heavy-handed interference. Her work for Sterling had been the first breath of freedom she'd ever known. It seemed oddly ironic that those experiences just might end up affording her the best chance of finding Sam.

Her bags were in a neat pile on the dock next to the *Nefarious* but Jones was nowhere in sight. His ship differed from some of the others anchored nearby, appearing to be as much pleasure craft as it was fishing boat. Ana looked up and down the docks and considered the risk of going aboard while he seemed to be absent. At some point she wanted to thoroughly check the ship for any evidence that Sam had been there. Although it was a remote possibility that he would have been careless enough to leave signs of his presence behind, she had to start somewhere. All she had was her brother's planned itinerary, which had included the charter to Laconos with Jones, and Sterling's certainty that Sam had docked at the neighboring island before his disappearance.

Analiese sent one more glance around, still seeing no sign of Jones. Tucking away a thread of trepidation, she went to the ladder on the side of the ship and climbed up, balanced precariously at the top. Turning carefully, she began to descend the other side.

"It's customary to wait for an invitation before boarding someone's ship."

The sound of that sleep-roughened voice startled her. She twisted around in the direction it had come from, and her foot slipped. Arms windmilling wildly, Ana toppled from the step and had a moment's view of the ship's deck rushing up to meet her before two hard arms broke her fall. Her breath rushed out of her anyway, as she found herself staring into Jones's enigmatic gray gaze.

He was very close. Near enough for her to note, with a degree of fascination, that his gray eyes were the color of smoke today, without the flinty hardness that had been apparent yesterday afternoon. Close enough to observe the freshly shaven jaw, with just the smallest nick below his chin. And definitely near enough to appreciate the effortless ease with which he held her against his bare chest.

"I was just…"

"Making a hell of an entrance." He set her on her feet on the deck and took a step away. "I noticed that. Very graceful."

Really, the man lacked even basic rudiments of civility.

Giving a small sniff, she straightened her sleeveless striped top and made a point of brushing off her white shorts, wishing she could brush away the memory of his touch as easily. "I didn't expect to see you about this early."

He moved past her, climbed the ladder to the dock beside them. "Don't know why not. We discussed the time we'd leave last night."

With an interesting display of muscle rippling across his bare back, he hefted her bags and heaved them carelessly over the side of the ship. But it wasn't the ease with which he'd lifted the bags that held her attention, it was the scar in the center of his shoulder blades. Even to her untrained eye, it looked suspiciously like a bullet wound. She didn't know how she'd missed noticing it the day before.

He was beside her in the next moment, and she strove to recover thoughts that had become strangely fragmented. "From your state last night I thought you might be… impaired this morning."

"You thought I'd be hung over," he interpreted correctly. "Guess you were wrong." He gestured to her bags. "Is this all you've got?" At her wordless nod, he picked them up again and began striding away. "I'll put them below. Follow me and I'll show you to your cabin."

Ana trailed behind him to a small door, which he pulled open to reveal the companionway. Making certain to maintain a safe distance between them, she waited for him to descend before she attempted to follow. With the way her luck had been going, she'd slip and land right on top of him.

Below deck, her impatience quickly turned to appreciation. The area was compact but outfitted with gleaming teak trimmed with polished brass. There was a galley tucked into one corner, with a large table and chairs, couch and TV fitted into the rest of the area. Jones led her down a narrow hallway. "You can stay in here." He opened one of the doors and strode in ahead of her, slinging her bags onto the double bed.

"How many does she sleep?" she asked curiously, entering the small space and looking around. Her oldest brother, James, had a sailboat that slept six. At thirty feet, it was less than half the length of the *Nefarious*.

"She sleeps ten total. The head is in the stem."

Ana flipped through her mental files, searching for the ship lingo she'd picked up from James. "In front, right."

"Since you're the only passenger, I'm just bringing along one crew member. Pappy's a pretty fair cook, and he'll also help me with the navigation. If you need anything, he'll get it for you."

Analiese was finding it increasingly difficult to focus on his words. The quarters were *small*. There was only the bed, bolted to the wall, and a closet on the opposite wall, with a dresser inside it. The space was shrunk even more by Jones's presence. The ceiling was low enough that he had to slightly hunch his over-six-foot frame, which put his face alarmingly close to hers. "Okay, then." She manufactured a brilliant smile in a sudden hurry to get rid of him. "I assume you'll want to check with the bank before we set out, so…"

Rather than take her hint, he remained in place. "They already called me. The transfer's complete. So if you're ready, we'll pull anchor."

"How far is Laconos?"

"Full throttle? Three hours or so. We can make it easily by afternoon, though, if you're not in a hurry, and there's no reason you should be."

With effort she switched her attention from the shape of his full bottom lip to his words. "There's not?"

He gave her a long look. "You said you weren't meeting friends until tomorrow."

"Right," she agreed, relieved. Really, didn't the man have things to do before they left? Starting with putting on a shirt? "Well, I'm sure you're busy. You must have a million things to do. I won't keep you." To her horror, the words tumbled out of her mouth like a waterfall. "I'm just going to put my things away. I packed in a hurry, and I think if I hung things up they'd be less likely to wrinkle."

To her relief he cut off her involuntary barrage of words by heading toward the door. "I'll leave you to it, then. Come up when you finish and I'll introduce you to Pappy."

"Okay, then. Good. See you later." The moment he exited the room she swung the door shut, leaned against it. Her knees were weak with what surely must be mortification. When she was uncomfortable she had a tendency to babble, and there was no doubt she'd outdone herself on that scene.

Blowing out a breath, she pressed her hand to her stomach, quelling the nerves that were still scrambling there. They were caused by nothing more than a minor case of claustrophobia, she assured herself. These quarters were small. Jones was big. Really big. Especially across the shoulders. And his chest was pretty wide, too, not to mention his biceps, which were…

Eyes widening with horror at her totally inappropriate train of thought, she pushed away from the door, crossed to her suitcase and began unpacking. She couldn't afford to be distracted right now. Especially by the man who might well have been the last one to see Sam before he disappeared.

Not for the first time, she wished she could afford to come right out and ask Jones about her brother. But the risk was too great. There was no telling how well the two knew each other, or what their relationship was. She had no idea, at this point, if Jones could be responsible for his disappearance.

No, remaining covert was in everyone's best interest. If Sam was all right, and for some reason had had to abort his mission temporarily, she didn't want to end up blowing it for him. That was the same reason she hadn't alerted her brothers. Cade was a New Orleans police detective, and James…well, James ran the family and their father's business with the same ruthless rein. Neither of the men understood the word *subtle*. They'd have torn the hemisphere apart looking for Sam, and in doing so would have destroyed his cover forever. Better that she make some discreet inquiries first, and determine whether they had cause for alarm. And then, she thought grimly, shoving her emptied suitcases in the closet, if she still was unable to find a lead on Sam, she would unleash her brothers.

After she'd stowed the smaller bag holding her toiletries beneath the sink in the minuscule bathroom, she went to the door and peeked out into the hallway. If there was a trace of Sam on this ship, it was likely to be somewhere down here. And with Jones and his crew member busy above deck, there was no better time to look around.

It didn't take long to explore the limited space. Unfortunately, her search yielded no hint that her brother had ever been onboard. But then, Ana thought, studying the last closed door, she hadn't finished her search. Not quite.

With a strange reluctance she reached out, turned the knob. The door swung open revealing what was obviously Jones's cabin.

The space was filled with a large bed, which was unmade, the pillow still bearing a slight indentation. Surprise surged. It occurred to her for the first time that Jones had slept on the ship. Maybe he even lived on it. Suddenly the area took on an almost suffocating intimacy.

To distract herself she gazed around at the cabin. It was more spacious than the others, but was filled by the bed and the rolltop desk tucked into the corner.

And it was the desk that had snared her attention now.

After throwing a furtive look both ways, she slipped into the room, leaving the door cracked so she'd hear if someone was coming. She went to the desk, picked up the shirt he had draped across it. Maybe he'd had intentions of getting fully dressed after all. She wondered if her arrival there that morning had interrupted him. The thought had her stomach fluttering. Forcing her mind away from the vivid mental image that bloomed, she tossed the shirt onto the bed and reached for the top drawer.

Locked.

A quick check proved that the drawers were similarly secured, which only made Analiese more determined. Straightening, she folded her arms, contemplating the lock's opening and wondered what a few twists of a hair pin would yield. She had some in her toiletry case. But before she retrieved one she grabbed the shirt off the bed again to replace it.

There was no sound to alert her, but suddenly she became aware that she was no longer alone. Sudden foreboding weighting her limbs, her gaze slowly went to the doorway. And saw Jones lounging, one shoulder against the jamb.

She released the shirt as if it were in flames. *Ohmygod*, she mentally groaned as she looked up to his unsmiling expression. With the vast amount of material her life provided, she thought fate could pass up the occasional opportunity to humiliate her. Since he wasn't moving, she gave him a weak smile. "Hey, I was just looking for you."

"I told you I'd be up on deck. Why would you be look-ing for me in my room?"

She tossed a quick look around. "Oh, is this your room?" Then she almost winced as she heard the disin-genuous tone in her words. "I was wondering…if you had anything for motion sickness."

"Motion sickness."

"I'm already feeling a little nauseous."

"Funny. We haven't pulled anchor yet."

Great. Where was a tidal wave when she needed a good distraction? "I meant I *will* be nauseous. Soon. When we take off."

He settled his weight more comfortably and crossed his arms. "You're planning on getting sick?"

"No, of course not." It took a great deal of effort to keep her smile in place. "I just mean that normally I do. So I thought if I took something now, before I really needed it, when I did need it I wouldn't need it so much."

With a vague sense of horror she realized the foolish drivel was coming from her. There seemed to be no end to the mortifying depths to which she would sink around him.

He hadn't moved, was still watching her with the ex-pression one might wear contemplating a strange breed of animal in a zoo. "So if you tend to get seasick, why would you charter a ship?"

It was on the tip of her tongue to deny any such weak-ness. She was an excellent sailor, had been going out on the gulf since she could walk. But she kicked pride aside to salvage what she could of the situation. "It's just the first hour or so out, then I'm always fine. And I meant to pick something up before I left home, but completely forgot about it. If you don't have anything…"

Silence stretched, taut with tension. Then finally he straightened. "I can probably find something."

Relief filled her. "Great." She could barely contain her eagerness to get out of his room. He disappeared into the head, and she took the opportunity to scurry across the narrow hall into her own quarters. Jones reappeared a moment later, holding two tablets and a paper cup filled with water. She took both from him, and said, "Thanks. I think I'll take these now and lie down for a while."

It seemed to take an interminable amount of time before he quit staring at her and backed out of the doorway. "That would probably be best."

Swinging the door shut after him, Ana gulped the water down. It didn't help. Her throat still felt strangled. Dumping the pills in the now-empty cup, she crumpled it in her hand. As far as her espionage skills went, she was scoring in the negative range so far. If she didn't get better at subterfuge than this, she wasn't going to be of much use to Sam.

She got the hairpin she'd come for and sat on the edge of her bed, waiting until she felt the ship begin to move. Although her nerves still hadn't recovered from her last encounter with Jones, she forced herself to cross the corridor again and ease his door open. Losing no time, she dropped to her knees before the desk and began to twist the pin into a decent pick.

Inserting it into the lock on the rolltop, she probed carefully. Although she had no experience at unlocking desk drawers per se, she had grown quite adept at picking the lock on the strong box in which Sam or James had hidden her car keys whenever they'd attempted to ground her. She could have just had extra sets of keys made, but she'd thought the idea had lacked finesse.

Her skills were rusty, so it took several minutes before she heard a tiny click, and she triumphantly removed the pin, easing the top upward. Excitement filled her when she saw the neat piles of papers and notebooks lining the cubbyholes. She'd hit pay dirt. Reaching for the first book, she withdrew it and began flipping through it. Something in here had to yield a clue about the trip Sam had taken with Jones. Whatever it was, she was determined to find it.

With the engine humming in the background, the sun on his back and the wind hitting him full in the face, Jones felt a measure of peace. The life he'd left behind five years ago could emerge, raw and vivid in his dreams, but the open sea always helped banish old ghosts. Of course, today the tranquility was marred by the presence of the woman below deck.

His mouth turned down. Damned if he knew why he'd taken her money. Well, hell yes, he *knew*...because he'd been unable to afford to turn it down. But no amount of money could compensate for some kinds of trouble, and he couldn't rid himself of the nagging suspicion that the word described Ann Smith. With a capital *T*.

"School of dolphin up ahead, Cap'n. Pretty miss like to see?"

Gazing in the direction of Pappy's outstretched finger, he followed the man's island dialect with little difficulty. "She's down below, sick. Let's leave her there."

"Ladies like dolphins," Pappy persisted. His wizened face was the color of walnut, burnished by his heritage and decades in the sun. "Pretty miss no different."

"She's more different than you think," Jones muttered.

Although the other man couldn't have heard his words from this distance, it was a sure thing he'd caught the tone. His voice split into a wide grin. "Cap'n show pretty miss nice things and mebbe she be nice to Cap'n." He cackled at the dark look Jones threw him. "I ask her. I bet she want to see."

Shrugging, Jones watched the other man disappear below. The woman wouldn't be coming above, he'd put money on that. He'd never met anyone yet who was only seasick the first hour of a voyage. She'd be confined to bed for at least half the day.

Which suited him just fine. The blonde was a distraction, one he didn't need. Even after she'd left the tavern last night, he'd been unable to stop thinking about her. Smoke hung thick in the place, so there had been no reason for her light, fresh scent to have lingered long after she'd left. And even less excuse for his mind to return to her, time and again that night, until he'd finally made an excuse to Lexie and gone home, alone.

He hadn't been drunk, not quite, so he couldn't blame his lack of concentration on liquor. No, it had been the woman who even now was probably retching below who was responsible for his sudden restlessness. That and a certainty that this was going to be the longest four days of his life.

"What you do with pretty miss, Cap'n? Toss her overboard?"

Although the idea had merit, he shook his head at Pappy's question. "I told you, she's in her stateroom."

The man swung his head in silent negation. "Not there. And not getting sick in head, either. Not in galley. You leave shore without lady?"

He stared at the man, impatient. "Of course not. C'mere. Take the wheel." When the man sprang to obey, he turned and went below. There wasn't much space below deck. The woman had to be somewhere. He just hoped if she'd gotten sick she'd made it to the head.

It took a few moments below deck to discern that Pappy had been right. Ann Smith was nowhere in sight. A wave rocked the ship wildly, and he mentally cursed his crew member's handling of the ship. Steadying himself with a hand against the wall, he opened the last remaining door.

And found the troublesome blonde in the last place he'd expected, the last place she should have been. In his cabin again, this time sprawled across his bed with her face buried in his pillow.

Ignoring the sudden knot that clenched in his stomach at the sight, he fixed her with a glare. Her head was bright against the navy sheets, and he had the sudden thought that now her scent would linger there, too, a tormenting reminder of her presence in a place she'd had no business being.

The glare settled into a scowl as she shoved herself upright in the bed, rose and turned for the door. Then sank slowly back down on the mattress when she saw him in the doorway.

"Hi." Her tone was the most timid he'd heard from her, but it did nothing to allay his anger. "That…that was a big wave, wasn't it? Did you feel it?"

"Must have been a big one to knock you out of your bunk, across the hall and into my bed."

"Oh, well…about that." She bounced up again, her hands twisting on the strap of her purse nervously. "I wasn't actually in your…hmm." Her gaze couldn't seem to find a place to land. "I just…I took the pills you gave me but my bunk is sort of small and uncomfortable. I thought I'd rest better in a bigger bed." She moistened her lips under his silent regard. "And I did. It's a very nice bed…."

Comprehension dawned slowly, and Jones felt like three kinds a fool. He'd really been gone from civilization too long if he was becoming this slow on the uptake. Jamming his hand through his hair, he muttered, "I don't believe this." It wasn't as if it hadn't happened to him before, but of all the sorts of trouble he'd half expected to encounter with the woman, this kind had been the furthest from his mind.

"Look," he said, turning his gaze back to her. "I think I know what's going on here."

She looked panicked. "You do?"

"Yeah. Damn." This was embarrassing, which was a crock. *He* didn't have anything to be embarrassed about. "But this thing between us is strictly business, okay? And that's the way it's gonna stay. I don't mix business with pleasure, ever." He'd learned his lesson about that the hard way and still had the scar to prove it.

Her expression was a mask of horrified fascination. "You…you think I want to have an *affair* with you?"

"Yeah, well…sex, anyway. And you seem like a very, uh, a real nice person. But I'm not interested in you that way." Jones was proud of his tact. Although it wasn't a skill he practiced on a regular basis, he thought he'd managed pretty well. Which didn't explain her suddenly thunderous countenance.

"Let me get this straight. Even if I were offering casual no-strings sex, you wouldn't be interested."

What was it about women that they had to belabor everything? He thought he'd been damn clear, and it was something more instinctive than diplomacy that had him refraining from pointing out that she didn't look like a no-strings kind of woman. "That's what I'm saying."

"It's because I don't have big boobs, isn't it?"

"What?"

"Boobs." Her tone was disgusted. "I've got brothers. I know a man's brain cells drain away the moment his hormones kick in. If I had a pair of thirty-six D's you'd be drooling all over me."

He couldn't believe they were having this conversation. "For your information, I never drool."

"All men drool when their tongues are hanging out of their mouths, which seems to be a universal reaction of your gender when faced with a huge set of mammary glands."

There was a dull throb beginning in his temple. "Look, I was trying to be polite, and you're missing the point."

"Oh, I got the point all right. If I was contemplating having wild tempestuous sex with you, you wouldn't be interested. I got that loud and clear."

How the hell she'd managed to make him feel guilty when she'd been the one to sneak into *his* bed was beyond him. "Okay, then. I'm glad we got that out of the way."

"Did we ever," she muttered, shoving past him and marching down the corridor.

He followed her, feeling at a loss. "You know, at your weight, if you had big b— If you were big busted, you'd probably topple over every time you got up."

She was ascending the ladder in record time. "Yeah, yeah. I told you, I know what men like."

"You don't know me," he said flatly, tearing his gaze away from the curvy hips preceding him. Because if she did, if she ever found out that he was developing an inexplicable interest in delicately made blondes with backsides shaped by an angel, well then God help them both.

Chapter 3

As mortifying events went, it ranked right up there with the time Sally Ann Bunston had announced to the boys in their seventh-grade class that Analiese Tremaine stuffed her bra. But having to endure three straight years of taunts about whether she was "packing" each day paled in significance to the scene in Jones's stateroom.

Staring out at the school of playful dolphins, she concentrated on deep breathing and vengeful thoughts. She wondered if there was a knife onboard sharp enough to carve Jones into shark bait. The other crew member could handle the ship, and hadn't she heard once there was no law at sea?

She supposed she ought to be grateful. Just the thought had her grinding her teeth. After the impact of that wave had dumped her headfirst onto his bed, and she'd looked up to see him standing in the doorway, her mind had gone completely blank. He'd seemed suspicious enough the first time he'd walked in on her there. How in heaven's name was she going to explain a second time?

Then he'd handed her a perfect explanation, at least one that his colossal ego had seemed to buy. She'd had no choice but to play along, even while she'd wanted to go for his throat. Was the man actually used to women hiding under his bedcovers in order to seduce him?

She threw a dark look in his direction. The answer, quite obviously, was yes. And why that should make her want to hunt for that carving knife again was a question she really didn't want to face. Lord knew she had plenty of experience dealing with formidable male egos: she'd grown up with three brothers. The walls of their home had practically dripped testosterone.

It didn't help, she thought glumly, as the dolphins faded from view, that her outrage over his ''rejection'' hadn't been totally feigned. No woman wanted to hear that a man found her unattractive, and despite his protests to the contrary, she knew exactly what she lacked that would have snared his interest. She'd seen for herself the type he went for last night when he'd been pawing that waitress. He'd be the kind of guy who liked his women available, inventive and gone in the morning.

Based on the supply of condoms she'd found in his bottom desk drawer, he was either overly optimistic or very well prepared. It was probably the latter, which made his rejection smart even more. It didn't matter that she didn't want him, on any level. It was the principle of the thing.

Blowing out a breath, she reached into her purse for sunscreen. Smoothing a generous amount over her bare arms, she repeated the action on her legs. After rubbing a small amount of lotion on her face, she settled her sunglasses on her nose, dropped the bottle back into her purse and stretched out on the chair. The breeze kept her from being too warm in the sun, and she could feel a measure of tension seeping from her body. Until she thought of the disappointment Jones's desk had yielded. Then her muscles tightened yet again.

She'd found a log in which he apparently kept track of his business dealings. The charter she'd set up with him hadn't appeared in it yet, but two others had in the past month. The person's name who'd scheduled the trip had appeared, along with the number of days, nature of the trip and payment. However, there had been no entry dated around the time Sam would have crossed to Laconos. Its absence would suggest that Jones and her brother had never hooked up at all. Except that another notebook had listings for dates of fuelings, the gallons and prices. And Jones had fueled up the ship more than once after the last documented charter.

Ana stretched out on the lounger watching the gulls wheel overhead, and wondered what the discrepancy meant. Did the man take the ship out himself when he didn't have paying clients? It would seem reasonable to expect that he might. She found it equally reasonable to think that maybe he hadn't logged Sam's trip because her brother had asked him not to. Or that he knew the secretive nature of Sam's job and realized it was best to leave no traces.

It was a long shot, she admitted silently, but Sterling knew that her brother had docked at Laconos, and that he'd arrived by ship. And although she had no more proof than before that she was retracing her brother's steps, she remained convinced. She needed to start planning how to gather information once she hit the island. Sterling had been very definite about the parameters of her assignment. She, of course, had some ideas of her own.

A shadow fell across her chair. "You feel better now?"

Opening her eyes, Ana saw a blinding smile in a seamed,

weathered face. The man standing above her was no more than her height, and she'd guess that he wasn't much heavier. His friendly expression was a welcome contrast to the scowl Jones usually graced her with, and the lemonade he was holding was tantalizing.

She tipped her glasses down. "Yes, I'm feeling fine."

The frosty glass was thrust into her hand. "For you. Good to drink liquids in sun."

Ana took the lemonade and indicated a seat beside her. This, then, was Pappy, the crew member Jones had mentioned. He was obviously a native islander, and it was equally obvious that he had a much sunnier temperament than his boss. "Won't you join me?"

"Cap'n say you go to beaches." Pappy sat on the edge of a lounger next to her. "Lots beaches near, and Cap'n know them all. You be pleased."

To save herself from answering, she raised the glass to her lips. Right now she'd be most pleased if the captain happened to fall overboard, preferably in shark-infested waters, but she hated to douse this man's enthusiasm. "Have you worked for Jones a long time?"

At the man's exuberant nod, she felt a measure of pity for him, followed by a nebulous idea. "So I guess you know him pretty well."

Pappy bobbed his head again. "Cap'n good man. Keep his ship in good shape. And—" his expression went sly "—ladies like Cap'n. Cap'n like ladies."

Some ladies. Analiese wanted to correct him. Women whose obvious charms were matched by looser morals. In that, he was much like most of the men in her acquaintance. It was plain to see where Pappy believed her interest lay. And she was willing to let him believe just that if it meant she could get him to divulge a bit more information about the mysterious Jones.

"He said you did the cooking and helped navigate. Do you join him on all his trips?"

The man squinted against the rays of sun. "All trips. Only small crew for some, but Cap'n, he need to eat."

"Have you been to Laconos lately?" she asked daringly. "Jones seemed worried about my safety there."

"Pretty miss be safe on beach. Cap'n make sure." He shrugged. "No one want to drive away tourists. Bad for island."

Which still didn't answer her question. She phrased the next one more pointedly. "When was last time you were on Laconos?"

Pappy rubbed his jaw. "Me? Last month, mebbe. Most people, they like fishing. Many other beaches. Laconos not beautiful like Bontilla."

Which meant, Analiese thought, her stomach knotting, that if Jones had taken Sam to the island, the trip had been kept secret even from his trusted crew member. She manufactured a smile and drank again. Her throat had gone suddenly dry. "A ship this large must take a lot of fuel. How many gallons does it hold? Enough to get us to Laconos, I hope."

The man chortled. "Two big tanks, pretty miss, plenty to go to Laconos. Each tank hold two hundred gallon. Only take three hundred to get to island." He rose, smiling widely. "I go make lunch. You need food, so you not get sick again."

She gave a vague smile in response, and he walked away, his stride adjusting automatically to the pitch of the ship. Reaching down, she opened her purse and took out the notebook she kept there. She'd taken some notes while thumbing through Jones's logs, using a coded shorthand that no one but her would be able to make sense of. Checking them, she determined that Jones had refueled the ship three times in two days well after his last documented charter. Which would have readied the ship for the trip to Laconos, refueled it for the trip back, and then again to prepare it for the next charter. She added and subtracted gallons for several minutes, before she sat back, satisfied. Given the fueling history, this ship could have been the one to carry her brother to the island.

It was thin, she acknowledged, amidst a growing sense of certainty. But it was something. And since she'd discovered that Pappy hadn't accompanied them, the man would have no other information for her. Which meant, of course, that any other details would have to be pried from Jones himself.

Despite the heat, her skin prickled. The thought of having to play along with his egotistical belief that she was hot for him, in return for stray tidbits she might glean, was about as appealing as having surgery without benefit of anesthesia. But finding Sam was worth the sacrifice, wasn't it?

Jones would be less likely to be suspicious of her questions if he thought she was using conversation as an excuse to get close to him. She scowled at the thought, but the truth of it couldn't be denied. He'd handed her a perfect opportunity, and she'd be a fool not to use it.

She could always, Ana thought, consolingly, consider the exercise as practice. God knew she needed the experience at flirting, and since Jones had said in so many words that he was immune, he was a safe enough target. And besides learning information about her brother's disappearance, maybe before this trip was over, she'd have Jones eating his rejection of her, word by demoralizing word.

She smiled, stretched more languorously on the deck chair and raised her face to the sun. The idea was one to relish.

* * *

"Brought you something to eat," Ana said, strolling toward Jones with a tray Pappy had prepared.

His gaze flicked from her face to the food, then back again. "Is it poisoned?"

"Do you trust your cook so little?"

"It's not Pappy I don't trust." His meaning wasn't lost on her, but she chose to ignore it. Although earlier in the day she would have given a great deal to see him choke on a chicken bone, she was beyond those feelings now. Almost.

"You were right, Pappy is a great cook. I already ate and it was wonderful." And when she'd finished, she'd offered to relieve the crew member of the plate he'd prepared for Jones, uncaring of the conclusion Pappy had drawn. She *was* eager for an excuse to approach the other man. Just not for the reason that Pappy and Jones seemed to think.

Setting the tray down on a nearby table, she removed the napkins covering the food and pulled up a chair. Jones watched her carefully. "What are you doing?"

"I thought I'd keep you company while you ate," she said artlessly. "You've been up here all morning alone. I figured you wouldn't mind a little company."

He reached for a piece of chicken. "I like being alone."

She refrained from pointing out that with his personality, he was likely to spend a great deal of time in that state. Despite her efforts, her gaze lingered on the puckered scar on his back. She'd spent more than an hour formulating ways to finesse needed information from him before approaching him with lunch. But instead of the discreet questions she'd settled on, she heard herself say, "What happened to your back?"

"I lowered my guard."

His stark answer sent a chill through her. She'd be willing to bet that for Jones that particular error had been rare, indeed. Ana wanted to ask who had gotten close enough to him to gain his trust, only to betray it. But she knew intuitively that he'd never tell her. "Tell me about Laconos," she said instead, forcing her gaze away from him and out at the shatteringly blue water before them. "The State Department has cleared it for U.S. citizens' travel, but you seem to believe that it's still unsafe."

He turned back to the wheel and adjusted its position. "I just think there's cause for caution there, that's all."

"The scandal six months ago was like a Shakespearean tragedy. The crown prince of Laconos must have been desperately in love with his girlfriend to be so devastated by his family's disapproval of their marriage." The world had been shocked to learn that the prince, Owahano Bunei, of the royal family, had shot and killed his parents and siblings before turning his weapon on himself one night at dinner. And all because his parents had refused to give him permission to marry the woman he loved. "I'd heard, though, that the transition of power passed easily enough to Owahano's uncle."

"That kind of transition is never effortless." It was his total lack of expression, rather than the words themselves, that alerted her. What Jones wasn't revealing was of far more interest than what he did say.

She hadn't asked Sterling about the nature of Sam's mission on Laconos. It would have been futile. The man made even the taciturn Jones seem verbose. But she'd drawn her own conclusion from the information she'd managed to glean from her brother's encrypted files. The United States government was taking a keen interest in the island's new government, especially now that the current king was jockeying for more clout with the Global Trade Organization.

Ana thought Sam had been sent on assignment to see, first-hand, if Laconos's request should be opposed. Given her brother's disappearance shortly after he arrived there, she wondered if he'd found a reason for that opposition.

"It probably won't matter much to you and your friends one way or the other." At Jones's voice, Ana shifted her attention back to their conversation. "You're just planning on enjoying the beaches, right? A day or two there, and you'll be off to another island."

She steered him away from a discussion of her fictional friends by saying, "I've heard that Laconos has a fabulous beach on the north side."

"You may want to avoid that one." Was that a tinge of embarrassment she heard in his words? Ana studied his profile searchingly. "There's a great beach on the south-west side, too."

"Why? What's wrong with the north one?"

"It's topless."

"Sounds great." With a provocative air she braced her hands on the table behind her and leaned back. She'd bet that Jones's knowledge of topless beaches was firsthand. So to speak. "Is that the beach you go to?"

"I have better things to do with my time than to laze around on the sand all day." He dropped the chicken bone back on the tray and reached for another piece.

"But what do you do when you don't have a charter?" Not even to herself would she admit that there was a hint of personal interest in his answer.

He gave a shrug of one well-muscled shoulder. "Work on the ship."

"You don't ever take it out by yourself?" she prodded. Prying information from the man was like arm wrestling an alligator, but then, she hadn't expected it to be easy.

"Sometimes."

''Where are your favorite places to go?''

He slanted her a glance. ''You know, you're wasting valuable sun time in here with me. I'd think you'd want to be working on your tan.''

''I got enough sun this morning.'' Let him think that she was in here to change his mind about taking her to bed. It might annoy him, but it would also allay his suspicions about the true reason for her interest. She made a production of crossing her ankles. ''Are you going to show them to me? Your favorite spots, I mean?''

''Nope.'' He'd polished off the second piece of chicken and exchanged the bones for another piece.

''Why not?'' She imbued her voice with a deliberately sultry note. ''Maybe they'd become my favorites, too.'' As long as she was engaged in the pretense, she may as well pull out all the stops. Ana might not have had near the occasions she'd like to practice her feminine wiles, but she was a world-class observer. She knew the moves—the head toss, the pouty lips, the fluttering eyelids. Jones was given the full treatment, causing him to stare hard at her.

''Do you have something in your eye?''

She stopped fluttering them to glare at him. ''No, you dolt.''

He looked unconvinced. ''Maybe you should leave your sunglasses on. The sun is pretty bright on the water.''

With jerky movements she grabbed the sunglasses from atop her head and perched them on her nose. Okay, so her wiles were rusty. Come to think of it, they'd never exactly mesmerized any man, with the exception of Billy Ray Mc-Intire, who'd barely qualified as such. But she couldn't help believing Jones was being deliberately obtuse. Was she really so lacking in appeal?

Steering around the obvious answer to that question, she concentrated again on getting the man to part with a bit of information. "So, where do you go to get away from it all? Beaches? Fishing? Deep-sea diving?"

He rolled his shoulders, clearly impatient with her questions. "I don't have a lot of free time. A ship this size takes a lot of upkeep."

So that line of questioning was a dead end. If there was another explanation for the discrepancy in his log other than the one she chose to draw, it certainly wasn't forthcoming. She changed the subject. "Osawa Bunei, that's the new king of Laconos, isn't it? Did he choose to keep the former cabinet or replace it with his own?"

Slanting a glance at her, he took a bite of the piece of chicken he held. After he'd chewed and swallowed he said, "What are you after on the island, a sun tan or a history lesson? From what I've heard he's replaced most of the original cabinet, and no surviving family members were chosen, which led to some dissension."

Ana frowned. "I thought the family had all been killed with the exception of Osawa."

"Not all the extended family. There were two other uncles and an aunt, as well as many cousins left. Osawa was just the next in line for the throne."

The scenario he'd described wouldn't have raised eyebrows in most countries, but in the small island nation of Laconos, nepotism was a time-honored custom. Osawa had probably had to remove family members from cabinet posts to replace them with his own picks, which didn't strike Ana as a good way to keep your relatives happy.

"Do you go to Laconos often?" she asked daringly. Heck, subterfuge didn't seem to work with him, so perhaps the direct route would prove more successful.

"No." He dropped the chicken bone on the tray and reached for a napkin to wipe his hands. "Most of my charters are for deep-sea fishing, a few families who want to go out for a day, that sort of thing.''

The ship rocked against a particularly large wave, and Ana clutched the edge of the table in an effort to remain upright. Since it was bolted to the deck, it was as stable an anchor as she'd find. Jones merely adjusted his footing and leaned into the pitch of the ship, riding the motion in much the same way as a jockey melded his body with a horse's moves. His position drew her attention to the muscles that clenched and released in his back, and then lower, where the faded denim of his cutoff jeans clung faithfully to his masculine backside.

Ana tipped her glasses down to better contemplate the sight. The man's buns were as extraordinary as the rest of him, which really didn't seem quite fair. There ought to be a physical flaw somewhere. The scar didn't count, as it only added to his aura of danger. When the gods had been handing out bodies, she thought judiciously, this guy had been at the front of the line. Too bad the same couldn't be said about his personality.

He glanced her way then, and her gaze jerked upward guiltily. ''Thanks for bringing the tray up. You'd better get it back to Pappy so he can wash it.''

As a brush-off, it was offensively transparent. She reached for the pitcher of lemonade and poured some into a glass. ''After I finish my lemonade.'' Pouring a second glass, she offered it to him. ''Want some?''

Grudgingly he took it. ''Look, I don't mean to be rude...''

''It must be an innate response, then.''

''...but entertaining the guests isn't part of my duties as captain.''

''I think we've already covered that.''

"Neither is sleeping with them," he went on, earning a glare from her.

"Well, I've gotten over the disappointment of knowing I'll never bear your children," she announced sweetly, restraining an urge to toss the lemonade in his face. "Do you have something against polite conversation?"

He turned back to the sea, squinted into the distance. "Yes."

"Well, that's no surprise." She sipped and followed the direction of his gaze. She couldn't see what would warrant such close attention. "How about if I talk and you just point and grunt. We don't want to tax your abilities."

His mouth twitched in what might pass as a smile. "You are a smart-ass, aren't you?"

"That depends on your perspective, I suppose." Her brothers had always thought so, especially James, who still operated under the assumption that she was a precocious twelve-year-old. "Miss Emmaline back home at the public library would share your view, but then she never had much of a sense of humor. So when I posted a screen saver on the library computers of her kissing Goofy, she definitely overreacted."

"When was this, last week?" He passed his empty glass to her, and she filled it up again, before handing it back.

"I was fifteen. It cost me the better part of my summer vacation, too. I had to help computerize the entire library collection as restitution."

"So you'd think you'd have learned to curb your outrageous behavior."

"I learned not to get caught," she corrected absently. Leaning forward, she gazed at the instrument panel above the helm. "Can I take the helm for a while?"

From his horrified gaze, she thought aggrievedly, you'd think she'd asked him for his kidney.

"No one handles the *Nefarious* but me."

"You said Pappy does."

"He's crew. You're not."

"I handle my brother's sailboat all the time." It was a stretch of the truth, but not totally. She had, but only with James hovering behind her. He was as protective of his precious ship as Jones seemed to be of his own.

"Well, this isn't a sailboat, and guests don't take the helm." From the flat tone of the words, she knew that wheedling would have no effect. "Maybe you should have stayed home and sailed instead of trotting all this way looking for a good time."

"I had to get away for a while." Ana was on familiar ground now, having practiced this story before leaving the States. "I just broke up with my boyfriend, and I needed to put some distance between us. The restraining order won't hold him off for long, and I didn't want any more trouble."

She was just warming to the rest of her story when he said, "Yeah, okay."

"What do you mean, 'yeah, okay'? You don't believe I could have a boyfriend?" The accuracy of that guess didn't make it any less insulting.

His gaze had returned to the waters ahead of them. "It means I don't care. About your boyfriend, restraining orders, or library pranks. I think it's time for you to go below." He reached for binoculars hanging on a hook nearby and raised them to his eyes.

It never occurred to Ana to do as he asked. She had a natural curiosity, and it was roused now. She stared in the direction he was studying and discovered what had snared his attention. There was a ship approaching at top speed. "Do you know who that is?"

Instead of answering, he issued another order. "Go get Pappy."

Ana threw him a look. Jones still held the binoculars in one hand, and his profile could have been carved from granite. He didn't answer her; he didn't need to. Whoever was on that ship, Jones wasn't looking particularly welcoming. Without a word she hurried away to do as he asked.

Pappy was in the galley scrubbing a frying pan when she popped her head in. "Jones wants you on the bridge right away."

The man dropped the pot scrubber he'd been wielding and wiped his hands on a towel. "He need me to take helm?" He strode after her down the narrow hall.

"There's a ship heading our way. He doesn't seem happy about it."

The islander looked around when they got on deck and spotted the approaching ship. He quickened his stride. Ana practically had to jog to keep up with him. "I thought shippers were friendly people."

"Most be." Pappy climbed the stairs ahead of her. "But some be pirates. We take care."

Pirates. Ana's jaw dropped. Of all the dangerous scenarios she'd considered before setting out on this trip, piracy somehow hadn't occurred to her. She'd think the older man was pulling her leg if she hadn't noted Jones's reaction earlier. She quickly followed Pappy onto the bridge and saw Jones step away from the helm to allow the crew member to take over for him. Then he stepped aside, swept up a shirt and pulled it on, without bothering to button it. The sleeves were torn out of it, but that wasn't what held Ana's attention. It was the snub-nosed revolver that Jones tucked into his waistband at the base of his spine. He turned, stopping short when he saw her in the doorway.

She moistened her lips. "Pappy said it might be pirates."

Jones cast a condemning glance the other man's way, but said, "That's always something we have to be prepared for, but this looks like a government cutter."

"Government? Whose government?"

He brushed by her and prepared to descend to the deck. "That's what I plan to find out. Follow me."

The invitation, though couched more as a command, surprised her. She'd expected him to order her below deck. Falling in step behind him, she asked, "Do I get a gun, too?"

"Do I look stupid to you?"

"I'm going to assume that's a rhetorical question."

He stopped on the starboard side, his stance relaxed, at odds with the muscles she could feel bunched in his arms when she halted beside him. "Listen. This is important, and I want you to follow my lead. Don't open your mouth unless I tell you to. Got it?"

Under normal circumstances his terse undertone would have gotten her back up, but nothing about this scene was normal. "Got it."

The cutter reduced its speed and veered slightly away, to swing beside *Nefarious*. Ana stole a glance at Jones and nearly choked. Nothing but polite interest showed on his face, an expression that had been noticeably absent during the time they'd spent together.

Schooling her countenance to reflect the same, her efforts were hampered by shock when Jones casually laid his arm around her shoulders. The unfamiliar weight of it made it difficult to concentrate on the four men aboard the other ship.

"Ahoy. Nice day for a cruise," Jones called out.

Ana saw the four men on the other ship exchange some words, then one of them stepped forward. "Ahoy, *Nefarious* captain. May we ask your destination."

"Laconos." The arm around her shoulders tightened. "Gonna check out the beaches there."

"You have chosen well." The spokesman's English was university precise. "Our country has the finest beaches in the hemisphere." The man smiled as his companions stared silently. "We are looking for a lost tourist. He went missing several days ago and we believe he was injured. Have you seen any other water craft near here today?"

"Yours is the first one," Jones replied. He brushed his fingers along Ana's shoulders in what would appear to be an absent caress. Nerve endings torched in the wake of his touch, and it was all she could do to suppress a shiver of reaction. Her involuntary response had her longing to grind her sandaled foot onto the top of his bare one, but she couldn't remove her gaze from the men on the other ship.

All of them were armed.

None had taken the pains to hide it that Jones had. Each had a shoulder harness with a gun snugged inside it. She somehow doubted those were the only weapons on the ship.

"If you should be approached by such a man during your stay on Laconos, we ask that you alert the local police. We have questions to ask of him before we allow him to go."

"Sure," Jones replied. He glanced down at Ana, his hand shifting from her shoulder to skim down her back. "But we're gonna be keeping pretty much to ourselves while we're there."

His meaning couldn't have been clearer. The other men smirked, one elbowing another and saying something that made all of them laugh. That, coupled with her involuntary reaction to his touch, compelled Ana to treat Jones with some of his own medicine. Turning toward him, she smiled up in his face, running her hand up his bare chest and then down again, skating her fingers along the tight skin of his belly above his waistband.

Jones's free hand came up to grasp hers, lover-like, but his grip was anything but caressing. His gaze dropped to hers, a warning in his eyes, one she chose to ignore. He'd started this charade. She was just playing along at his request.

''Enjoy your stay on Laconos,'' the man called, as the cutter began to move away.

''Stay put,'' he muttered, raising his hand to wave. ''I think they need more convincing.''

Frowning, Ana tipped her head back to ask what he meant an instant before his firm, sculpted lips covered her own.

Chapter 4

Shock held Ana immobile. The pressure of Jones's mouth against hers sent a frisson of sexual awareness skipping through her system. Logically she was aware of the pretense he was engaged in. Emotionally she was struggling with her own knee-buckling response. The man knew how to kiss. Somehow she wasn't surprised.

Even through the haze of her own heightened senses she was able to discern the air of detachment in his touch. While his lips moved persuasively against her own, inciting her pulse to riot, he held himself aloof. And the realization heated her temper as surely as the kiss was heating her blood.

She could feel the exact moment when he'd decided the farce had gone on long enough. His hands dropped to her waist to set her away from him. Ana would never know just what inner demon drove her to press up against him, go on tiptoe and open her mouth beneath his.

He went still. Pressing her advantage, she slipped her

hands into his open shirt, skated them up his bare sun-warmed skin. Muscles jumped beneath her touch and a purely feminine sense of satisfaction curled through her. She may, to her constant regret, lack much experience, but the man wasn't immune to her. The realization made her bolder, made her want to discover just what it would take to make Jones lose that iron control of his. While she doubted she'd ever see it, she was driven to force more of a reaction from him.

Her arms twined around his neck, and with one hand she found the thong that kept his hair tied back and released the knot. She threaded her fingers through the freed strands, marveling at the thickness and texture.

His fingers clenched on her waist, and Ana braced for the moment he would push her away. But instead, Jones pulled her closer, drew her bottom lip into his mouth and scored it with his teeth.

The deck seemed to tilt beneath her feet, and weakness permeated her limbs. When his tongue boldly swept into her mouth, tasted her own, the kiss became all too real, all too devastating. It became abruptly clear to Ana that she'd never really been kissed before. Not like this. The press of his mouth was demanding, explicitly carnal. His taste was that of an aroused, primal male, and it traced through her senses leaving a trail of fire in its wake. One of his hands slid lower, found her bottom and squeezed. Shivering, she pressed closer to him, cupped his hard jaw and gave herself over to feeling.

Sensations were colliding inside her, too varied to be individually identified. There was the sun high overhead, bathing them both with warmth. The heat of Jones's body pressed tightly to hers, her breasts flattened against the sculpted muscles in his chest. The dark sensual flavor of his kiss and the tidal wave of response that told her she knew nothing about wanting. Of desire. But there was no doubt that this man could teach her.

The raucous screech of a gull overhead shattered the building desperation between them. As Ana was jolted back to reality, she was aware of the sudden tightening of Jones's body. Fighting a crippling sense of loss, she forced herself to be the first to step back, and manufactured a careless smile to hide the emotions still crashing inside her. "Well, if that didn't convince them, nothing could."

"What?"

She half turned away. It was easier, far easier, to play her part when she wasn't facing him and longing to dive back into his arms. "You wanted them to believe we were lovers looking for a secluded beach, didn't you? They shouldn't have any doubts after that display. Good thinking."

His answer was slow in coming. "Yeah, that's what I'd planned. But I think things got a little out of hand."

Something in his voice alerted her. It took a great deal of effort to meet his eyes, and what she saw there had her swallowing involuntarily. "Well, you told me to follow your lead, so I did. You were very good, by the way. I'm sure they didn't suspect a thing."

He shrugged, the gesture rife with frustration. "Yeah. Maybe it wasn't such a great plan, after all. I mean, I don't want you getting the wrong idea."

On a ten-point scale for offensiveness, that remark warranted at least a fifteen. Ana welcomed the anger that began to bubble in her veins, dissipating the desire that still lingered there. "The wrong idea?" She pretended confusion. "Oh, you mean about you wanting to go to bed with me. I thought we were beyond that. We were just acting, right? It's not like either of us *felt* anything."

The flinty hardness in his eyes was all too familiar. "As long as you realize that."

"No problem." Lifting a shoulder, she turned away, wandered toward the bridge. "You've got nothing to worry about. I put more effort into kissing Robby Marlowe in fourth grade. While he lacked your technique, he made up for it in enthusiasm." She felt, rather than heard, him fall into step behind her.

"You must have been pretty precocious."

"Not really. It was a just a game of spin the bottle. Didn't you ever play games as a kid?"

"Not those kind." He quickened his stride and reached the staircase before her, started up it. The sight of his hard buns encased in faded jean cutoffs had her throat going dry. What the man did to denim was positively sinful. So, surely it was that sight, in addition to the kiss, that had short-circuited her brain. Because once conscious thought struck her again, she froze in her tracks.

If the government officials were looking for just a lost tourist, as they claimed, why would they all be armed? Weapons suggested they expected danger, or at least a fight from the man they sought. Which meant he wasn't just an ordinary tourist.

A chill coursed through her. Could the man they were searching for be Sam? The thought filled her with dread.

We believe he may have been injured....

Ana cautioned herself not to jump to conclusions, but she had to face facts. If the "missing tourist" was Sam, the Laconos government had no intention of letting him off the island. Which made it all the more imperative that she find her brother. Before the police did.

Intent on getting some answers from Jones, she hurried in his wake up to the bridge. When she appeared, he and Pappy broke off the conversation they were holding in undertones and looked at her. "It wasn't pirates, Pappy," she announced as she strolled into the room. "It was just a government cutter from Laconos. Did Jones tell you?"

She didn't miss the warning look Jones shot the other man.

"Not to worry, miss. Laconos government very friendly to tourists."

Not so friendly, Ana thought, if they were responsible for wounding the man they sought. Rather than voicing the thought, she said disingenuously, "They must be if they're going to the trouble of trying to find an injured tourist. But I don't understand why they would be looking for him so far from shore. If he got this far, he obviously isn't hurt badly. He wouldn't need their help."

Taking the helm from Pappy, Jones turned his back to her. But she was certain the lack of expression in his voice would be mirrored in his face. "They're just being cautious. If he got hurt in their country they're probably going to want to file a report."

Pappy slipped from the bridge and went down the stairway. Ana didn't spare a glance for the older man, however. She needed all her wits about her to deal with Jones. "If that's all it was, why did you feel compelled to enact that little scenario for them?" She watched his back stiffen, one vertebra at a time. But his tone was even enough when he answered.

"Just didn't figure you'd want to be delayed any more than necessary. A ship can get tangled up in a lot of red tape if government officials take an interest in it or its passengers. Might take hours to answer all the questions they have about your plans and frequency of visits." He shrugged out of his shirt, tossed it aside and took the gun from his waistband and put it back in the drawer before him. With an obvious desire to change the subject, he said,

"It's another hour to the island. Do you want to try one of the beaches?"

"No, I think I've gotten enough sun for the day. Let's just put into port and I'll explore the city for a few hours." She didn't believe his explanation for a minute. If Jones was anxious to avoid questions with the Laconos government, it didn't have anything to do with delaying her. It was much more likely that he wanted to avoid having his ship under scrutiny.

And right now she could only guess at the reason for that reluctance.

The Laconos port authority seemed to have doubled their paperwork and questions since the last time Jones had put into port there. He'd been dealing with a couple of the agents for fifteen minutes when the two men appeared to get distracted. Following the direction of their gazes, he silently cursed when he saw the object of their focus. Ann Smith was descending the plank board to the dock.

He analyzed the subject of their fascination with a critical eye. The woman certainly wasn't beautiful, although her looks probably defined the word cute. Short straight nose, wide blue eyes and lips that had a tendency to pout when they weren't curved as they were now. Her bright head of hair gleamed in the sun. She ought to be wearing a hat. She was too fair-skinned to have built up much of a resistance to the sun.

One of the agents made a token attempt to shift his attention back to Jones, but the other seemed unable to take his eyes from the woman approaching them. He felt a swift surge of annoyance. Was the woman being deliberately provocative, or had she always had that noticeable sway to her hips? It called a guy's attention to the very respectable curves there, and unwillingly Jones had a brief mental re-play of the feel of them.

That recollection led to another, when he'd briefly for-gotten his excuses for staging that kiss and tasted her in earnest. Because he wasn't a man given to impulse, it was difficult to fathom the reasons for letting his control slip, even a little. Except that he hadn't expected the sweet, fresh flavor of her. Hadn't anticipated the spike of need that had pierced his usual impenetrable restraint. She'd taken him by surprise, and so had his response to her. And he didn't like that fact at all.

His displeasure sounded in his voice. "You need to get something to keep the sun out of your eyes. The last thing I need is you getting heatstroke."

She raised that pointed little chin of hers and he knew instantly he'd taken the wrong tack with her. He was be-ginning to believe that the best way to get her to do some-thing was to tell her to do the exact opposite.

She disputed his words with a careless shrug. "I'll be all right. I'm used to the sun."

He gave her a long look. True enough, her skin bore a light golden tan, but was hardly the color of the seasoned sun worshiper. Deliberately he let the subject drop. He made it a point to remain uninvolved. It was nothing to him if she keeled over from heatstroke. Except if Pappy had to fuss over her sickbed he wouldn't be available for his other duties. Not that Jones expected the man would mind. From what he'd noticed, his crew member was about as dazzled as the two men before him.

"I'm going in to town to sightsee." Ana aimed a smile at the two agents. "Do you have any recommendations?"

It was pathetic, Jones reflected, as the men fell over each other to be helpful, how the woman used those big guileless eyes to reduce the agents to babbling idiots. He slitted his gaze. He was beginning to believe there was a whole lot more to her than he'd first believed. No woman could be so full of contrasts. The way she had these two men eating out of her hand spoke of a woman comfortable in the knowledge of her own appeal. She'd been blatantly obvious in her machinations to get into his bed, but once he'd had her in his arms she'd seemed damned inexperienced. He hadn't missed her slight gasp when his tongue had gone in search of hers. Her nipples had been tight little knots stabbing into his chest, and no matter what she'd pretended later, she hadn't been able to hide her very real response to their kiss. Which somehow didn't make him feel any better about the involuntary response *he'd* had.

The memory made his gut clench, and he scowled in her direction. "We're busy here," he said, interrupting what seemed to be becoming a cozy coffee klatch. "So if you're finished…"

Although her eyes flashed, her voice was still warm as she thanked the men for their help. Her tone when she addressed him, however, was glacial. "I may dine while I'm out. Tell Pappy not to fix anything for me."

She'd started to walk away when he said, "Make sure you get back here while it's still daylight." Although there was no way she could have avoided hearing him, she gave no indication that she had. Which was just as well, because the remark definitely hadn't sounded as detached as he'd meant it to. He switched his attention from her to the agents, who were watching her stroll away with avid interest. "Could we get done here, gentlemen?"

One of the agents turned back to him with a broad smile. "I can understand your hurry to join your woman, sir. We will only be a few more minutes."

Jones opened his mouth to correct the man, and then shut it again. Wasn't that exactly the impression he'd sought to give the government officials? A couple looking for romantic hideaways was apt to garner little attention. And although the thought of pretending to be Ann Smith's lover wasn't the most comfortable to contemplate, if it served to lessen the suspicion that incoming ships were being subjected to, it was a necessary pretense.

In less than fifteen minutes he'd dispensed with the formalities, and the agents went on their way. He went back onboard and took a quick shower before changing into khaki shorts and a T-shirt. Shoving his feet into a pair of sandals, he grabbed some sunglasses and headed off the ship.

Joining the throngs of people on the street, he walked quickly, keeping an eye out for a familiar face. He'd been to the island often enough to have a few contacts here, and he wouldn't be returning to the ship tonight before he'd spoken to all of them. Something about the story of the missing tourist had sounded off to him, and he wanted to learn what the rumors on the street were. He was starting to get a real bad feeling about this whole thing.

"Jones." The tall thin man behind the counter of the diving shop nodded a friendly greeting. "Been a long time."

Jones was content to wait until Hector, the owner of the place, finished with the group of tourists he was speaking to. The conversation he'd be having with the man was best accomplished in private. Several minutes passed as he examined the equipment displayed in the store, until the customers finally made an exit, their purchases in tow.

"Hey, mon." Hector came out from around the counter and clapped a friendly hand on Jones's shoulder. "Where you been hiding, huh?"

Grinning, Jones gave a shrug. "Heard you were busy

keeping all the women on the island happy. Didn't figure you'd have time for an old friend.''

"It is a big job," Hector agreed, his dark eyes alight with amusement. ''My ladies demand much of me.'' He patted his flat stomach. ''That is how I keep trim.'' When Jones only laughed, he turned, motioned for him to follow. ''Come. I will find us beers and you will tell me your adventures, yes?''

Minutes later there was a Closed sign hanging in the window, and the two men were enjoying beers in back of the shop. The breeze from the ocean stirred the air, and Jones could see his ship in the distance, rocking gently against the pier. The sight reminded him of his reasons for visiting Laconos twice in the last couple weeks. The memory had him frowning. ''Hear you had some excitement on the island recently.''

Hector's expression stilled, and he cast a quick glance around the area. With the exception of a matronly woman taking laundry off a line several properties away, there was no one in sight. That didn't prevent the man from lowering his voice. ''There has been excitement on the island for many months now. No one is sure what the future holds for our country.''

Jones tipped the bottle to his lips and drank. ''A government cutter stopped me an hour from shore. Wanted to know my purpose for visiting the island.''

Hector looked unsurprised by the news. ''They seek a man, that much I know. For days now officials have come to all the shops, always asking questions, showing a picture. Wait.'' He rose, went through the back door of the shop and returned a few minutes later with a folded sheet of paper. Handing it to Jones, he sank down into his seat again.

Jones straightened the paper and stared at a sketch that,

despite its crudeness, was startling in its familiarity. It was the man he'd brought to the island on his last trip here. Expressionlessly he creased the paper again and gave it back to Hector. "What's he done?"

The other man shrugged. "That we are not told. Just that he is wanted for questioning and that he is injured."

"*Is* injured? Or *might* be injured?" The officials had made it sound that morning like they hadn't been sure.

"The man was hurt. Stabbed in the thigh and lost much blood. I know this not because the government says so. But I keep my ears open and hear many things. Some say this man they seek, he fought with a high-ranking cabinet member and was injured in the fight. No one seems to know what they fought about."

"Does anyone say where this man might be?"

"No one has seen him. No one dares ask questions, for fear the soldiers come to question their loyalty." At Jones's sharp look, Hector went on grimly, "As I said, much has changed. No longer do we live our lives and let the royal family run the government. Now the government begins to run the people. There is unrest growing."

Jones drank in silence, contemplating his friend's words. Before Owahano Bunei had shocked the country and the world with his actions, the island of Laconos had been historically conservative, steeped in tradition. It had been a major event fifteen years ago when they'd begun welcoming, even courting the tourism industry. Although friendly with the Western nations, the Laconos government had been traditionally neutral in all world conflicts, shunning any foreign influences that would threaten their customs and way of life. From what Hector was saying, the new government here was far more controlling of the citizens' lives than the last one had been.

"Any rumors about why the man was on the island?"

When Hector shook his head, Jones pressed on. "If you hear anything, can you get word to me? I'll be docked here for another day."

Hector looked uneasy, throwing a look over his shoulder. "It is not wise now to be seen with outsiders. Too many officials watch and accuse." When Jones's hand went to his wallet, the man's face went from uneasy to offended. "But I do not need money to help a friend. If there is something to tell, I will find a way to send a message."

"I'm grateful." The two men's gazes met and held, before each raised their bottle in a silent salute. Friendship didn't always supersede fear. When it did, Jones knew, it was to be valued all the more.

Ana didn't have to pretend a fascination with her surroundings as she made her way through the busy marketplace. She had a feminine appreciation for the display of wares, and a competitive instinct for a good deal. Engaging the clerks in a conversation about their goods was an excellent way to lead into other topics.

With ruthless efficiency she wended her way among the tables, stopping to ascertain the clerks' level of English before deciding to stop and spend time there. But while several of the vendors were well versed in her language, few of them had anything to share about the man the government was searching for.

She thought even Sterling would have to admit that she was using the utmost discretion as she probed for information. After an hour or so, she grew even more comfortable with her task, masking her interest behind a guise of interested tourist. She stopped to admire a table of brightly colored scarves, catching the owner's eye as she held up a brilliant blue and pink one. "These are different. Are they made here on the island?"

The female clerk bobbed her head. She had one of the scarves woven in an intricate braid in her hair, which was pinned on top of her head. "We dye scarves, my daughters and me. You like? Pretty lady can use many scarves. One to wear ever day."

The woman's English was understandable enough to keep Ana in place. "I like them very much. I just can't decide which ones to get." As she slowly looked through the piles of scarves, she drew the woman out about her three daughters and the upcoming grandchild one was expecting. By the time Ana had selected three scarves, they were discussing the names being considered for the anticipated newborn.

Ana haggled over the price with the woman, settling on one before reaching into her purse. "I'd like to do more sight-seeing this evening, but I'm a little worried about this man everyone is searching for." She handed over the money and the woman busied herself with wrapping the scarves. "Do you think it's safe for me to be downtown at night while this guy's on the loose?"

Ana thought it was interesting that the woman appeared to know exactly what she was talking about. And equally intriguing was the quick look she threw around her before lowering her voice to answer. "As I tell my husband, the man the government seeks will not be found. Some say he is already dead from loss of blood. Others say he was not human at all, but a *dieu païen,* a pagan god who the government has angered. Either way, he will not be seen again."

Ana's hand had become alarmingly unsteady as she held it out to collect her change from the woman. It was as if the woman had plucked her darkest fears about Sam's situation and put voice to them. It took conscious effort to put her money away and collect her purchases, schooling her expression to a polite one. "So it would be safe to come down here at night?"

"Very safe, miss. The military is everywhere these days. And there is much show of security since some of our new government officials frequently enjoy the nightlife." She leaned even closer, more than a tinge of disapproval in her voice. "It is to be hoped that they work as hard for our people by day."

Hiding her curiosity at the woman's words, Ana prepared to leave. "My friends and I would like to find a place with music and dancing. Where should we go?"

Other tourists were stopping nearby, and the vendor, with an eye on her trade, began drifting away. "There are only two places like that in the city, Le Dauphin and Laval's. Both are down the street from here." The woman beamed a welcoming smile at the newcomers, and Ana walked away, her mind swirling.

She wondered if the woman's opinion mirrored that of other islanders. If so, it seemed as though the people were becoming dissatisfied under the new rule.

It was more comfortable to dwell on what the woman had revealed about the government than on her suppositions about Sam. Ana had no doubt that her brother would relish the rumor about him being a god, but she didn't even like to consider the woman's other guess.

Dread twisted with worry in a greasy tangle in her stomach. As much as she hated to contemplate it, it was clear that Sam had been injured in some way during his mission. But he'd managed to escape from Laconos's military. That fact didn't do much to lessen the sick concern she was feeling, but it offered a thread of hope. The government officials obviously thought he was well enough to make his way off the island, so his wounds couldn't be as serious as the woman had indicated.

Ana continued her way down the marketplace, hoping for further information. Rumors abounded about the mysterious man the government sought, but no one seemed to have any facts about him. As the hours passed into early evening, she decided that there was nothing more to be learned there and decided to turn back for the ship.

Ana strolled with seeming aimlessness until she was nearing the shoreline. When she found a collection of large boulders on the beach, she ducked behind them, pulled out the cell phone from her purse and punched in Sterling's number. She hoped the man agreed that the Laconos government's continued search for Sam meant good news for her brother's well-being.

But moments later, after the number had rung incessantly, she was forced to cut off the call. Sterling hadn't answered.

Trepidation swirled inside her. This had never happened before. He'd always been there in the past, a disembodied voice on the other end of the line, one she had imagined all sorts of identities for.

The sun was sinking lower over the horizon of the ocean, turning the water into ripples of rainbow. But Ana was unable to appreciate the beauty of the scene as she grappled with this newest development. Not only had Sam disappeared, but the man who'd assigned her brother to this mission couldn't be located either. For the first time since she left the States, she felt totally alone.

Chapter 5

"Very pretty, miss. Beautiful like the moon on the ocean."

At the sound of Pappy's unusual babbling, Jones frowned and headed in the direction of the man's voice. As he turned the corner of the deck, he stopped short as he watched Ann twirl around before Pappy's admiring gaze.

"You like it?"

Unfortunately, Jones did. Very much. He doubted there was a man alive whose hormones wouldn't stand up and salute at the picture she made. She'd done something to her hair so that it fluffed around her face, inviting a man's fingers. The figure-hugging strapless black dress she wore followed her curves faithfully before ending well above midthigh. Made of some sort of stretchy material, it looked as if it could be peeled down her body if one took the notion.

He scowled. It looked like, he thought grimly, she was

inviting a man to do just that. "Where are you going in that getup?"

At his voice she turned, and he had the renegade thought that a dress like that wouldn't allow for her wearing much beneath it. Swallowing hard, he shoved the thought away.

"Getup? What a quaint phrase. Back home we call this a dress." She reached into her oversize black purse and withdrew a compact, opening it to check her lipstick in the mirror.

He folded his arms across his chest. "This isn't a cruise ship. We don't dress for dinner on the *Nefarious*."

She slipped the compact back into her purse and looked him up and down. "Really? And here I thought the pains you'd been taking with your appearance were for my benefit."

Rubbing at a streak of grease across his chest, he scowled at her. After returning to the ship, he'd done a little work on the engine and was exceedingly aware that he hadn't yet cleaned up. "I'm just saying, you're dressed a little fancy for a quiet meal onboard. It isn't necessary." And it wouldn't change anything. Though she'd succeeded in catching his eye, and his attention, more than once in the past several hours, hormones had never been allowed to interfere with logic. She was wasting her time.

"You and Pappy can have your quiet meal together. I have other plans."

Her words succeeded in dragging his attention from her slender thighs. "Other plans?"

"I'm going downtown for a while. I understand that there's quite an active nightlife and thought I'd check it out."

"I don't think so."

The words were out of his mouth before he'd even considered them. Where the hell had they come from? The woman's actions were no concern of his. But even as he formed the thought, it sounded like a lie. He shifted uncomfortably. As his client, he owed her a certain protection, that was all. Especially since her own judgment didn't seem to be the greatest. Although the explanation didn't totally satisfy, it was the only one he'd admit to.

He was beginning to know her well enough to expect the flare of emotion in her eyes at his statement. But he was unprepared for the tiny smile she gave him. "It's all right. I already checked, and there are cabs available to travel back and forth to the ship. I'm not completely unaware of safety precautions."

Jones figured if the woman had one ounce of sense about her safety, she'd never have worn that dress. But rather than pointing out the obvious, he reached for a discretion he rarely used, to say, "If you want to go downtown, I'll take you."

He didn't know which of them was more shocked by his words. He definitely didn't want to spend any more time than necessary with the woman, especially in a setting that she could construe as a date. The last thing he needed was to provide her with encouragement and find her in his bed again. The thought had his loins tightening.

"No, thanks."

He didn't respond right away; he was too busy combatting his involuntary reaction to that recent mental image. When he did register her meaning, saw her turning to walk across the deck, he strode after her. "Hold on. I said I'd take you. Give me some time to clean up."

She turned, gave him a considering look. "Somehow I don't think you're the type to enjoy a night out on the town. At least, not in places I'd care to go."

Since her words were true enough under normal circumstances, he saw no reason to dispute them. Especially when he didn't care to reflect too hard on his reasons for making the offer. "You shouldn't be out on your own in a strange country at night. Give me fifteen minutes to change and I'll meet you back here."

Again her lips curled in that tiny little smile. He didn't know what to make of that expression, not then. Going below deck, he shaved three minutes off the promised fifteen and headed back up dressed in clean khakis and a dark shirt. The deck was empty.

Throwing an impatient look around, he expected to hear voices alerting him to where Ann and Pappy were talking while she waited for him. What he didn't expect to see was the cab at the end of the dock pulling away.

Ana handed a bill to the waitress and took the fruit juice she'd ordered. It was her second at Le Dauphin, and her stomach was already sloshing with the water and juice she'd imbibed this evening. Had she been ordering alcohol tonight, she'd have been comatose an hour ago.

Impatiently she sent another look around the dimly lit interior of the place. Like Laval's, it was loud, noisy and filled with people grouped around tables or gyrating on the tiny dance floor. Although there had been a steady stream of customers through the place, most looked like tourists. And none of those who appeared to be native islanders seemed old enough to be government officials.

The plan that had brought her here tonight was clearly a long shot. But the only chance she was going to have to question government officials about the mysterious stranger they were seeking would be in a setting where they wouldn't suspect her interest. As time went on, however, that possibility seemed to be growing more and more remote.

Stirring her drink idly, she glanced at the slender watch

on her wrist. The glowing numbers revealed it was barely eleven. Stifling a yawn, she resigned herself to a late night. She'd already learned that the bars here didn't close until near dawn.

"Did you buy that drink for yourself, my lovely? I told you I'd be happy to get your next one for you."

Giving an inward sigh, Ana pasted a disinterested smile on her face and turned to the man addressing her. It was the third time he'd approached her since she'd entered the place, and he seemed to get more forward with each drink. Italian, she thought, given his accent, and very close to total inebriation. Clutching her chair as much for stability as for proximity, he leaned closer to her.

"Thank you, I'm still waiting for someone."

"A man is a fool to leave you alone for so long. He does not deserve you." He swayed, nearly landing in her lap.

Curbing an impulse to elbow him where it would do the most good, she merely gritted her teeth. "Please go away."

Instead of obeying, he pulled out a chair and sat down near her. "It is not safe for a woman as beautiful as you to be left alone in such a place. Better that I stay and keep away the bothersome men, hmm?"

It was on the tip of her tongue to let him know that he was the most bothersome of all the men who'd wandered by her table that evening when the door to the bar opened again. Habit had her glancing that way, shock had her freezing.

Jones stood in the doorway, his gaze sweeping the area. Ana's heart, which had seemed to stop for an instant, began pounding. What in heaven's name was he doing here? She would never have imagined that he'd choose such a noisy, crowded venue to spend his free time. The tavern she'd found him in on Bontilla bore no resemblance to this place.

She watched as he chose a section close to the door and

began pacing it. A frisson of warning shot down her spine. Jones hadn't ducked in for a nightcap. He made no attempt to catch the waitress's eye. He was prowling the area with the deliberate air of a panther stalking prey. It had never occurred to her that he would come after her. He'd made his lack of interest in her blindingly clear. Except, of course, when he'd issued orders.

He slipped between crowded tables with an effortless ease, despite the crowd. Ana noted the way people stepped away from him, allowing him passage. She didn't blame them. He looked more than a little dangerous, not to mention extremely pissed off. He would cover the dim, crowded club, one section at a time until he found her, or until he was convinced she wasn't there. It would be only moments before he spotted her. And his presence by her side for the rest of the evening would put paid to her plans.

The realization propelled her to action. "I feel like dancing," she said brightly, jumping up from her chair and reaching for her purse.

"I have a better idea, *mi cara.* Let us leave this place and find one quieter."

Ignoring the man's slurred suggestion she turned to make her way to the dance floor, intent on losing herself in the crowd there. But while she might have escaped Jones's notice, she didn't succeed in evading the amorous man at her side. Despite his uncertain equilibrium, he followed her.

The lights above the dance floor sent spinning splinters of color over the mass of gyrating bodies. Ana slipped into the crowd and began moving to the music. She maneuvered around her companion until his back shielded her from Jones's gaze. And then she craned her neck to locate the back entrance.

With a studied movement she swung her purse to deflect the Italian's roaming hands. Although Jones was no longer in view, she didn't fool herself into believing he'd left the club. He didn't strike her as the kind of man who did anything by half measures.

The crowd swelled around her, pressing her closer to her companion, who took the opportunity to pull her into his arms. The bass of the music seemed to well up from the dance floor and pound its way through her body. She used her elbows to wedge some space between her and the Italian, who was using the opportunity to lean heavily on her in a move owing more to inebriation than desire. Squirming away, she checked the path toward the exit again. The place seemed to be filling up with even more people, but she'd have a clear shot. If she was going to avoid Jones, it was now or never.

She stopped moving and let her body go limp. The Italian, who had begun using her for support, stumbled, nearly fell. Ana used the opportunity to slip out of his arms and push her way through the throng of people until she got off the dance floor.

There were numerous disadvantages to being short, all of which she'd been enumerating since she was fourteen and it had become apparent that nature wasn't going to bless her with the height her brothers enjoyed. But for once her stature worked in her favor. She pushed and twisted, ducking between people and squeezing through the narrow aisles until she finally was able to reach the back door. She burst through it to lean against its other side.

The outside air seemed fresher than normal, in contrast to the smoke-infested atmosphere of the nightclub. She filled her lungs with it once, twice, and ordered her raging pulse to calm. It was only then that she focused on the frozen tableau before her.

Two men were staring at her, one hunched over a satchel that looked like those sold in the marketplace, adorned with colorful sea birds. Except that it wasn't filled with shells or gaily patterned scarves. There were white bars spilling out of it, glistening in the moonlight.

Cocaine.

She recognized the substance in an instant. Cade had shown her pictures of busts he'd made working narcotics in New Orleans. The man with the satchel held a knife. She assumed he'd been in the act of using it to shave off a corner of one bar, to test its authenticity. In the next moment he shifted the knife in his hand, turned to face her and raised it threateningly.

"Vlados, chita."

With his gesture, she understood the command, if not the words, but there was no way she was going to obey. Keeping her back to the building, she began a frantic search with her hand behind her, until she found the door handle and yanked.

Nothing happened. The man with the knife started coming toward her rapidly, a steady stream of what was certainly curses falling from his lips. His companion was frantically raking the goods back into the satchel. Ana tried the door again but it had obviously locked after her. A precaution to ensure that all patrons would have to pass through the front and pay the cover charge, while still obeying any fire regulations the island might have.

There was no other way into the building from here. It was unlikely that anyone in the noisy bar would hear a woman screaming in the small courtyard out back, so she didn't waste her breath. Instead she threw herself sideways as the knife-wielding man reached for her, thrusting her hand into her purse and searching frantically until she withdrew the small cool cylinder. She held it up as the man lunged toward her and sprayed a long blast of pepper spray in his face.

The knife dropped as the man cried out, brought both hands to his eyes. Ana swung around, brandishing the canister, but she didn't have to worry about the second man. He was already running in the opposite direction, the bag clutched to his chest. Because the idea had merit, she did the same, fleeing around the corner of the building toward its entrance.

The street in front of the nightclub was jammed with people, and it was toward the mob that Ana headed. She threw one quick glance over her shoulder to see if the man with the knife had recovered enough to follow, and only when she ascertained that there was no one trailing her did she dare slow down to a fast walk.

Letting the crowd of people swallow her up, she was content to allow herself to be eddied toward the entrance of the club she'd left only minutes ago. She watched until another throng exited the club and drifted toward them, heading in the opposite direction, toward Laval's.

She never noticed the man step out of the shadows to fall in step behind her.

Ana spent a half hour in Laval's, but her concentration had been shot. Stumbling upon the drug dealers had spiked her adrenaline to a fever pitch. But that peak had long since faded, leaving her shaky with nerves. She'd once had a narrow escape when a courier job had gone very, very wrong, and was familiar with the way adrenaline faded into shock. She would get very little else accomplished this evening.

For the dozenth time she looked toward the bar, considered summoning the local police. For the dozenth time she discarded the idea. She couldn't afford the scrutiny the revelation would bring her, and especially didn't want to alert any law enforcement official to look more closely at her forged papers. The man she'd acquired them from had assured her of their quality, but there was no use inviting trouble. She rose, ready to admit defeat for the evening.

Intent on hailing one of the taxis that waited, lined up at the curb, she left her fruit drink and started for the doors. The club was as crowded as Le Dauphin had been, although more spread out. There were two levels to the place, with the dance floor and band on the bottom and extra seating above. It seemed to her that the entire area was filled with shouting, laughing people intent on drinking themselves senseless.

She got as far as the doorway before she felt a hand on her elbow. Operating solely on instinct, she drove it backward and spun around even as her free hand went in search of the canister in her bag. She heard a rush of indrawn breath, telling her that her elbow had found connection, and then a strangled voice.

"Pardon, je manque."

The man she turned on wore a pained expression. Short and slender, he had thick, dark hair ringing a rapidly receding hairline and eyes as droopy and sad as the hound dog she'd had as a child. Whether in response to the look on her face or to the blow she'd already landed, his hands were raised in a gesture of surrender.

"Please, I mean no harm." His English was halting. "There is one who would speak to you." He stopped then, as if searching for the words, before shrugging helplessly. "If you would please."

"Who?" Ana hadn't released her grasp on the canister in her purse. No one else seemed to be paying attention to them.

"Icanno Shala. *Il est un homme très important dans notre gouvernement."*

The name meant nothing to her. Drawing on long-ago

memories of high school French, she struggled with the translation. An important man in the government? A bud of interest unfurled.

"Please." The man was becoming more insistent, if not braver. He didn't touch her again, but he was attempting to subtly herd her along with him.

Ana's mind was racing. Her nerves from the drug deal she'd stumbled upon hadn't completely dissipated, but if this Shala was a government official she might be able to learn some information about Sam.

Her mind made up, she looked at the man and said, "Wait." Then she walked to the long, gleaming mahogany bar and gestured to the young bartender. Wiping his hands on a towel, he approached her, smiling flirtatiously.

"What can I get for you, beautiful lady?"

"Can you tell me who Icanno Shala is?"

Her words succeeded in wiping the smile from his handsome face. "He is a cabinet minister, miss, for the Laconos government."

"And is he here tonight?"

The bartender nodded slowly. "Upstairs."

Smiling her thanks, she turned to the man who'd approached her. "Let's go."

If he was surprised at her sudden acquiescence, he didn't show it. As a matter of fact, his face, as they made their way toward the back of the club and up the steps, bore an unmistakable stamp of relief.

It wasn't until they had walked across the upper level and stopped before a large booth that the man spoke again, not to Ana, but to another sitting inside the dimly lit booth.

"Là voici."

Although the booth was filled with people, men and women alike, Ana's gaze arrowed unerringly on one. Icanno Shala. He would be the man who wore an aura of power as easily as he did the fine linen shirt and the designer watch on his thick wrist. Although he made no attempt to rise, she thought he wasn't tall—no more than three inches taller than she. He had the swarthy complexion and stocky build of a native. One who enjoyed sampling the finer things in life.

At a casual wave of his hand, the other people in the booth rose and wandered away, to be followed by the man who'd been sent to retrieve her.

"Thank you for agreeing to see me. I hope you have not been inconvenienced." Unlike his employee, Shala's English was perfect. His smile a moment later revealed a crossed incisor. "I am Icanno Shala. If you would do me the honor of sitting…?"

Remaining where she was, Ana said, "Do you have any identification?"

The man's dark eyes blinked once. *"Pardonnez-moi?"*

"Identification. I'd like to be sure who I'm speaking to." She gave a shrug. "You can't be too careful."

Shala looked as though he couldn't decide whether to be offended or amused. He must have decided on the latter, because his smile turned rueful as he reached into his back pocket. "I suppose you are right."

She took her time looking at the ID in its glossy black case, not because she doubted its validity but to more closely examine the government seal. Isle of Laconos, it read, depicting an unsmiling Shala as minister of interior.

Snapping the case closed, she handed it back to him, along with a dazzling smile. "Forgive me if I seem overly cautious."

"Not at all." He gestured for her to sit, and she did so. "A woman traveling alone cannot be too careful."

Caution bloomed at his words. Did he assume she was alone because she was without escort, or because she'd garnered some closer attention? She wasn't given time to comment on his statement because he was already going on.

"And now you have me at a disadvantage. You know who you are speaking to, but I know only that I'm talking to a beautiful woman."

"Smith." Politely she offered her hand, watching him carefully. "Ann Smith."

He took her hand in his, holding it longer than necessary. "From your accent, I would assume you're an American. Are you enjoying your visit to our country, Miss Smith?"

"Your island is very beautiful."

He inclined his head. "I am happy to hear you say so. But even a country as beautiful as ours is not completely without problems, is it?"

His cryptic words did nothing to explain his motive for this meeting. Weighing the odds, Ana made a swift decision. "Apparently not. I believe I stumbled on a drug transaction earlier this evening."

The lack of surprise in his expression told her that her surmise had paid off. Somehow this man had learned of the scene. "So I am told. Might I ask why you did not contact our police about what you saw?"

Having made her choice, Ana gave it all she got. She shifted her gaze uneasily. "May I be perfectly frank, Mr. Shala?"

"Please."

"I'm in a strange country with a rather tumultuous recent history. I know little of the new government, and nothing of the criminal element. It would be difficult to know who to trust. Beautiful beaches can be found on any number of islands nearby. I don't want any trouble."

"Of course not." He surveyed her for a full minute, during which time she strove to look apprehensive. It wasn't much of a feat. Her heart was pounding like a locomotive.

"You didn't know if our police force was corrupt."

"I didn't mean any offense—"

He waved away her protest. "None taken. You were quite right. In some of the islands nearby graft is a very real threat for the local police. Not here, of course, but you could not know that."

It was as if something inside him relaxed as he spoke the words. Although it was barely discernible, she thought a measure of tension seeped from his frame. "There is no reason for you to become involved, of course, but I would appreciate your help. We know of the two men engaged in the transaction, you see." His teeth flashed briefly. With his crossed tooth he gave the impression of a saber-toothed tiger who had bitten off more than it could chew. "Among my responsibilities is protecting our country from unlawful drug activity. We have had the men under surveillance for some time, seeking enough information to put them away for life. The Laconos government deals with drug runners very severely."

Ana's eyes widened. "Oh, don't tell me I interrupted some of your agents when they were about to make an arrest?"

At the distress in her voice he reached across the table to pat her hand. It did not escape her notice that he failed to remove it. "No, the agents were not going to make the arrest tonight, merely gather more incriminating evidence. We hope to be led to their superiors, you see. The more carefully we prepare the case, the more far-reaching our arrests will be."

His hand felt heavy and moist on hers. Forcing herself to leave hers motionless, she wet her lips. "I just went out for some air," she lied. "I'll never forgive myself if I messed up your investigation by blundering into the middle of it.''

"We will continue. The men may go further underground, however. It may become more difficult.''

Shrugging helplessly, she said, "I feel bad about that.''

"You mustn't.'' His fingers squeezed hers in a grip that was meant to be reassuring. They felt like a vise. "However, if there is anything you can tell us about these men, perhaps our investigation will be aided.''

Nodding excitedly, she leaned forward. "I can describe both of them—oh.'' She pretended to be crestfallen. "Of course you don't need a description if you've had them under surveillance.''

Shala's voice lowered, as if soothing a dull-witted child. "No, but that is just the kind of help you might give us. Perhaps you heard them speak. Were you close enough to hear their conversation? Could you identify the language they spoke?''

"No,'' she said honestly. "I didn't hear what they said to each other. They saw me before I noticed them. Only one of the men spoke to me.'' Her shudder wasn't totally feigned. "I didn't have to understand his words to know they were threatening. He came after me with a knife.''

The hand on hers turned stroking. The look in Shala's eyes was at odds with his paternal tone. "That must have been quite frightening. How did you get away?''

She relayed the experience for him, beginning with the pepper spray and closing with how she'd lost herself in the crowd heading toward here. And all during the telling he continued to caress her hand, in a gesture that missed soothing when coupled with the way his gaze drifted over her bare shoulders and lower.

"You are a very brave woman. Very…resourceful. Many

in your situation would have frozen. How did you know what to do?''

The admiration in his tone didn't cover the fact that he was still not sure about her. Was he using a personal interest in her to disguise a more professional one? She decided he was, because it was exactly the thing she would have done in his position.

She wasn't about to tell him she'd started carrying the defensive spray when she'd commenced doing courier work for Sterling. ''I live alone in a large city in the United States.'' The address on her phony passport would verify her lie. ''It pays to be careful.''

He used the opportunity to change the subject, to ask about her fictitious life in Atlanta. He asked questions, let her talk a bit, and then switched back to the men she'd seen earlier. What language did the man address her in? How much French did she understand? After fifteen minutes of conversation it was clear to her that she was being efficiently interrogated.

Shala was smooth about it. If she hadn't had an NOPD detective for a brother she might never have realized that his sudden shifts of topics were designed to take her off guard. As it happened, she'd been interrogated by the best on enough situations to make her cognizant of what was happening right now. Cade could squeeze information from a garden hose.

''I must admit that my experience tonight has affected my decision about staying on Laconos.'' Ana steeled herself to ignore the way Shala's gaze lingered on her chest. ''I can't say I feel completely safe here.''

He protested, as she'd thought he would. ''Please do not let one unfortunate episode ruin your stay here. I can assure you it will not be repeated.''

She acted unconvinced. ''I wish I could believe that. But

yesterday while I was in the marketplace I heard rumors of some man on the loose, running from the government. Coupled with what I saw tonight…'' She shook her head. ''I don't feel comfortable being alone here.''

He followed the path she set. ''I do not mean to belittle your fears, but they are unfounded. Remember, the man who threatened you tonight is under our constant surveillance. He would not be allowed to harm you.''

''But what of that man wanted by your government? No one seems to know for sure what he's sought for, but I have my suspicions.'' She threw a quick look around, lowered her voice conspiratorially. ''Was it…murder?''

Shala gave an indulgent laugh. ''I am afraid our diligence in the search has given rise to many unfounded rumors. No, the man is merely a nuisance. He breached the security of the capitol, that is all.''

''Oh.'' Ana made a moue of disappointment. ''So he was just a thrill seeker of sorts.''

''Perhaps. At any rate, we wish only to question him about his intentions before allowing him to go on his way.'' The smile he gave was sharklike, and convinced Ana that if Shala had his say, there was no way Sam was ever going to be allowed off the island alive. She wondered what damaging information her brother had discovered that had the government so anxious to find him.

Shala lifted her fingers to his lips. ''If you remain unconvinced of your safety, perhaps I shall have to personally assure your security.''

Her first reaction was to yank her hand from his. Although his words were innocent enough, the look in his eyes was not. She ground her teeth together and smiled at him. ''You would do that for me?''

''It would be my pleasure.'' Was that his tongue touching her palm? She suppressed a shudder of revulsion. ''Tomorrow, once I am done with work for the day I would be free to escort you wherever you wish. Perhaps we could dine together and later go dancing. There is a place on the other side of the city that you will enjoy.''

She was tempted to decline. Though she lacked experience, even she knew that entrusting herself to Shala would be danger of a different sort. But before she could respond, he frowned, as though just remembering something.

''First, though, there is a government function I must attend. If you would do me the courtesy of joining me, we could dine afterward.''

Senses humming, Ana leaned forward and called on all her feminine wiles. She could only hope that Shala was more impressed by them than Jones had been. ''I would love to accompany you to the function. And then later... you could have me all to yourself.''

Her deliberate wording had his fingers tightening around hers. ''You will not find drinks and conversation with cabinet members frightfully dull?''

''I can't think of anything that would be dull with you, Icanno.''

It had taken remarkably little convincing, Ana reflected later in the taxi, for the man to agree. And far less imagination to picture the ending he had in mind for their evening together. But she thought the opportunity the evening afforded was worth the personal risk. After dinner she'd fake an illness that would have her going back to the ship, after promising to meet the man the next night. A promise she had no intention of following through with.

It could work, she thought with satisfaction, as she watched the taxi approach the dock area. And the plan allowed her access to government officials that she would normally never have. Perhaps one of them would let something drop about the hunt for Sam, or about the reason for the search.

She paid the driver and walked up the dock toward the *Nefarious*. Lights winked along its side, but it was dark aboard the ship. She wondered if Jones had returned. For the first time, she thought about what she would say to him. Even if he'd spotted her in Le Dauphin she could always pretend she hadn't seen him. The crowd there would make the excuse seem reasonable.

Still, she was glad she was going to be given time before facing him again. Slipping off her shoes, she tiptoed down the companionway into the narrow hallway below, finding her cabin in silence. The stealth required made her smile. She was a master at sneaking into the house after breaking curfew, although she'd been caught as often as not.

The door to Jones's cabin was closed. He must have given up his search and returned to the ship much earlier. Soundlessly she opened the door to her room, slipped inside and closed it behind her. She let out a little breath of relief, and set the shoes soundlessly on the floor. Her arms were at the bodice of her dress preparing to peel it down her torso before a low, angry voice pierced the shadows.

''Where the hell have you been?''

Chapter 6

Slapping one hand to her heart, Ana sought to keep it from jumping through her chest. "My God, you scared me to death. Give you a mustache and a rosary, and you could be my grandmother."

The small wall lamp above her bed was snapped on, and then Jones rose from the edge of the bunk, his face a grim mask. "If she had to keep track of you, prayers probably came in handy."

Faced with his implacable expression, Ana was once again aware of the way his presence seemed to shrink the area. Involuntarily she retreated, until her shoulders met the door. "There was no reason for you to wait up. I figured you'd be asleep." In fact, she'd counted on it.

"You're not at Disneyland," he said grimly. "You're a woman in a strange country, one that's had more than its share of unrest lately. Only an idiot would go out at night alone."

"Idiot?" The word burned, even if it served her purpose.

She wanted him to believe her a harmless ditz out for a good time, didn't she? So there was little point in telling him she was a black belt in karate and an expert marksman. Especially since neither of those facts had helped her much tonight.

"Sorry if you were worried. I just wanted to—" she swallowed as he came closer "—experience the nightlife on my own, you know? Besides, you wouldn't have liked the places I went, believe me. Too crowded."

"As it happened I did experience those places," he snapped. "Looking for you."

She let her eyes widen. "Why would you come looking for me?"

"Maybe because you seem to have the sense of a gnat and a gift for trouble."

Okay, the ditz pretense was wearing a little thin. Or maybe it was just his ready belief in it that burned. "Look, I'm sorry if you were worried, but there was no reason—"

His hand slapped the door beside her head. She winced at the restrained force behind the action. "There was every reason," he disputed, shoving his face close to hers. "Do you have any idea what can happen to a woman on her own in a place like this? Something could be slipped into your drink and you'd be out in a matter of minutes. The white slave trade is thriving these days, did you know that? Or maybe you'd be targeted for robbery, instead. People have been known to get their throats slit for the contents of their wallet."

Ana swallowed, partially at the vivid scenes he was painting, partially at his proximity. His other hand had joined the first against the door, on the opposite side of her head, effectively caging her. And she couldn't be sure whether the wild pumping of her pulse was due more to his words or to his nearness.

She had as much practice at soothing male tempers as she did at rousing them, and she called on it now. "You're right, of course. It can be dangerous for a woman out on her own. But believe it or not, I do take precautions."

Rather than mollifying him, her words seemed to enrage Jones further. His eyes slitted and his voice went low and smooth. "Do you?"

Swallowing hard, Ana forced herself to maintain his gaze. "Yes. I don't take chances, and I'm not without some self-defense training."

"Prove it."

Ana blinked. "What?"

The note of mockery in his voice was at odds with the dangerous light still burning in his eyes. "Let's see those self-defense moves of yours, baby. You've got a man cornering you, wanting more from you than you care to give. Stop me." As he spoke he moved even closer, until his shoulders blocked the rest of the room from her view. There was barely an inch between them, and the scant space was filled with a vibrating tension that simmered, warning of imminent eruption. "Maybe he's trying to seduce you out of that sexy little dress of yours." He reached down, traced one index finger across the bare skin above her breasts, where the dress ended.

He lowered his head so his voice sounded beside her ear, his breath caressing her neck. "Or maybe he doesn't care about seduction at all. Maybe he's just going to take what he wants." He hooked his finger in the top of her dress and tugged lightly. Ana shivered violently. The callused pad of his finger was grazing the top of her breast, the light contact making it all but impossible to concentrate on what he was saying. "What're ya gonna do, Annie? Huh?"

She started at his use of her nickname, her gaze flying to his. How had he known that her brothers insisted on calling her that, despite her threats of bodily harm? But in the next moment she realized her error. There was no secret knowledge in Jones's eyes, he hadn't discovered her true identity. The look she did discover there, however, turned her bones into warm, soft putty.

It took all the strength she could muster to manage a response. "Back off, Jones, before I have to hurt you." Admittedly, her words lacked conviction, but she managed to wedge her arms between them, pushing hard at his chest. He allowed himself to be moved, but only slightly.

"Talk is cheap, honey. I don't think you know how to—"

Her strangled gasp interrupted him, and he looked down, then froze. He'd dropped his hands when she'd pushed him, but hadn't remembered to disengage his finger, taking a corner of her dress with him, exposing her breast.

Ana reached to cover herself, but Jones's hand was there first. And he wasn't making any move to restore her modesty. Instead, he traced his finger around her breast, trailing a line of fire as his path moved to her nipple, before taking the taut nub between his index finger and thumb.

"Ah, damn." The muttered words seemed to be torn from him, and then he wasn't speaking at all, but kissing her, with the same restrained force that had marked his actions earlier, only with much greater effect.

The ship seemed to pitch and shift beneath her feet, although it was rocking gently against the dock. Jones's mouth ate at hers, weakening her knees and shredding her resistance. Coupled with the shockingly intimate touch on her breast, Ana's senses whirled, then imploded. The stateroom became steamy with heat.

She clutched at his shoulders as he crowded her against the door, her lips parted beneath his, as desperate longing flashed through her. She'd wanted this, from the first time he'd kissed her. Wanted to see him lose control, to react without that careful caustic guard of his. The reality shattered anything she could have imagined.

His touch wasn't controlled at all this time, but a little rough, a little wild. This wasn't a man like any other she'd known, whose timid or grasping touch had annoyed or disappointed by turns. Jones knew exactly what he was doing, and the result was devastating.

Her tongue answered the demand of his and she shuddered as he sucked at it, tested it lightly between his teeth. It wasn't until she felt his second hand on her other breast that she realized he'd tugged the bodice completely down and held her half naked, pinned against the door.

And it wasn't enough. She raised one hand to thread through his hair and pulled him closer. Ever closer. With the other she tugged at his shirt, yanking it higher so she could feel his skin against hers. And then shuddered when he pressed his bare chest against hers.

She couldn't tell whose heart was pounding more loudly. She felt his hand shove up her skirt, smooth along her thigh, and almost sighed. When his fingers grazed her mound, a gasp was torn from her. Then his hand was on her bottom, squeezing the softness there.

A fist of desire clenched low in her belly. Her palms found the smooth skin on his sides, and skated down to the low-riding khakis on his slim hips. She brushed the back of her fingers beneath his navel and felt his stomach muscles contract beneath her fingers. His reaction brought a pleased hum of satisfaction, which turned to a strangled gasp when he lowered his mouth to her nipple.

Dark sensual colors exploded behind her eyelids when he sucked strongly from her, drawing a sob from her throat. She pressed closer, wanting more of the erotic torment, unsure if she could stand it. His other hand left her bottom and caressed her thigh, before slipping his fingers beneath the elastic in her panties and touching her intimately.

She jerked in shock, a violent, involuntary reaction that she regretted as soon as she felt him freeze, to remain shuddering and unmoving against her. Then a moment later he was releasing her, with a suddenness that left her bereft.

"Damn."

Dragging her eyelids open, she saw him jam a hand through his hair, take a step back. And although it was on the tip of her tongue to plead with him to return, she knew it would be in vain.

"Annie."

He didn't say any more. He didn't need to. With trembling hands she pulled the dress back up over her breasts, then smoothed the skirt down where it rode high on her thighs. She wished she could control the shaking in her limbs.

Jones looked away and muttered an expletive. Then with the air of a man faced with an unpleasant task, he turned toward her again. "Look…I'm sorry."

Sorry. Her incredulous gaze flew to his. He was *sorry?*

"This was my fault. All of it."

Desire, which had only moments ago been honed to fever pitch, turned neatly, irrevocably to anger. "Did you hear me assigning blame?"

"No, but you should. I was just trying to get you to see…" He had the grace to look uncomfortable. "Well, it doesn't matter. I should never have touched you, not like that."

"No, of course not." There was strength to be found in anger, Ana discovered, which she embraced. It was infinitely preferable to the hurt that threatened to bloom. "It wouldn't do for me to get the wrong idea, now, would it?"

"No." Because he was focused on tucking his shirt back

into the waistband of his pants, he missed the glare she speared at him. "I had no right to come on so strong. What I had to say could have, should have, waited until morning."

"Let's talk about rights, shall we?" She moved away from the door because she certainly didn't want to keep him from leaving. Far from it. "While you're apologizing, why don't we talk about your right to follow me in the first place, to tell me what I should and shouldn't do while we're in dock here."

He looked up, his gaze narrowing. "That's not about rights, it's about good sense."

"Oh?"

He must not have sensed the danger in the word, because he went on. "I don't make a habit of meddling in people's lives, but you…you need a damn keeper. I had to follow you for your own good."

Her simmering anger went to boil. How many times had she heard the same words from one of her brothers? "You know, as a general rule I've never cared much for things done for my own good."

His jaw hardened. "Most people don't, but I couldn't just stand by and let you put yourself into a possibly dangerous situation, could I?"

"Why not?"

Her blunt question seemed to take him by surprise. He stared at her a moment, then rubbed his jaw. "Damned if I know."

He may not know, Ana thought desolately, but she could guess at it easily enough. "Don't tell me you were trying to protect me?" He couldn't know how much she yearned to hear him answer in the negative.

"Yeah." The admission obviously pained him. He didn't

seem any happier with his answer than she was. "I guess I do. Feel kind of protective."

Bubbles of fury began to surge in her veins. It was a welcome contrast to the pain in her heart. "I see." She nodded wisely. "Sort of like the feeling a guy has for his sister."

He shrugged uneasily. "Maybe."

"Well, that brings up a rather interesting definition of family you must have, given the last few minutes, but we won't get into that."

It pleased her to hear a snap return to his voice. It was preferable to the note of regret that had been there earlier.

"Look, I'm not going to apologize…"

"That's a welcome change."

"…for my intentions. I was trying to make sure you didn't get yourself into a situation that you couldn't get out of."

"I'm going to assume that we're talking about me going downtown alone and not about what happened between us a few moments ago."

He had the grace to look chagrined. "I don't blame you for being mad. I said it was my fault, didn't I? It won't happen again." When she only looked away, blinking rapidly, he paused for a moment before starting for the door.

She let him reach it before crossing over to him. "Jones…"

"What?"

Rather than speak, she looked up at him, her eyes swimming with tears. Watched him swallow hard, saw his expression soften infinitesimally. Then she plowed her fist into his belly and gave a satisfied smile when the breath whooshed out of him. Her voice steady, she said, "That's a little sampling of my self-defense moves. Once you can breathe again, be sure and tell me what you think."

* * *

There was no cover over the porthole in his cabin. Jones had never wanted one. He liked being able to see the stars, liked even better to lie nude on the deck beneath them, with only the balmy night air as a blanket. But right now he wasn't contemplating the stars or the midnight blue of the sky they studded. He was merely using the view to wipe out the one that seemed branded on his memory.

Testing, he closed his eyes again. Once again Annie's image swam across the surface of his mind. He snapped his eyes open, rolled over and buried his head in the pillow. But he couldn't prevent the memory of the tiny gasps she made as he'd taken her nipple in his mouth. His palms tingled as if they still remembered the feel of her silky thigh, that tight round bottom.

And knew the torment was no less than he deserved. Where the hell had that violent welter of emotion come from? He'd spent so long feeling little or nothing at all that it had been a shock to feel the bubbling surge of protectiveness, of anger. Of concern. Even more shocking when that unusual level of emotion had turned so suddenly to a scalding, primitive desire.

With a groan, he turned over and propped his crossed arms beneath his head. He was losing his edge. It wasn't necessarily reason for alarm. He had the thought, and tried to believe it. Five years away from the dark alleys and furtive shadows, instincts were bound to dull a little, weren't they?

That was the least of his concerns at the moment. Where was the cool objectivity that had layered his instincts for so long? He shook his head, baffled. He hadn't expected a compact, tousled little blonde to slip under his defenses, even for a moment. The fact that she'd done just that still stung, but the sensation would serve as a reminder. It had been a miracle that he'd lived through it the last time he'd lowered his guard. He'd never been a man who made the same mistake twice.

Punching his pillow, he turned on his side and firmly closed his eyes. Since he wasn't one to believe in divine intervention, he wasn't about to tempt fate again. Ann Smith could do whatever the hell she wanted. Worship witches beneath the moon. Swim with sharks. Dance naked in the streets. He wouldn't interfere. All he had to do was hang on for the rest of this trip, then he'd never see the woman again.

And when his gut clenched at the thought, he did a damn good job of convincing himself that the sensation was one of relief.

The sun was high overhead before Jones went on deck. He couldn't remember the last time he'd slept that late, but sleep had proved elusive. The sky had begun to lighten before he'd dropped off. Even then his dreams had been full of a tempting pint-size blonde, so the slumber hadn't been particularly restful. It seemed, he thought morosely, as he took up a stance against the rail, there was no escaping the female. At least not for the next few days.

He was raising his second mug of coffee to his lips when he became aware that he wasn't alone on the deck. Glancing sideways, he saw the woman responsible for his sleepless night seated in one of the lounge chairs, purse at her feet, writing diligently in a notebook.

He studied her for a moment. He didn't know when the nickname had come to him, but she didn't look like an Ann. She was too diminutive for the more formal name. If she were his he'd call her Annie. It seemed to fit better, seemed to capture her bright spirit.

Derision filled him at the thought. He, better than anyone, should know just how little a name told about a person.

Alias Smith and Jones

And she wasn't his, at any rate. He wasn't in the habit of staking claims on women. And if he were, it certainly wouldn't be one who was part tempting seductress, part shy innocent.

Grimly he faced forward again. He'd known he was going to have to deal with this moment at some point, but would have preferred doing so when he wasn't still bleary from lack of sleep. Still, despite her ire when he'd apologized last night, he was responsible for what had happened between them. No doubt she was going to feel embarrassed this morning. Despite what she said about boyfriends and restraining orders, there was no question that his experience far outweighed hers.

She was probably dreading this encounter even more than he was. The thought had him feeling slightly avuncular. It wouldn't kill him to go out of his way to break the ice. Surely there was something he could say that would make the situation less uncomfortable for her.

"I thought you were going to miss it altogether."

Surprised at her words, he turned and lifted a brow.

"This beautiful morning," she explained. "I love days like this, don't you? The sky is absolutely cloudless. A day like this seems to hold promises."

Her sunny tone took him off guard. "Yeah, it's great." He searched her face carefully, but could discern only a lazy contentment in her expression. So much for the embarrassment he'd wanted to spare her.

A cowardly part of him was tempted to take the opportunity she was offering and pretend last night had never happened. But taking the easy way out often had a way of coming back to bite him on the ass. So he plowed ahead with what needed to be said. "Look, about last night…"

"Yes, I've been thinking about that, too." Tilting her glasses down her nose, she stared at him over the top of them. "I've deducted two hundred dollars from your fee for your behavior."

He felt as if he'd just been sideswiped by a tank. "Two hundred…"

"I thought that was fair, because, well, let's face it, you behaved abominably. You promised exemplary service, but last night really deserved a five-hundred-dollar deduction."

His jaw clenched. Was she actually trying to lowball his fee? "Listen…"

She went on as if he hadn't spoken. "But I wasn't blameless in the matter myself. I was kissing you back, and then there's that punch I landed."

Between set teeth, he ground out, "Don't worry about it. You hit like a girl."

Glaring at him, she said, "I certainly do not. And you're missing the point. I'm willing to accept partial responsibility for the whole affair. That's why I'm only deducting two hundred instead of the whole five. I've made a note of it." She indicated the notebook.

"What is that? Your little book of grievances?"

She slipped the glasses back up on her nose, then replaced the notebook in her purse. "If you're not able to discuss this reasonably right now, we can put it off until later."

His temples throbbed with a headache that had been absent until she started talking. "Fine. Great. Deduct your two hundred. But we forget about this now, right? It's all behind us?"

The smile she gave him was as dazzling as the sun on the water, and somehow made his head pound more. "It's already forgotten. As a matter of fact, I wanted to talk to you about trying out one of the beaches today. Whichever one you think. I need to be back here by four or so, though, so we should probably get started soon."

"Sure." At least the conversation had turned back to business. If they could keep it on this level for the rest of the trip, he might make it through the next few days without strangling her. "Are you meeting your friends here later?"

"My what?" Her tone was blank.

"Your friends. You said you'd be meeting them..."

"Oh, right. Yes, they should probably arrive later today. I've left messages at the hotels for them so they know how to get in touch with me. But this evening I have a date. That's why I need to get back, so I'll have time to get ready."

"A date?"

She nodded, raised her face to the sun. "Mmm-hmm. And I'm sure that won't be a problem for you, because you've already assured me that your behavior last night was an aberration."

His knuckles were white from the strength of his grip around the mug. Then it suddenly occurred to him what was going on here. Something inside him eased. "Okay. No problem. I'll be sure to get you home in time for this...date."

Something in his tone must have alerted her. She raised her head to look at him. "I do have a date."

"Sure you do. The nearest beach is only twenty minutes from here. You'll have plenty of time in the sun before you need to come back."

She sat up straight on the lounger, swept off her glasses and glared at him. "You don't think I have a date."

"Doesn't matter." He checked his watch. "We'll pull anchor as soon as I finish my coffee."

"You egotistical baboon." Sparks were spitting from her eyes. "You can't believe I'd make up that story just for your benefit, do you?"

"Actually…" He pretended to consider her words. "Yeah, I do. But it's not necessary."

For a moment he thought she was going to throw something at him. She looked around as though searching for weapons. "I don't know what kind of women you're used to—well, I have a pretty good idea—but I don't need to make up stories to impress men."

"It's okay," he soothed, feeling more cheerful than he had in hours. "We're starting over, remember? I'll let you know when we get there." He started toward the bridge.

"For your information, I'm meeting Icanno Shala this evening."

The name stopped him dead in his tracks. Disbelievingly, he turned back to look at her. "You're meeting who?"

"Whom. You've heard of him? He's minister of the interior, I guess. First we're going to a government function of some kind and then to dinner."

He retraced his steps. "Don't even joke about that."

"I'm not joking." Replacing the glasses, she slipped down to a more comfortable position in her chair. "I met him last night and he seemed…" Was that a slight hesitation in her voice? "…very charming."

Jones had to reach for calm. Strong-arm tactics weren't going to work. If he'd learned anything about her, it was that. "If you're serious, you need to rethink your plans. Shala doesn't have the best reputation with women." She didn't have to say a word. The lift of her brows said it all. "Okay, think what you want about me, but this guy isn't the most savory in the new government. And if he gets you alone, you aren't going to have a lot of options, have you thought of that? With his power he can get away with pretty much anything."

Her shrug was careless. "What makes you think I'll want options?"

"I'm not kidding, Annie." He crossed to her chair and towered above her. "This isn't some high school boy you can lead around by the hormones. You're way out of your league here."

"Is it my imagination or are you getting protective again?"

This time it was him plucking the glasses from her nose. "Knock it off. This is serious. Write a note making an excuse, and I'll have Pappy deliver it."

"No."

He squatted down beside her, his gaze doing battle with hers. "I don't know what games you think you're going to play with this guy…"

"And I don't know which is more offensive—the fact that you've already regressed back to the Neanderthal of last night or the fact that you think I'm a virginal idiot."

When he merely looked at her, she had the grace to flush. But her voice was stubborn. "I'm not totally inexperienced. There have been plenty of men. Scores."

The corner of his mouth lifted. "Yeah, right."

If the daggers shooting from her eyes were real, he'd be lying slashed and bleeding on the deck. "There have!"

"Save your stories for someone who cares. I'm just giving you fair warning. I'd do the same for any client of mine. If you don't want to listen—" he shrugged and rose "—that's your problem."

"I did listen. Now you need to listen to me. I can handle Shala."

"The way you handled me last night?" Where those words had come from he didn't know. But rather than eliciting the storm he'd expected, she merely shoved her glasses back up on her nose and reached into her bag for a paperback.

"Not exactly." She gave a delicate yawn. "Wake me up when we get there, will you?"

Without another word he turned on his heel and headed for the bridge. Three days, he consoled himself, tamping down his temper. Seventy-two hours. Four thousand three hundred twenty minutes. A mere drop in the overall concept of time.

Then why the hell did it suddenly seem so endless?

Chapter 7

The sand on the beach was as fine as granulated sugar and just as bright. The sun reflecting off the turquoise sea was blinding. Seagulls wheeled and slashed across the impossibly clear sky. And all of it was wasted on Ana.

There was a snake in her paradise.

Jones lay beside her on his stomach, head buried in his arms, for all appearances taking a nap. She measured the space between his prone body and the good-size piece of driftwood nearby. It would give her the utmost pleasure to brain him with it.

It had never occurred to her that he would need to accompany her to shore. The ship was too large, and the depth of water too shallow, for the *Nefarious* to be anchored nearby. Jones had directed her to follow him into a small dinghy carried on the side of the ship, lowered it to the water and fired up its small outboard motor.

Unable to remain still a moment longer, she jumped up, jammed her feet in her sandals, and strode off. There were a couple dozen people on the beach with them, scattered about in brightly colored dabs on the sand. Yet it wasn't the people who held her attention, but the rim where the beach met jungle.

She studied the tangled vegetation in the distance and wished she'd brought binoculars. From the research she'd done before she'd left the States, she'd discovered that Laconos had only one major city on the island, with a few other villages scattered about in the area. The towns were all close to the shore and to fresh water. Crystalline beaches bordered the island, while the center was covered with thick jungle.

And it was in that jungle where she thought Sam might be hiding.

There were few other possibilities. She hardly thought he could hide this long in town, and unless he'd already found a way off the island, what better way to elude the military than in the midst of that dense vegetation?

She didn't doubt his ability to do just that and survive. But without knowing how badly he was injured, there was no way of guessing whether he remained hidden because he was physically unable to leave or because he just hadn't yet devised a way off the island.

The key to the search for her brother, she thought for at least the hundredth time since last night, might well lie with Icanno Shala. She'd like to hear what the man thought about Sam's whereabouts—where they'd searched and where they were planning to look next. If it hadn't been for her thirst for information about her brother, she would never have accepted his invitation. She didn't need Jones's assessment of the man to guess his intentions.

Just the thought of Jones had her walking faster. She thought she'd done a passable job this morning covering the hurt, the anger that had so rapidly replaced her passion last night. Dismay at the memory simmered in her belly. She'd lived her life struggling beneath her family's suffocating mantle of protectiveness. Her brothers were motivated at least in part from the words emblazoned on the Tremaine family crest. Honor. Duty. Devotion. All three of her siblings devoted their lives to that code. But she'd never been able to make them understand that because of their interference, her life was devoid of the same sense of purpose. Their overprotectiveness had robbed her of any chance for independence. It was the last emotion she wanted to elicit from Jones. The very last.

Weary of her inner turmoil, she directed her attention to the matter at hand. Scanning the dense thicket of vegetation, she thought of Sam hiding in there somewhere. Almost definitely injured. Maybe even badly. But whatever shape he was in, he had to be looking for a way off the island. How was she going to help him with that if she had no way of knowing where he was?

"What are you looking for?"

The sleep-roughened voice startled her. Jerking around, she saw Jones at her side, watching her with an enigmatic expression on his face.

"No one." It took a moment before she realized what she'd said, and she hastened to cover. "I mean, nothing. I was just wondering…do they sell jungle tours?"

"Probably." He hadn't donned his shoes, she noted. Except for the damp denim shorts he wore, he was completely bare. "I wouldn't recommend one unless you were fully inoculated before coming here. It's not worth the risk."

She didn't care to reveal that inoculations of any kind had been the last thing she'd worried about before making arrangements for the trip. Somehow the dangers of contracting malaria didn't seem as real as her fears for her brother. "I don't want one of those touristy kinds," she said. "I'd rather go deeper, see more…" Her voice trailed off under his unswerving scrutiny.

"If I tell you how incredibly stupid that idea is, am I going to get written down in your little book of grievances again?"

"It was just a thought," she said sulkily. And upon closer consideration, probably not a very good one. What were the chances she'd find Sam's hiding place even if she could enlist someone to help her search? And there was no way she could conduct such a exploration with an islander's help without running the risk of her actions being discovered by the government.

The frustration she felt sounded in her voice. "You know, I'm surprised you have any customers if you constantly insult their intelligence."

"With most of my customers I don't find it necessary."

"Of course, you probably don't get many repeats, either," she muttered. She lengthened her strides as she walked the shoreline. It was maddening that he didn't need to adjust his own to keep up with her.

"What is it with you, anyway?" His voice sounded genuinely curious. "What's with this constant need to flit from one adventure to another? Do you just not have anything better to do with your time? Or more money than sense?"

This time he must have been prepared, because the elbow she sent into his gut didn't seem to faze him. The knowledge rankled almost as much as his words. "I never flit."

"From where I'm standing, you look like a world-class flitter. Island hopping, meeting friends in the tropics, jungle tours…not to mention cozying up to a world-class sleaze like Shala. Maybe it's time you got a bit of focus."

The message, the faint note of condemnation in his voice, summed up her growing restlessness with her life a little too neatly. She whirled on him. "Where do you get off judging me? You? As near as I can tell you're a dropout from society making a living by taking money from rich tourists. At least I have a real job.''

"Doing what?"

Belated caution tempered her response. It wouldn't do to blurt out her sensitive work for Tremaine Technologies. ''I work for a software company.'' The vague answer didn't hint at the highly confidential nature of her assignment for the encryption/decryption security division. The job was challenging. But it didn't stem her growing dissatisfaction.

And because that dissatisfaction circled, threatened to swamp her, she lashed out. ''So what about you? Is that scar on your back the reason you're hiding out in the middle of nowhere?''

He stilled, was silent for a time. ''I guess you could say that,'' he surprised her by saying finally. ''There's something about a bullet in the back that makes you reevaluate your choices.''

He seemed as startled as she by the revelation. She was silent, mulling over what he'd revealed. It hadn't taken a bullet to convince her that her life needed examining. Trouble was, the questions never seemed to bring any answers. How did she discover who Analiese Tremaine was without leaving everything she held dear, everyone she loved?

Sometimes she wondered if leaving Tangipohoa Parish wasn't her only option. There she was merely a compilation of others' perceptions, expectations. The trouble with the insulation she experienced at home was that it shielded her from making the kind of decisions, even the mistakes, that others learned from. Jones would never known how close his casual assessment had come to the truth.

Tired of the all-too-familiar path her thoughts were taking, she shifted her thoughts back to him, taking advantage of his unusual verbosity. ''Who shot you? A pirate?''

"No, my partner."

He wheeled around then, started back toward their blanket. She was left to stare after him, unable to follow. She didn't know what to say to him, anyway, after that disclosure. His tone had been flat, with no hint of the emotion that would have had to accompany such an event. She had vivid experience with memories that haunted in the night. Ana wished she hadn't pressed Jones to reveal his.

She felt an unusual trepidation as she came up on deck that evening, dressed for her date with Shala. The feeling intensified when she saw Jones sprawled out in a lounger, beer in his hands, dark glasses covering his eyes. Although she couldn't see his gaze, she could feel it as it traveled over her form clad in the pale yellow silk dress. It warmed her skin more thoroughly than the rapidly sinking evening sun.

Distracting herself from the sensation, she asked, "Who was that?"

"Who?"

She pointed at the man who was even now scurrying away from the ship. "Him."

"Just someone with a message for me."

It was clear that he wasn't going to offer more information. With a great deal of effort, she prevented herself from asking for any, and focused on the conversation ahead.

Steeled for another argument about her plans for the evening, she was nonplussed when he reached into the small cooler beside him.

"Beer?"

"I...no thanks." She did sit down in the chair he lazily shoved toward her, though, watching him carefully as she sat on its edge. "You seem...relaxed."

And he did. Obscenely so. Compared to the tense, terse mood that had enveloped him since his cryptic words on the beach, right now he looked about as energetic as a sloth.

Oddly enough, the pose had her instincts heightening. Nerves danced down her vertebrae. "Well, I'm leaving now."

Tipping the beer to his lips, he took a long swallow before lowering it and nodding. "Figured. I got you a cab."

Startled, she turned and gazed down the pier. "That wasn't necessary. Icanno was going to send a car for me." As if in response to her words, a black limo cruised to a halt next to the waiting taxi.

Jones gave a negligible shrug. "No problem. I can cancel the taxi."

Something was definitely off here. He was entirely too laid-back. She watched him suspiciously. "You're going to stick to our agreement, right?"

Again the bottle was raised to his lips, and when he finished drinking, he lowered it to his chest. She followed its descent with her gaze, noted the way the condensation from the bottle transferred to his bare skin. Inexplicably her throat tightened.

"And what agreement might that be?"

Senses oddly scattered, she replied, "No interference in my plans."

"You've got your plans for this evening—" he reached over lazily and indicated the cooler "—and I've got mine."

With difficulty she tore her eyes away from the moisture collecting on his chest. "Good. Great, then."

"You'd better go." Although the dark glasses shaded his eyes, she had the distinct impression he'd closed them. "Your driver's waiting."

Shala's driver. She took a deep breath, and her grip tightened on the handle of the oversize bag she carried in lieu of a purse. She'd be much better served if she focused on the upcoming evening and how to elicit information from Shala while evading his lecherous moves, than by focusing on the lone drop of condensation tracing a lazy path down Jones's torso. Not that she noticed that sort of thing as a general rule, but the man was the picture of sexy male indolence. So it was difficult to say why she had the impression of a lazy male panther ready to pounce.

Jerkily she rose, turned away. She was imagining things. Jones clearly had nothing more in mind than drinking himself into oblivion tonight. Which would fit beautifully with her own plans. At least she wouldn't have to worry about dealing with him once she'd eluded Shala at the end of the evening.

But making her way off the ship and down the dock, she couldn't shake the feeling that the man at her back was even more of a danger than the one she was about to meet.

The little government function that Shala had described proved to be something a bit more formal. The silent driver took Ana to the heart of the city, to a tall narrow white building flanked on either side by equally nondescript structures. When the guards checked the driver's ID and waved them through the iron gates, the car progressed up a curved, crushed-shell drive and pulled to a stop before the wide expanse of stone steps.

Icanno Shala descended the steps as a white-jacketed servant opened the door for Ana. "Miss Smith," Shala said, ducking to take her hand and help her from the car. "It is a pleasure to see you again."

"And you, Icanno." She made sure her smile didn't waver when he failed to relinquish her hand. "I feel a little disoriented. It occurred to me on the way over here that I had no idea where I was going."

The man at her side gave an indulgent laugh and tucked her hand beneath his arm. "Welcome to my country's capitol building. My offices are upstairs, as are many others. We are hosting a foreign dignitary this week, and this function is in his honor."

Foreign dignitary. Ana's senses sharpened. Despite her queasiness at Shala's attentions, the evening could prove to be more filled with opportunities than she'd hoped.

Shala led her into the open-air foyer of the building and through a series of hallways. The quarters were narrow, but opulently decorated. She recognized examples of native art interspersed with portraits. She would have liked to stop and examine them further, but Shala was propelling her in the direction of voices.

Ana found herself in a space large enough to swallow its hundred or so occupants. It was the first room she'd seen in the place without open-air windows. An effort, she supposed, at security.

She slowed, feigned uncertainty. "Icanno, are you sure I'm dressed appropriately?" The dress wasn't traditionally formal. Shala was wearing a dark suit and sedate tie, as were most of the men in attendance. The women, though, were dressed in brightly colored cocktail dresses that made Ana's look like nun attire.

His hand tightened around hers. "You are a vision, Ann. I promise our stay here will be brief. I am selfish enough to want you all to myself."

Smiling up at him, she said, "I certainly understand that a man of your standing must have pressing duties. I don't mind waiting until you've fulfilled your obligations here."

They were greeted then by a cluster of people, and Shala made introductions. As he reeled off the names, she wished she'd done more research on the island government. Boswi Awano, Serpitei Agahei, Teril Montai…within moments

Ana's head was whirling. Shala didn't bother with anything other than the names, so it was impossible for her to tell what the other guests' functions in the government were.

"Are you enjoying your visit on our island, Miss Smith?" Awano's English, unlike Shala's, was slow and halting. He was shorter than Ana, with walnut-colored eyes almost hidden in a deeply wrinkled face.

"Very much," she assured him. "Despite a rather frightening experience last night, Icanno has assured me it is quite safe here."

"She stumbled on some rather rough characters," Shala put in smoothly. "I assured her that our local police force would take care of them."

From the grip on her hand, Ana had the distinct impression that he didn't want her to discuss the matter in more detail. Her supposition was realized when he excused himself and steered her toward another group of people.

"I'm sorry, Icanno," she said, sotto voce. "I'm afraid I wasn't thinking. Would you prefer I didn't mention those two I ran into last night?"

"I am probably being overly cautious, but there is no reason to risk sensitive details of our investigation getting out," he said smoothly.

"I'm sure you're right." She gazed up at him, wide-eyed. "You must have a great deal of experience in matters like this."

"Dealing with unpleasantness is a small but necessary part of my job." She started when his hand rose to cup her bare shoulder, where it lay, heavy and moist. "But I am very committed to seeing to my country's continued well-being. The rewards far outweigh the challenges."

They drifted from one group to another for a while, engaging in small talk. It didn't escape her notice that he walked by one cluster in a corner of the room without stop-

ping, and she glanced at the people standing there. All
seemed to be listening to the man in the center of the group.
She wondered if he was the dignitary Shala had spoken of.
But as the moments passed, the question lessened in im-
portance as Ana's nerves strung even tauter. Maybe her
growing unease stemmed from the fact that Shala rarely let
an opportunity go by without touching her. A stroke of her
arm, a hand resting proprietarily at the small of her
back…it was getting increasingly difficult to smile and pretend she was unaffected by it. And equally difficult to shake
the feeling that his behavior masked a certain watchfulness.

Ana focused on smiling, answering when needed, laughing on cue, while she puzzled over Shala's behavior. If she
hadn't been observing him so closely, she might not have
noticed that his gaze went again and again to the doorway.
Or the way he stiffened a fraction when a man came in,
nodded in his direction, before moving toward the refresh-
ments.

Senses alert, she wasn't at all surprised when he bent
forward, murmured in her ear, "I am anxious for us to
leave here and spend the rest of the evening alone. Would
you mind one more introduction before we go?"

"No, not at all." She turned to accompany him and desperately hoped that her frayed nerves didn't show. "I have
to admit to being a bit hungry myself."

Forcing her limbs to relax was made harder by the pos-
sessive hand he stroked down her spine, before settling on
her hip. "Soon we will take care of our…appetites. First
there is someone I'd like you to meet."

They moved down the hallway and turned, mounting
some stairs. Ana noted her surroundings surreptitiously.
Rows of closed doors dotted the hallways, making her believe she was being led to the office area of the building.
They turned and mounted another set of stairs, and she

pretended to listen as Shala pointed out the artwork that adorned the walls, featuring portraits of ancestors of the royal family. She would have liked to stop and study the one of Owahano Bunei, the prince who'd recently wiped out his entire family before taking his own life, but she was guided past it and down the marble hall before Shala stopped and rapped on a door, announcing himself.

Opening the door, he ushered her inside a huge richly decorated room. It seemed as much living area as office. Couches and chairs were scattered at one end, while an acre-wide desk of polished walnut stretched across the opposite wall.

It was the man behind the desk who commanded Ana's attention now. Tall and exceedingly thin, he had the still, watchful air that reminded her, fleetingly, of Jones. There the similarity ended, however. This man's cheekbones were prominent above sunken cheeks, giving him a cadaver-like appearance. When he rose, he towered over her by at least a foot.

"Our Royal Highness, Osawa Bunei." Shala bowed his head. "Please meet Miss Ann Smith."

The king extended a hand. "How good of you to come."

Ana managed a properly awed smile as the king's cool, dry palm closed over her own. But inside the adrenaline was pumping. "It is an honor, Your Highness."

He indicated for both of them to take a seat before his desk. "Minister Shala has informed me of your unfortunate episode yesterday evening. I trust you were not injured?"

Mind rapidly working, she replied smoothly, "No, I was shaken up, but Icanno…Minister Shala has convinced me of my safety here on your island."

A look flashed between the two men. "As well he should. Although not completely without crime, our country has a low tolerance for criminals. Rest assured that the man who attacked you will be brought to justice very soon. We do, however, feel badly about your misfortune.''

"I hold no lasting fears about your wonderful country. Icanno has assured me that the scene I witnessed is very rare.''

"He is correct." The king reached out one long, narrow hand to pick up the gold pen on his desktop. Twirling the pen between his slender fingers, he noted, "And I am quite pleased to hear that your fears have been allayed. The tourism industry is becoming more and more important to our economy. We wouldn't want anything to negatively impact our future in that area.''

Nerves were rapping at the base of her skull. "I can assure you that my lasting impressions of your country will center on its beauty and the charm of the people.''

"Good." He gave a slight wave of his hand, and a servant sidled forward with a tray of drinks. Ana accepted one, wondering when the woman had entered the room. She'd been so engrossed in the scene playing out that she hadn't noticed.

"Although I've been to your country, I am afraid I have never visited Georgia. Is Atlanta a large city?''

Tension spiked through her limbs. Because even as she answered the question, she was certain that Shala had already briefed the king on her background. And much like the minister had the night before, the man used the seemingly congenial conversation to extract more information from her. No, this wasn't her first trip abroad, she answered once, remembering Ann Smith's phony passport documents. But she'd never been to this country before. Yes, this was the first time she'd witnessed a crime. She'd been quite shaken by the experience.

"In your fright, Miss Smith, did you recognize what type of transaction you had stumbled on?''

Truth, as much as she could afford, seemed the most reliable option. "It looked like a drug transaction, Your Highness. Our papers in the States are full of accounts of successful busts. I recognized the bars of cocaine."

The gold pen was threaded through those long narrow fingers. "I hope you recognize how fortunate you are. A lone woman escaping two dangerous criminals..." He shrugged. "It could have gone much differently."

"The experience was harrowing. I realize how lucky I was."

The conversation began to take on the aspect of a verbal tennis match. And as she warded off the questions she became convinced that this meeting was the real reason behind her presence here tonight. Perhaps she hadn't convinced Shala of her reasons for not going to the police the previous evening. Or maybe he'd failed to convince the king of her harmlessness.

Or perhaps her imagination was working overtime and she was conjuring up problems where none existed.

She sipped from her drink to ease the dryness in her throat, found it difficult to swallow.

"Tell me, what do you do in Atlanta, Miss Smith?"

"I run a small antique gallery," she lied. "I've been blessed with some modest success."

His deep expressionless eyes reminded her of a shark's. "Ah, a businesswoman. I have always found the American career women to be very...pragmatic."

It was another twenty minutes before the king rose, clearly dismissing her. "It was a pleasure meeting you, Miss Smith." His dry voice sounded like the rustle of fall leaves. "I will leave you in Minister Shala's capable hands. I trust you will enjoy the rest of your visit."

Overcome with relief, she murmured a goodbye and turned toward the door.

"Icanno, I'd like a word with you before you leave. Perhaps you can have someone escort Miss Smith downstairs."

Senses sharpening, Ana smiled at Shala and said, "I think I can find my way." His absence, even for a few minutes, might give her an opportunity to snoop around some of the offices on the floor below them for information on Sam.

In the next moment that tenuous plan was dashed when the king said smoothly, "That won't be necessary." He leaned forward and pressed a button mounted on the side of his desk. Seconds later a man entered soundlessly, making Ana wonder where he'd been lurking earlier.

"I won't be long, Ann." Shala turned to her, took one of her hands in his. "Jamal will return you safely to the party downstairs. I'll join you shortly."

She followed the silent Jamal out of the room and down the hallway. But her attention wasn't on the stiff posture of the man before her. It was on the closed doors lining the hallways on the floors they descended before they reentered the formal gathering room. She looked at the unsmiling man and said, "I think I'll sit down and wait for Icanno."

Her words were meant to send him on his way, but he remained at her side. "I will wait."

Seconds ticked by. "That isn't really necessary," she said firmly.

He didn't respond, but neither did he move.

Ana mentally kissed away her plans for exploring the upper floors. There didn't seem to be any way to extricate herself from the stoic man at her side. She shot him a sideways glance. Unless…

Pressing her hand to her stomach, she took a deep breath, arranged her features into a distressed expression. "You… you wouldn't be able to find me something for nausea, would you? I'm afraid that champagne on an empty stomach wasn't a good idea.''

Jamal looked at her, clearly torn between two equally distasteful prospects. He didn't want to rouse Shala's ire, but neither did he look excited at the possibility of having her throw up on his shiny black shoes.

To help make up his mind, she raised her hand to her lips and gave a low moan of discomfort. Jamal swallowed hard, sidled away. ''I will see what I can find.''

Ana watched him leave the room with ill-disguised haste, and mentally dusted her hands together. She'd stayed home from school more than once with that little play, until Cade had come home unexpectedly one day and found her eating chocolate-covered cherries while she danced to MTV. Her brothers had been a little more difficult to convince after that.

Losing no time, she leaped from her chair and rushed from the room, hopefully leaving the impression of a woman in desperate need of the nearest rest room.

When Ana got to the hallway she walked swiftly toward the stairs and slipped up them. If someone stopped and questioned her, she could always continue with her illness story.

Since Shala had indicated his offices were on the second floor, it was toward that area she headed now. She half expected to meet him coming down, but the halls were empty and dimly lit. Her footsteps sounded loud to her own ears, the lone sound eerie in the near darkness.

She tried the knob on the first door. Locked. Moving on, she tried the next ones, and hit pay dirt on the third. Easing it open, she slipped inside before closing it behind her and leaning her shoulders against it. Now it was her heartbeat that sounded raucously in the darkness. It felt as though it were practically jumping out of her chest.

Taking a deep breath, she reached into her bag and fumbled for the penlight flashlight. She hadn't been quite sure what she'd need for this excursion tonight, so she'd thrown in anything she could think of that might be helpful. It took several moments before her fingers found the flashlight and she withdrew it, clicking it on.

There was no way to tell who the office belonged to. Not wasting any time, Ana went to the desk, knelt before it and began pulling open the drawers and rifling through them.

A few minutes later she called it quits. The office obviously belonged to someone in charge of city services. There would be no information about Sam to be found here.

Snapping off the flashlight, she eased the door open a fraction, listened carefully. Not hearing anything, she peeked out and saw nothing but darkness. She pulled the door shut behind her and headed for the next one. To her surprise, this one was unlocked, too. Blessing her good fortune, she slid inside and closed the door behind her. This time she had a little more luck. The correspondence on the desk indicated its occupant was connected to the military. Hadn't Shala indicated that the military was engaged in the search for Sam?

The top drawer yielded a thick sheaf of pages labeled *Sécurité: Rapport du Incident.* With shaking hands, she withdrew the document. Flipping it open, her euphoria quickly turned to dismay. It was written in French. She sighed. She might have known. And her high school French was certainly not up for the task of interpreting it.

Unwilling to give up, she skimmed the pages, picking out stray phrases she recognized. The more she read the more certain she became that the document denoted the efforts to find Sam.

She had to piece together the information she could glean from her limited French. There was a date noted that matched the day after Sam had come to the island. She understood the words capitol, *intrus*. *Risque* was *risk*. Ana puzzled for a moment over *la recherche de la ville*. It meant *search of the city,* she finally decided. *Aucun signe* was *no sign*. And then the word *dangereux*. She gave a silent laugh. If they thought Sam was dangerous, he must have inflicted some damage on the men he'd fought with.

She flipped to the last page and scanned it. They appeared to be concentrating their search to the jungle now. Ana dropped the papers back in the drawer, dread mingling with relief. It was good having proof that the government had no idea where her brother was, but she was no closer to knowing how to find him and help get him off the island.

Her reverie was shattered when she heard a noise outside the door. Ana's head snapped up. Were those voices?

She cracked the door open and peered out. Three figures, men, were coming down the hallway toward her. Only one voice could be heard, and it was speaking rapid French. From the odd words she caught, the speaker wasn't happy.

"Idiot négligent!"

Tension spiked through her limbs. Something about the voice sounded familiar, but she couldn't waste time figuring out who it belonged to. The footsteps were drawing nearer. What if they were headed for this office?

Pulling back into the room, she shut the door silently. Looking around wildly, she considered possible hiding places. There were blinds rather than drapes at the sliding-glass doors, but a quick look outside showed a tiny terrace that she could use. Unlocking the door, she opened it enough to slip through if the door to the office should begin to open. With held breath, she waited as the footsteps came nearer, drew even with the door…and then moved on.

Relief swam up in a dizzying flood. Ana bent over, drawing deep breaths into oxygen-starved lungs. After a few moments she closed and locked the sliding-glass door and crossed the room, pressed her ear to the office door. When she didn't hear anything she eased the door open, looked both ways. Seeing no one, she swiftly exited the room, intent on making an escape.

Except, to return the way she'd come she'd have to walk by whichever room the three men had gone into. Surely, she reasoned, there had to be more than one stairwell in the place. Logic said there'd be another on the opposite end of the corridor.

As silently as she could she made her way down the hallway. But she'd gotten no more than a few feet before a door behind her suddenly opened, and light spilled out.

"Arrêt!"

The urge to flee was strong, but logic won out. Even as ice filled her veins at the command, Ana stopped. A woman who'd lost her way searching for a bathroom was much less suspicious than one who ran away.

Quelling her screaming nerves, she turned quizzically, recognized Shala in the doorway. Making an immediate decision, she retraced her steps, saying querulously, "Honestly, Icanno, I've been looking all over for you. I'm feeling ill and haven't been able to find a rest room and…" The rest of her spiel slid down her throat as she drew near enough to catch a glimpse of the man ducking behind Icanno.

It was the man from the courtyard. The one who had threatened her with a knife.

For an instant nobody moved. Her blood went glacial when she saw the grim purpose on Shala's face the instant before he lunged for her.

Ana whirled, ran back the way she'd come. There was no effort to quieten her steps now. She ran as swiftly as she was able, ignoring the shouted commands behind her.

When she came to a corner she dodged around it, hoping it wouldn't lead her to a dead end. Where was that damn staircase? The frantic thought pounded in her temples as she passed the darkened doors without a sideways glance. There had to be one around here some—

Ungentle hands yanked her backward, a hard arm was crossed over her throat and a callused palm slapped to her mouth. Without ceremony, she was dragged into one of the darkened rooms.

Chapter 8

"Scream and we're both screwed." The man's whisper was no less fierce for lacking volume. He released the arm around her throat, kept the hand over her mouth as he reached out to lock the door. In the next instant he was stifling a curse as nails raked the back of his hands, and her elbow found his gut. He'd forgotten those self-defense moves of hers.

Spinning her around with a cautious grip on both arms, he shoved his face close to hers. "Dammit, knock it off or I'll shove you back out there and let them have you."

Her voice, when it came, was uncertain. "Jones? What are you doing here?"

"Looks like I'm saving your ass." He didn't see any reason to sugarcoat it. Whatever she'd been doing up here was about to land them both in a whale of trouble if they didn't get out of there, fast.

Hauling her by the arm, he pulled her over to the sliding-glass door, unlocked it and slid it open. The voices could be heard outside the door. It was only a matter of minutes before they were discovered. He didn't intend to wait for that to happen.

Shrugging swiftly out of his backpack, he unzipped it and withdrew a long cable with a hook on one end. It had provided his access to the building, but he'd never considered having to use it to get them both out. Securing the hook to the wrought-iron railing around the small terrace, he tossed the cable over the side. Ana came closer, watched it tumble into the darkness, and swallowed hard.

"I hope you're not going to suggest that we climb down that."

Grabbing her bag, he shoved it into his pack, rezipped it and shoved his arms through the straps. "Unless you know how to fly, we're using the cable." He pressed his hand to the small of her back to urge her closer to the railing. She remained stubbornly in place.

"I think there's something you should know," she began.

But he really wasn't listening to her. He was focused on the sound of footsteps racing by the door. It would be only moments before the men discovered that Ana hadn't gone down the stairway, and then they'd be back to search every room on the floor. He was going to make damn sure they weren't there when that happened.

"The cable will hold both our weight, but we don't have much time." His voice was pitched to an urgent whisper. "I'll go first, then you climb right in front of me. Once you've got a good grip I'll let the line out. Ready?"

"I don't think so." Her voice was thready, but there wasn't time to coddle her, even if he'd felt like it. He jumped nimbly to balance on the edge of the railing, then gripped the cable in both hands and swung his body around to slide down it about three feet. He stopped then, waiting.

He'd need to remain as close as he could to the top so he could reach the release button.

"C'mon."

Her figure was rigid. "I can't."

Precious seconds were ticking away. "Look if you're not wearing underwear or something, don't worry. It's dark. I'll never see a thing."

"Underwear!" The word was strangled. "It's not that, I'm just…"

Jones could hear the voices again. Damn. They were either coming back already or the men had split up. They'd just run out of time.

"Either I clip you on the jaw and take you down unconscious or you go under your own power. But make your decision *now!*"

Maybe it was the certainty in his voice that decided her. But she finally scrambled over the railing, her breathing coming in harsh, ragged pants, and clung to the cable. One of her feet caught him in the jaw before she pressed her knees to the line, and he muttered a string of imaginative curses under his breath.

"Hang on," he said between clenched teeth. She didn't appear to need the reminder. She had a death grip on the cable. He reached up to shove his night-vision goggles back in position before stretching beyond her to the release switch. He flipped it, and the mechanism's motor began to whir. He clamped his hands above Annie's as the cable made a descent to the ground two stories down.

Scanning the grounds below for signs of activity, Jones wasn't unaware of the shudders racking her delicate form. He was practically wrapped around her. But though her breathing was loud and labored, she made no other sound.

"When we get down, be prepared to follow me and run

like hell,'' he instructed, sotto voce. ''No questions, no arguing…just run. Got it?''

She failed to respond, which didn't surprise him. All her effort seemed focused on their descent. The ground a safe foot below him, he let loose and jumped, waiting for her to join him. But he had to reach out and unwrap her fingers from the cable, even once she was standing on solid ground.

''You okay?'' he asked, a reluctant tinge of sympathy rising in him.

Her head bobbed jerkily. He remained unconvinced, but they didn't have time to discuss it further. He picked up the end of the cable and flipped a button. The hooks keeping it secured to the balcony above retracted, and the line came tumbling down. Grabbing it, he thrust it into his pack with one hand, even as he grabbed her palm in his other.

He started running, tugging her in the direction from which he'd breached the fence at the back of the property. He wasn't unwise enough to try one of the buildings on either side of him. There was no doubt in his mind that the government occupied those spaces, too. They were too close to be good security risks, otherwise.

Annie was keeping up with him with a surprisingly long stride. He supposed adrenaline kept her going, and he wanted to put as much distance between them and the capitol as he could while it lasted. He had the experience to know that once the adrenaline faded, shock would take over.

At that moment lights blazed throughout the building. Floodlights snapped on, sweeping the property with their beams. Cursing, he reached behind him and pulled out the gun he had tucked in his waistband. Voices sounded in the distance a moment before a spotlight caught them in its glare.

Annie stumbled, and he pulled her upright. The voices were joined by others, and the light remained fixed. He heard her gasp and knew she'd finally noticed what they were running toward.

A ten-foot wrought-iron fence with pointed spikes topping each rail.

"Jones," she hissed.

But he already knew what she was going to say. "Hope you were a tomboy, sugar."

"What?"

There was a sharp crack, and then another. Dammit, they were shooting at them. And using something with a bit more range than the Beretta he carried.

They'd reached the fence. The spotlight pinned them against the wrought iron, moths struggling against a certain death. He crouched down. "Step on my shoulders," he commanded. She didn't argue, but scrambled awkwardly up, one hand holding her dress in a ridiculous effort to save her modesty. He had the fleeting impression that modesty was pretty crazy, considering the fact that she'd all but invited him to her bed on more than one occasion. Or been in his.

With a mental shake he dislodged the thought and secured her feet with his hands. "Hang on." He rose, staggered once, then righted himself. She was a featherweight, but he wasn't in the same kind of shape he'd been five years ago. "Grab the top bar, beneath the spikes. Got it? When I count to three, I'm going to heave you up. Swing your legs over the fence, and get them safely on the other side before you slide down. Ready?"

From her strangled protest, it didn't sound as though she was anywhere close to ready, but they didn't have time for arguing. The shots were coming closer, the last near enough to kick up dirt three feet away.

"Go!" He gave her feet a mighty push, and she took care of the rest. Once he was certain she'd cleared the top, he turned and raised his gun, fired off a round. He didn't kid himself that he would hit anyone at this range, but it might dissuade them from coming quite so close, so fast.

Flipping the safety back on, he shoved it back into his waistband and distanced himself several yards from the fence. With a running start he leaped skyward, grabbing the bars as high as he could, and hoisted himself up the remaining distance. His ascent wasn't pretty, but within moments he'd swung over the other side, slid partway down and jumped to the ground beside Annie.

"They're shooting at us!" she shouted, sounding half panicked, half amazed.

He grabbed her by the arm and started racing away. "Then you better keep your head down."

Swiftly he considered their options. Shala knew Annie had come by ship; he'd had his car pick her up at the dock. So he had to get word to Pappy to pull anchor and get the *Nefarious* the hell out of there. Shala would alert the police to stop the ship if they got to it in time.

They dodged in and out of the labyrinth of deserted alcoves and alleys of the marketplace. Stairways spidered up aimlessly from some of them, leading God knew where. Strolling passersby looked at them curiously, but no one made a move to stop them. Shala hadn't gotten his force formed yet. Jones knew they didn't have much time.

He ducked into the maze of connecting alcoves and stopped, leaning heavily against the wall. Tugging down the goggles, he shrugged out of the backpack and unzipped it. Digging around inside, he found the hand-held short-wave radio by touch.

"Jones…" Annie's voice was ragged.

"Quiet." He switched the radio on, winced when the

static seemed abnormally loud in the darkness. "*Nefarious* 172-651, come in. *Nefarious* 172-651."

"But, Jones…"

"Dammit, be quiet!" He threw a glare at her, noting the way she'd collapsed, sliding down the wall.

"*Nefarious* 172-651. Over."

"Pappy?" Relief washed over him in a wave.

"Cap'n?"

"Pull anchor. Immediately. Full throttle it back to Bontilla. Hire Ranachek to meet me on the north side of Laconos, near the beach there. I'll contact him with further orders."

"You all right, Cap'n?"

Jones didn't bother mentioning that right now he and Annie were far from all right. But he was determined that his ship would be. "We're fine. Just get moving."

"Aye, aye, Cap'n."

"Jones?"

Jones switched the radio off, replaced it in his backpack and put his arms through the straps again. Only then did he glance at Annie. "What?"

"Those sirens you hear? They're headed our way."

He lifted his head, listened for a moment. Damned if she wasn't right. "How much farther do you think you can go?"

Annie looked at him and rose, brushing off her dress. "As far as I need to."

He felt an unwilling tug of admiration. Her chest was still heaving, her dress was damp with perspiration, torn in a couple places and smeared with dirt. But her expression left no question that she was willing to press on. Which was good, because in another minute those police cars would be on top of them. He held out a hand, waited until her fingers closed around his. "That's good. Because we don't have a lot of choices."

Going to the front of the alcove, Jones peered out. The flashing lights of the police cars were already on the streets coming toward them. He heard more sirens in the distance, and hoped like hell Pappy had wasted no time getting the ship moving. Looking out again, he saw that uniformed police had piled out of the cars and were running toward the marketplace.

"C'mon," he said, and pulled her back inside the labyrinth of alcoves.

"What?" She balked. "Are you crazy? We can't go back inside there. There's no way out."

"Hate to tell you, sweetheart," he said grimly as he yanked on her hand to get her moving again. "But there's no way out in that direction, either."

He chose a stairway in one corner and they ran up it, turned the corner and found themselves in a narrow passageway lined with open-air windows. A quick glance inside the lone door showed a crude latrine.

The sound of shouts, of running feet could be heard below them as the area was searched.

"It's only a matter of time before they head up here," Ana said with a surprisingly even voice. She stuck her head out the window, looked down. She didn't have to tell him that it was too far to jump. He already knew what their only option was. He gave her a long look, and her gaze widened. Apparently she'd just figured it out as well.

Minutes later there was the sound of footsteps in the corridor. Curses, shouts, then the noise receded, fading in the distance. Jones turned his head carefully. Annie's face was deadly white, her eyes screwed shut, and her hands were clutching the roof tiles with a death grip. "I think it's safe to get down now."

"Are you sure?" she said, without opening her eyes. "I mean, we just got up here."

"Yeah, it's a shame to waste the view," he agreed dryly. "But we need to get the hell out of Dodge."

Reluctantly she opened her eyes, but he noted that she kept her gaze trained on his face. "I think it's only fair to warn you that when this is over, I'm really going to kill you."

He was already sliding toward the edge of the roof, hanging on to the edge as his feet sought the purchase of the windowsill below. "Get in line, sweetheart. But first we have to escape. Preferably alive."

Ana had never been so exhausted in her life. She huddled next to the building on the outskirts of the city, her arms clasped around her legs, chin resting on her knees. Her body was shaking with a mixture of weariness and shock. Jones was seated next to her, digging in that infernal backpack of his once again.

Her head was spinning, so she closed her eyes. The pounding adrenaline had long since drained. Her limbs were weak and achy. Her heels had been rubbed raw by her sandals, which owed more to fashion than to comfort. It seemed a lifetime ago since she'd had a moment of sleep. Or a glass of water. She'd kill for either.

Without opening her eyes, she muttered, "You don't happen to have a canteen in that terrorist handbag of yours, do you?"

"No. Sorry."

She opened one eye, looked at him. The shock of discovering who'd grabbed her in the offices, coupled with the escape amid a shower of bullets, had shifted her surprise at his appearance to a much lower priority. But delayed curiosity rose now, and wouldn't be stifled.

"Does Rambo know you've stolen his outfit?"

His voice was sour. "Funny."

"No," her voice was reflective, "what's funny is you appearing in the capitol, dressed like a second-story man, complete with the tools of the trade." He was clothed completely in black. Black jeans, black long-sleeved T-shirt, black watch cap on his head. Even the pack, from which he'd just withdrawn a—she needed to open the other eye to get a closer look—compass, was black.

She straightened, regarded him quizzically. "Mind telling me just what you were doing in the capitol offices?"

"Not at all." His gaze remained trained on the compass. "Just as soon as you tell me what *you* were doing there."

A moment ticked by. Then another. In the next instant he looked up, caught her gaze on him. She realized belatedly that she hadn't responded. "I...I was looking for a bathroom."

He surveyed her steadily. "And I was looking for dance partners for the Ice Capades." Their gazes did battle, at impasse. She looked away first. That narrowed flinty stare was too hard to face while her mind was racing furiously. For the first time it occurred to her that she was going to have to come up with a reasonable explanation for what had gone down tonight.

"Well, there's a bit more to the story, I guess."

"Yeah, I guess."

She ignored his caustic agreement, still piecing her story together. "The night I went to the nightclubs, I kind of stumbled on a drug deal outside, and one of the guys had a knife—"

"What?"

Uh-oh. She sent him a cautious glance. The dangerous look in his eye matched the lethal tone of his voice. "It's okay. I got away. And that's how I met Shala. He'd heard

about the scene—at least," she finished grimly, "that's th
line he gave me." It was glaringly apparent that Shala ha
been hiding as much from her as she'd been from him.

There was silence from the man at her side, the kind tha
promised an impending storm. Then "You'd better tell m
the whole story."

She could only partially comply. Giving him a carefull
edited version of the drug transaction, her escape, the er
counter with Shala and then the strange conversation wit
Bunei this evening, she finished, saying, "I was looking fc
a bathroom when I happened to see Shala with that man..
the same one who'd threatened me. And it didn't appear a
though he was in danger of imminent arrest." It ha
seemed, she thought, as though they were having an ar
gument about something at first, but when the two men ha
been coming toward her, they'd acted pretty chummy.

The creative oath he muttered when she'd finished ha
her brows raising.

"Pardon me?"

"You need to be locked up," he said succinctly. "Unde
armed guard 24/7. You're a danger to yourself, not to men
tion those stupid enough to get involved with you."

Anger snapped through her veins, dissipating a bit of th
exhaustion. "If we're referring to your involvement, I ca
certainly attest to the stupid part."

He went on as if he hadn't heard her. Perhaps it was jus
as well. "You come to a strange country where you don'
know a soul. You proceed to traipse around at night o
your own, almost get your throat slit by a drug dealer, ac
cept a date with one of the shadiest guys in the new gov
ernment and, golly gee, he just happens to be in on th
drug deals up to his eyeballs and turns around and tries t
kill you. I gotta hand it to you, lady. You really know hov
to vacation."

Her fists curled. He was back to calling her lady, like the first day on the dock. As if he hadn't called her more informal endearments on their wild trip across the city evading the police. It was a ridiculous thing to focus on, when her primary emotion at the moment was wanting to give him a swift kick. "There's a bit more to it than that."

"Really." He folded his arms across his chest and stared at her, giving the appearance of a man prepared to wait. "This ought to be good."

"I'm through explaining things to you," she snapped. Actually, she was out of facts that she could afford to reveal to him. "It's your turn. What were *you* doing there?"

There was a beat of silence. Then another. Finally he said, "I went to make sure you were all right."

She gave him a get-real look. "Yeah. That'll fly. You had no way of knowing where I went, and it's probably too obvious to point out that you didn't exactly come outfitted in your party togs."

"What the hell's a tog?"

"Never mind. You're stalling." She ought to know, she'd perfected the art. "If your story is true, how'd you know where I was?"

"We're wasting time." He made a point of checking his watch, touching the button that illuminated the face. "I just wanted to give you a few minutes to catch your breath before we discussed our next move."

But his effort to distract her didn't work. "It was that taxi you hired, wasn't it?" If she'd had the energy, she would have smacked her forehead at the conclusion. Better yet, she'd have smacked *his*. "After promising me that your protective crap was over, you had me *followed*."

His mouth was flattened to a tight, grim line. "Yeah, so?"

Dismay and anger mingled to form a tight knot in her

stomach. What was it about her that elicited this kind of reaction in men? Did she put out some sort of vibe that made every man of her acquaintance believe she was someone to pat on the head and set aside while life marched by? It was enough to make a woman scream. Out of all the emotions to claim to feel for her, protectiveness was the one guaranteed to wound.

"I didn't need protecting," she said in precise tones. "I'm not completely without resources of my own." He wasn't the only one who had a few surprises in his bag.

"Yeah, I saw how well those resources were working for you tonight. Not to mention your sense of direction. You spent a lot of time in those rooms before discovering that they weren't bathrooms."

The mockery of his words escaped her. Sudden understanding bloomed. "How would you know that? Unless you were watching the whole…that's why those doors were open! You'd already been in them."

He adjusted his goggles again to peer down the street. "They don't lock when exiting without a key."

She reached out and grabbed his arm. "And you thought you'd find me upstairs in those rooms?"

"I did find you upstairs in those rooms," he pointed out.

"Not because you were looking for me." Her certainty in that fact was growing. "Is that the story you're sticking to?"

He turned and looked at her, the goggles making him look utterly foreign, utterly dangerous. "Are you sticking to your story?"

Her mouth snapped shut. "Yes."

"Then so am I. Let's hit the road."

She rose, silent only because she needed to think about all the inconsistencies in his tale. There was plenty he wasn't telling her, that was for sure. Even more than what she wasn't telling him. And it occurred to her, as she brushed the grit off her dress, that the man standing next to her was a stranger. And a much different person from the one she'd assumed he was on the day she'd hired him.

She wasn't any too certain what to make of that.

"They'll post guards around the edge of town." He was talking again, his voice low, cool and emotionless. "But before we try slipping by them we need to get you some different clothes."

She couldn't agree more. When she'd bought this dress, it hadn't been with the intention of climbing over fences or on top of roofs—she gave an involuntary shudder—or hiding in grimy alleys. "What do you have in mind?"

"I'll take care of it while you wait. It's easier for one person to get in and out undetected than for two. Wait for me here. If you hear anything," he pointed to the large, steel garbage bin behind them, "hide in back of there."

He was gone before she could form a protest, a black, silent wraith in the night. The darkness immediately closed in around her, lending a feeling of isolation.

Shaking off the gloomy feeling, she waited until she was sure Jones wasn't coming back and then got up, moved farther back into the alley. It was a dead end, and the stench from the garbage didn't make it the most desirable of places to wait. The faint scrabbling sounds she heard around her were certainly from rodents who found the aroma more tempting than she did.

But it afforded her a measure of much-needed privacy, one she wasn't likely to get again. She reached into her bag and took out the phone, rang Sterling's number again. He hadn't responded the last three times she'd called. She waited five rings, then ten. Switching the phone off, she grimly folded it up and returned it to her purse. She'd done the occasional courier job for him, jumping at the chance for some excitement in her otherwise quiet life. But that work was very low priority, she knew. She had no idea of his function or position for whatever alphabet agency he and Sam worked for. She had no inkling what his continued absence from his phone meant, outside the obvious. She couldn't depend on him for advice.

She raised her head sharply in the act of dropping the phone in her bag. Were those footsteps? Her skin prickled despite the balmy night air and she edged closer to the receptacle. Unless Jones had been very quick indeed, he couldn't have returned so soon.

Reaching back into her bag, she drew out the small derringer. It wasn't the size she normally practiced with, but there had been no question of getting her gun through airport security. She'd had to wait until she reached Bontilla to purchase another. Though small, it was lethal enough to stop someone at close range. And from the faint sounds that seemed to be drawing nearer, the range was going to be close indeed.

Quickly she grabbed her bag and moved behind the bin, wedging herself in between its filthy metal exterior and the stone wall of the building face. It was tight, even for her slim form. In order to fit she had to keep her head turned to one side. There wouldn't be room to change position which would render even her gun partially useless. If someone thought to look behind the garbage receptacle, they would have to get very near to see her. But for her to have a fighting chance, they'd have to approach from the side on which she carried the gun.

Holding her breath, she waited as the scuffling sounds came closer. She hoped it was rats. That had to be the first and only time in her life she'd experience that particular desire, but moments later she knew the hope was in vain.

Although they were trying for quiet, she could hear whispers, breathing. At least two people.

Nerves were doing a screaming race up her spine. She couldn't visually assess what kind of danger was out there, and somehow that made it even worse. She could only wait, listening to the stealth with which the people moved, wondering at their identities, afraid she could already guess.

They were coming closer. Stray pebbles and debris crunched beneath their feet. Ana swallowed, released the safety on her gun with a smooth, silent movement. The close fit didn't allow her hand to tremble. But she was shaking inside, tension spiking her nerve endings.

One of the men finally moved past the garbage bin and into her range of vision. He wasn't clad in police uniform, though, but in military garb much the same as the guards at the capitol. Panic churned viciously in her stomach. She watched as he searched the length of the alley, kicking over boxes, disturbing the nightlife feasting beneath. He turned, uttered a command in French.

The bin jostled as a second man began to pull boxes and bags from the metal receptacle. Ana gritted her teeth, wondering at the wisdom of her hiding place. If the bin were pushed back too far, she may well end up with a few crushed ribs, if not worse.

The minutes stretched interminably, as the men thoroughly examined the contents of the bin. Finally giving up in a disgusted exchange, they left, their exit not nearly as silent as their entrance had been.

Her pent-up breath was released in a silent stream. Only her close proximity to the metal and the stone wall kept her upright. She was certain without the support she'd have slid to a limp, boneless heap. Sliding the safety back on her gun, she waited until she thought at least ten minutes had passed. Then waited another five before she deemed it safe enough to attempt to wiggle from her position.

And found it impossible.

She struggled harder, pressing her body against the metal side of the receptacle in an attempt to move it away from the wall. It didn't budge. She was held in place tightly, with little more than an inch in which to move.

She'd never been claustrophobic, she assured herself, even as the oxygen seemed jammed in her lungs. There was no reason for the sensation to occur now. Of course, it was easy not to be claustrophobic when you had freedom of movement. When your limbs weren't restricted and when your face wasn't caught snugly between two equally unyielding objects.

It was due to her inner struggle that she didn't hear the first sound. But she definitely heard the second.

"Annie? It's Jones."

She had to swallow a couple times to moisten her dry throat before answering. "I'm back here."

He must have already been making his way toward her, because moments later he was flattened against the wall, gazing in at her. And from the look on his face, he was none too pleased to see the muzzle of her gun staring back at him.

Chapter 9

"Dammit, that thing better not be loaded," Jones muttered savagely.

"It wouldn't do me much good if it wasn't."

"It doesn't look like it's doing you much good now."

He had a point, Ana acknowledged. "The safety's off. But I don't think I can get out on my own. It was pretty tight going in, and there were two guys here not too long ago checking for us in the garbage bin."

His expression changed. "Police?"

"Military."

Jones disappeared from view, and moments later she felt the receptacle move a few inches, allowing her some much-needed space. When she reached for her bag, she cracked her head smartly against the wall. Stumbling out into the alley, she raised her free hand to rub the bump already forming, while Jones reached toward her, and plucked the gun from her other hand.

"Hey!"

"I'll hang on to that for you."

"I was hanging on to it just fine by myself."

"Call me paranoid, but I've got a thing about letting people behind me with a gun."

Ana recalled the scar on his back, his stark admission. *It was my partner.* But even knowing the motivation for his high-handed behavior didn't lessen her reaction to it. "How about if I stay in front, then?"

"How about if I'm the only one armed? I feel safer that way."

"You Tarzan, me Jane," she muttered.

"What?"

It wasn't worth repeating because she had every intention of getting her gun back. Soon. And because she finally spotted the bundle he held in his hand. "For me? Gee, Jones, you shouldn't have."

"I'm sure the owner of these will think the same thing."

Her gaze flashed to his. "You stole them?"

"No, I waltzed into Saks Fifth Avenue and picked something off the rack."

He was, she noted, becoming something of a smart-ass himself. "There's no need to be snippy about it." She thought she heard him snort as she reached for the clothes. "After my proximity to rats and garbage, I'm a bit anxious to slip into something a little more comfortable. Not to mention something in one piece."

She waited, the bundle clutched to her chest but he made no move to leave. "I'd like to change."

"Yeah. Make it snappy."

Her brows raised. "Some privacy?"

She could hear the smirk in his voice. "Aren't you the same one who was willing to try out that topless beach?"

"Get over on the other side of the garbage bin, Jones! And don't put those goggles on, either."

"They're not X-ray," he reminded her, but he moved away with a studied reluctance.

She wasted no time in exchanging the dress, which now sported a pungent ripe odor, for a loose-fitting dark tunic top and some matching baggy drawstring trousers. The socks and boots that completed her stolen ensemble were too large, but she was glad enough to be rid of those blasted sandals that it didn't bother her.

"Here."

His approach had been silent, and, she noted, he hadn't waited for her to give him the okay. He handed her a bottle of water, which she looked at in amazement. "So you did go shopping."

"That's one word for it. Figured there were a few things we were going to need. I got sandwiches, too, but we'll leave them for later."

Twisting off the cap of the bottle, she tipped it to her lips and drank greedily.

"I scouted things out a bit. It looks like the local police force is charged with guarding the perimeter of the city now. From what you said, I'm guessing the military has taken over the search for us."

She lowered the bottle. "I heard you order Pappy away from the island. How do we get off it?"

"I've got a ship coming. All we have to do is make our way to it."

"But..." She stared at him through the darkness. "You said the ship should meet us on the north side of the island."

"That's right." He took the bottle from her hand and raised it to his lips. "Which means we'll be heading straight through the jungle."

Jones watched from his hiding place and prayed Annie remembered the instructions he'd given her. He'd feel a helluva lot more comfortable if he was the one distracting the guard. But the man would be more suspicious of another man than he would be of a woman. At least, he was banking on that.

Trepidation twisted viciously in his stomach. He didn't like sending her into certain danger. Not that she seemed to mind. She'd appeared only too eager to enact the plan. He'd actually stopped once as he'd been mapping strategy out loud, ready to scrap the whole thing and find another way, one that would have kept her a safe distance away from the action. But she wasn't having any of that.

You're still trying to protect me!

He shifted uneasily at the memory of her razor-sharp, whispered accusation. From the ferocity in her voice, she could have been accusing him of stomping kittens. And she was wrong, completely. At least mostly. He just preferred to do jobs himself, that was all. He'd always worked best alone. Bystanders had a habit of getting in the way, getting hurt. He just hadn't wanted to chance that happening with her.

She'd been like a bulldog after that, he recalled. He'd been unable to shake her from her stubborn insistence on helping. That, coupled with the fact that his first plan had seemed the likeliest to succeed, had convinced him to give in. But he hadn't given her back her gun, as she'd insisted. He might be out of options, but he wasn't crazy.

His hand tightened on the binoculars when she moved into his view. She'd donned the vividly colored head scarf he'd brought her, which would cover, at least for a time, that bright head of hair. He was hoping that would help her avoid identification for valuable moments. His stomach clutched as she staggered, cradling her arm to her chest and keening loudly. The guard stationed across the street from her straightened, reached for his weapon.

Muscles tensing, Jones forced himself to remain motionless. So far things were working like a charm. She was sticking to the strategy. She hadn't ventured beyond the corner of the buildings to the street. She'd be visible only to the one guard, not to any stray militia officers who could be searching nearby.

Dread pooled nastily at the base of his spine. The policeman was tersely ordering her to halt as he left his post to approach, but Annie was ignoring him, stumbling farther this way. Jones balanced on the balls of his feet, waiting for the guard to pass his hiding place.

"S'il vous plaît m'aider. Je suis blessé."

From the pain sounding in her voice, he would believe that she was hurt himself, if he didn't know better. He just hoped her statement didn't come true in a few more moments.

"Arrêt. Comment vous appelez-vous?"

Jones watched as Annie turned at the policeman's order, staggering back a few more steps as if in near faint. The man was no more than three feet from Jones, his weapon still drawn, an ominous threat.

"Enlever le foulard."

Annie moved to obey the tersely worded order to take off her scarf, her hand going to her head. Jones picked that moment to spring. With two quick silent steps he was behind the man, one arm wrapped around his throat, jerking him off balance. "Get back," he ordered Annie, as the man's weapon tipped skyward. A moment later it clattered to the ground as the officer doubled over, sagging limply in Jones's grasp from the well-placed kick Annie had sent to the man's privates.

Muttering a curse, Jones dragged the man's head back

and delivered a punch that would put him out of his misery
for a few minutes. Then he dragged him back to where
Jones had waited earlier, out of sight of anyone happening
by. "Don't even think about it," he advised grimly when
he saw her bend over, reach for the policeman's weapon.

Her small nose went in the air, and she raised her hands
in surrender. "Fine. I was just trying to help."

After dumping the unconscious body in a doorway, Jones
crossed and picked up the weapon. "Did it ever occur to
you to stop trying to help and just follow directions for
once?" He emptied the automatic of its magazine and
shoved it in his pack, before tossing the gun on top of the
limp policeman.

"I don't take orders well," she said, her voice sulky.

"Honey, you don't take orders at all." He squatted to
remove the radio clipped to the man's belt, transferring it
to his waistband. Then he rose, gripped her elbow in his
hand and pulled her down the street to peer around the
corner of the building. "You were supposed to lead him
past me, then get the hell out of the way."

"What are you complaining about? I just made it easier
for you to overpower him. Now even when he regains consciousness he isn't going to be moving too fast."

Recalling the lethal power behind the kick she'd delivered, he almost winced. The man was going to have much
more serious concerns than the two of them when he woke
up. He waited for the lone taxi driving by to get a couple
of blocks away before he said, "Let's go. Stay down."

In a crouch they ran across the deserted street. The next
nearest guards were stationed about a block on either side
of them. All it would take was for one of them to look their
way at this exact moment, or to have seen the incapacitated
policeman leave his post, and they'd be dodging bullets
once again. But the silence that greeted their maneuver was

absolute. It was almost eerier than the gunfire he'd half feared.

In front of them was a small park backed by thick vegetation. It was toward that vegetation that he headed now, releasing her to free his arms. Shrugging out of the pack he carried, he swung it around front and dug for a flashlight and the heavy, curved machete he'd stolen from the store he'd broken into. They came to a halt at the back of the park, their path blocked by the snarled vines and dense vegetation.

"Here, hold this." He shoved the flashlight in her hands.

"What are you going to…Jones!"

The blade flashed in the darkness as he hacked away at the thicket, cutting a path for them to enter.

"This has got to lead straight through into the forest."

"That's the general idea."

"You can't be planning for us to go in there at night!"

Even as she protested, she kept the light shining unwaveringly on the area before them.

"You have a better idea?"

"Have you considered waiting until daylight?"

"The object is to get a head start on the militia before they figure out where we've gone and come after us." He didn't bother to keep the sarcasm from his tone. He couldn't afford to get distracted by the thin thread of panic in her words. Now was a time to concentrate on what needed to be done. And that meant getting whatever head start they could on whoever would be coming after them.

He'd slashed enough of the strangler vines and thick plants to allow them to enter a couple of feet. He plunged forward, stopped to hack some more. "I need the light. Get up here."

"This is ridiculous." He reached back, grabbed her tunic and pulled her forward. She never missed a beat. "You can't expect to cut your way all the way through the forest."

"Actually, I just plan to clear a few feet." He cast an eye up and down the street. It was still quiet. He wondered how long they had before someone came by and sounded the alarm. "Once I slice away the stranglers and vines we'll be able to enter the forest itself."

"Yeah, right."

There was a decided note of disbelief in her voice, one he couldn't blame her for. They were close enough to hear the night noises coming from the thicket of dense vegetation: the eerie cry of howler monkeys at the top of the canopy and the distinctive cough of a jaguar calling its mate. It wasn't especially tempting, to race into the primitive night scene, but what waited behind them was even less attractive. The Laconos government had already had their security breached once. They wouldn't be inclined toward leniency over this latest attempt.

"C'mere."

Annie obeyed reluctantly. "I still think we should talk about this."

He went behind her to the entrance he'd made, and started scooping up the hacked undergrowth. Arranging it across intact vines, he did what he could to disguise the damage he'd done. Rejoining Ana, he began cutting with renewed effort. How long since they'd taken out that guard? Fifteen minutes? Twenty? Tension knotted at the base of his skull. Instincts, well honed from years on the street, sprang to life. Time was running out.

"This is ridiculous. It'll take us months to get through the forest at this rate."

"No, it won't." Already the vegetation was thinning. "The outside is dense from strangler vines and lianes, but once we get through this, the forest floor itself can be traveled pretty easily."

A gibbon's screech sounded from somewhere directly overhead. The sound had an undeniable effect on Annie, bringing her close enough to grab for the waistband of his pants. But it was the noise at his waist that sent a chill down her spine.

The radio he'd taken off the guard spit static, then voices could be heard speaking urgent French. The guard they'd disabled had been discovered.

"We just ran out of time," he said grimly. "Hang on to me and keep the flashlight trained in front of us." He took her rare silence for agreement. As a siren sounded in the distance, he forged through the last of the vines he'd cut until they stumbled onto the forest floor.

"Do you think they're desperate enough to search the jungle at night?" she asked, trying to keep the trepidation she felt from her voice.

When something in him tried to soften at the sound, he deliberately hardened it. "We're desperate enough, aren't we? Now run!"

For once she did exactly as he asked.

Dawn had come and gone, but it made little difference in the forest. The upper canopy blocked most of the sunlight, and what little did get through was blocked by the second or third canopy of smaller trees. Only the dimmest light would be available in full day, but Jones had had Annie snap off the flashlight, anyway. She supposed he wanted to conserve the batteries. He hadn't mentioned how long their trek across the island would take, and she hadn't yet summoned the courage to ask.

Tossing down a pile of ferns he'd cut, he arranged them with his foot and ordered, "Sit."

Her descent qualified more as total collapse than simpl
obedience but she was too exhausted to care. They'd reste
at regular intervals but never for long. Her body had gon
through stages, first of adrenaline-fueled energy, followe
by a zombielike automatic pilot that had carried her th
far. Now, however, she was afraid she'd entered anothe
stage of bone-deep weariness that wouldn't allow her t
rise again.

Jones shoved his goggles back and squatted down besid
her. He reached for his pack and unzipped it. A memor
roused her enough to demand, "Give me my bag back.
can carry it."

He spared her barely a glance. "You can hardly put on
foot in front of the other. I'll keep carrying both of then
I don't suppose you have a permit for that gun you wer
carrying."

"I have a permit." Not for this gun, exactly. And not i
the name she was currently using, but she didn't think thos
facts were worth mentioning. From the look on his face, h
wouldn't agree.

"Mind telling me why you thought you needed a gun?"

She caught the wrapped sandwich he tossed her, alread
salivating. It was hard to be high-minded about his thiever
earlier that night when it meant she was finally going t
get fed. "No, I don't mind. If you don't mind answering
question for me."

Oh, he minded. She bit into the sandwich with huge en
joyment, finding the expression on his face almost as plea
surable. He liked being in control and calling the shot:
What he didn't like, judging from his countenance, wa
having the tables turned on him.

"Okay, what's the question?" He bit into his own sand
wich with a little more ferocity than could be blamed o
mere hunger.

"What's your real name?"

An innocent enough question, she would have thought. Certainly not one that should have had him freezing, the sandwich raised halfway to his mouth. Then in the next instant he recovered, took another bite. "What makes you think it isn't Jones?"

Until his answer it hadn't occurred to her that his last name could be as phony as hers. But the way he'd worded the question suddenly made her believe differently. "You have to have a first name," she pointed out logically. "No mother in her right mind would hold her newborn in her arms, look down lovingly and say, 'He's the picture of Grandpa Jones. That's what we'll call him.'" As a matter of fact, she couldn't quite imagine him as a newborn at all, but she was willing to give him the benefit of the doubt and believe he'd come into existence in the usual way.

"I just go by Jones. Where'd you get the gun? You couldn't have gotten it through Customs."

Studiously ignoring the question, she continued eating, ignoring his thunderous expression. The sandwich was unlike anything she'd ever eaten before. It actually consisted more of a thick tortilla than of bread, and the meat filling wasn't recognizable, either.

"You said you'd answer my question if I answered yours."

"I meant truthfully. Unless you want me to tell you that Santa brought me the gun last Christmas."

"Christ," he muttered, chewing ferociously.

"No, I doubt that's your name," she said, deliberately misunderstanding him. "You're not in the least godlike. How about if we start off easy. Just give me your first name." As silence stretched, with him avoiding her gaze, she felt a small measure of disappointment. Ridiculous, really, to let such a little thing mean so much. Especially in light of the fact that she was keeping so much from him.

Not for the first time she considered telling him everything. Her relationship to Sam, his disappearance, her search for the smallest clue that might lead her to her brother.... And not for the first time, she held back. She could trust him now less than ever. Okay, maybe he'd saved her skin back at the capitol, but he'd never told her what had driven him to violate the security there to search the offices. Nor what he'd been searching for.

Indelicately, she licked her fingers, savoring every crumb of sandwich left there. No, trust wasn't something she could afford to give him. Which was a pity, really. Because she really, really wished she could trust Jones.

She looked at him then and nearly gasped. He was watching her, arrested, with such heated intent in his eyes that her heart immediately began to gallop. Belatedly she realized his attention was on her mouth, as her tongue was in the act of cleansing the pad of her forefinger. Maybe she wasn't displaying proper jungle etiquette. The next thought bounced crazily in her head in rhythm to the wild pounding of her heart. Or maybe, just maybe, he was having to restrain himself from reaching for her. From licking those last crumbs himself. From tasting her, with an altogether different sort of hunger than the one he'd displayed for his dinner.

The moment spun out, the two of them transfixed in the dim humid heat of the forest. Ana's chest grew tight, and her lips parted, her tongue creeping out to moisten them. Jones's gaze tracked the movement, and in one euphoric moment she knew. He wanted her. The way he had on the ship that night. The way he'd made her want, too...a sudden violent longing that seared the blood and sharpened the senses. The kind that made any thought of control laughable.

Then he looked away, and the moment was over. He spent several minutes searching for something in his pack. Ana released a great shuddering breath and took the water bottle he handed her with a shaky hand. Raising it to her lips, she drank. Had she thought he was about to lose control? Hah. The man could have invented the term. She hardly presented a picture guaranteed to inspire lust in the man.

Ana handed him back the bottle and gave herself a rueful look. The shapeless black top and cotton trousers weren't exactly haute couture, even for wear in the rain forest. The boots, though functional, were rather clumpy looking, and she'd long since wound the scarf high around her neck to ward off mosquitoes and other insects. Given the fact that she was probably at least as sweaty as he was, she was certain she fell somewhat short of every man's jungle fantasy.

And that, she told herself grimly, was familiar territory indeed. "I'll bet it's Percy."

"What?" He looked up with a frown from stowing the water back in his pack. "What's Percy?"

"Your name." Annoying him was a great way to get her mind off what she'd felt like doing to him a few short minutes ago, so she threw herself into the task. "It must be something you're embarrassed about. Or else you'd tell me." She pretended not to notice the way his eyes narrowed. "It could be Ambrose. Or Dilbert."

"Dilbert." His tone had gone low and menacing.

She nearly grinned. Getting a reaction from him at all was rewarding. Nearly as rewarding as if he'd told her the truth.

"Listen, I want to know where you got the gun and how long you've had it."

Swatting at a mosquito the size of a Volkswagen, she tilted her head to look at him curiously. "If I tell you, will you give it back?"

"If the time comes that you have to use it, yeah, maybe. If I can be assured you know how."

"I can put a round in a target at forty yards," she answered simply. "Care to find out firsthand? Put a coconut on your head and stand against that tree over there."

He didn't look particularly eager to comply. "Firing at a target is quite a bit different than firing at a human being, and a moving one at that."

She gave an involuntary shiver as his words recalled the precariousness of their situation. "I know," she replied in a subdued tone. "But if the time comes, I'll do what I have to."

Evidently something in her expression must have convinced him, because he gave a short nod, then pulled out the directional finder from the backpack again, squinted at it.

"Are we still headed the right way?"

"We're moving more northeast than straight north, but there's no help for that."

She nodded her understanding. The terrain hadn't made their trek easy, by any means. They'd had to swerve around deep ravines, and hack their way through thickets of jungle. Once they'd scrabbled down a slope so steep she'd been grateful for the near darkness. If she'd had to try it again in broad daylight, she was afraid she'd disgrace herself.

"What will happen to those friends you were supposed to meet?"

Swallowing became difficult. "I...I don't know. We

never hooked up. I meant to check in with them tomorrow. I mean, today.''

He didn't look convinced. ''Won't they sound the alarm to someone when they don't see you? Maybe call your family?''

The shrug she gave would have done Hollywood proud. ''No, why would they? They'll just figure we missed each other.'' Deliberately changing the subject, she asked, ''How much farther?'' She watched a brilliantly colored butterfly, as big around as her fist, dance above their heads and disappear in the trees.

''Seven miles or so, the way I figure it,'' he answered. Her stomach dropped. Seven miles. At the moment she didn't think she could make it seven inches.

''You're doing pretty good, considering.''

He said nothing else, only looked at her. Growing discomfited, she made a show of checking the laces on her boots. She wanted to keep them tied tightly enough that nothing could seep inside them. Or crawl. ''Considering what?''

''Considering…I had you figured for a college girl out for a good time with her daddy's money.''

Her smile was forced. ''Well, my daddy has plenty of that, all right.'' The pang in her heart was a familiar enough weight. She'd lived with it all her life.

''Something about you doesn't add up.''

''Me? I'm not complicated.''

He was studying her as if solving a particularly complex puzzle. His gray gaze was piercing. With the goggles pushed atop his head, his hair pulled back in its usual thong, and the black form-fitting clothes, he looked like a warrior. Half-tamed and primitive. The day's growth of beard only added to the picture. She gave an involuntary shiver at the image.

"There's the gun. And the way you've kept up on this trip." He looked fierce, as if he was on the trail of something he couldn't quite put a finger on. "You're in pretty good condition for someone who…what'd you say? Worked in a software company?"

"Step aerobics," she said airily, secretly quaking inside. Once she'd begun doing jobs for Sterling she'd made sure she was in good shape. She wasn't exactly leaping tall buildings with a single bound, but she'd added weights to her martial arts training. "If it makes you feel any better, every muscle I have is whimpering."

"Yeah." The doubt in his voice said he remained unconvinced.

In an effort to distract him, she said challengingly, "You know, you're not exactly what I'd figure for a charter ship captain, either."

That shrewd look faded from his eyes to be replaced with a familiar wariness. "How many charter ship captains do you know?"

She waved the question away. "You carry a gun. Not to mention a bag of stuff that would do a burglar proud. And you didn't get into your kind of condition by swabbing decks."

As a diversion it worked admirably. But it failed to acquire any new answers. "You'd be surprised. Swabbing decks is pretty physical." He stood, indicating that their rest was over. Taking her hand, he pulled her to her feet. Then he reached down for the ferns she'd sat on and flung them into the underbrush.

"That radio has stayed pretty quiet. There's been nothing but static for hours." Okay, she admitted, she was stalling. She'd rather eat that disgusting mold thing on the tree next to them than start walking again. "Do you think that's good news?"

"It probably doesn't mean anything," he said. "It's going to be the military searching for us in here, not the police, and this is a police radio. The only way we're going to hear something on it now is if the military use the same frequency, which I doubt."

He turned and started walking again, and with a sigh, she began to trudge after him. The sandwich and drink had made her feel half-human again, but lack of sleep was catching up with her. Her legs felt wooden. Because the upper canopy blocked most of the sunlight, the forest floor was surprisingly clear. Occasional fallen trees blocked their path, but mostly there were only leafy ferns and rotting vegetation. This made a thick spongy carpet of muck that clung to her boots and made every step an effort.

She hadn't lied about her muscles. Every time she picked up her foot she felt the ground sucking at it, making the backs of her legs tremble with exertion. To make matters worse, she thought she could hear a low rumble in the distance, which sounded suspiciously like thunder. She supposed she should count herself lucky that they hadn't been rained on yet, but she wasn't in the mood to count her blessings. "Do you think they have parties trying to pick up our trail?"

"Hard telling." It gratified her to note that walking seemed to be a bit difficult for him, too. Of course, he was also carrying both their bags and hacking through any vines that blocked their way. "If they got really fortunate and figured we'd head for the forest, and found the exact place we entered it—we'd have no more than an hour head start, tops." At her gasp, he looked back at her. "But that's the worst-case scenario. They're going to figure we'd head for the docks. They'd need special equipment to hunt for us in the jungle at night. And it would take a while to put a team together."

"Unless they already had men in the jungle that they could get in contact with," she said, half thinking out loud. When he only looked at her, she added, "That guy they're searching for. What if they have a party already in here trailing him?"

They exchanged a look, and Ana knew she wasn't saying anything he hadn't already thought of. There was more than the danger behind them to fear. They could just as easily be walking into the enemy's arms.

Chapter 10

The ominous sound Ana had heard earlier increased, a rumbling in the sky that sent the parrots and toucans screeching in flight, blinding streaks of brilliance through the forest. There wasn't time to appreciate the sight. Moments later the sky opened up in a torrential downpour. If she thought she couldn't get any more miserable, Ana was quickly proven wrong. The rain turned the vegetation beneath their feet into swampy muck that tugged at their boots like a vacuum with each step. The humid air became a tropical steam bath, an exotic sauna from which there was no escape. Soaked to the skin, wiping the moisture from her face, she could only think that the mosquitoes were going to be worse than ever after this.

It was all she could do to put one foot in front of the other. So intent was she on that task that when Jones stopped in front of her, throwing out a hand warning to be quiet, her dulled reflexes had her plowing into his back.

He grabbed her around the waist to steady them both.

Ana's first thought was that he didn't let go of her immediately. His hard arm was unyielding around her, keeping
her plastered to his side. His body threw off a heat that had
nothing to do with the outdoor temperature but was
uniquely his own. And for a moment she wanted nothing
more than to turn in to that heat, to claim some of it for
herself.

The strength of that longing was staggering. Intellectu-
ally she could blame it on the situation. Didn't they say
that danger was a powerful aphrodisiac? Add bone-deep
weariness to the mix, and her sudden desire to rip his
clothes off would be reasonable, wouldn't it?

The fuzzy, barely formed thoughts were shocking
enough to have her pulling away from him. Apparently,
proximity shredded her common sense. Despite the fact that
he was her only chance off this island, she trusted him less
than ever. He'd made no attempt to explain his presence in
the capitol. And until she could puzzle that out, she
couldn't afford to feel anything toward the man but caution.

"Quiet." His near-silent command succeeded in shaking
the wayward thoughts from her mind. She became aware
of the rigidity of his muscles. Peering ahead, she could see
nothing that warranted his sudden attention.

"Stay back." Jones slipped out of the backpack and
reached inside it, taking out the pair of binoculars he'd used
earlier. Unscrewing the night scope lens first, he handed
that to her before raising the binoculars to look at something up ahead.

Ana squinted through the pouring rain. The vegetation a
hundred yards or so in front of them grew denser again.
Jones would have to hack his way through it. But try as
she might she could see nothing that would warrant his
sudden caution.

When he lowered the binoculars, she snatched them from

his hand. "Let me see." At first she saw nothing but an up-close sight of the vines and bushes ahead. But eventually, once she shifted the angle of the glasses, she saw what he'd been looking at.

"A village!" The collection of huts barely qualified as such but surely they'd provide shelter. There might even be beds. Food. Maybe Sam had found this place in his flight, and sought help. Perhaps he was even there now.

Hope jittered oddly in her chest. Granted, it was a long shot, but the people there would know of other villages in the jungle, wouldn't they? And chances were she and Jones would be coming across more than one of them on their way to the north shore.

"We'll have to veer right to avoid the village and revert to course on the other side of it."

Dropping her hand with the binoculars, she jerked to face him. "What? Why? Maybe someone down there can help."

"That's doubtful. These people live off the land and sea. They'll be among the poorest on the island. And the villages would be the first place the militia will check if they're combing the jungle."

The tiny thread of hope she'd been harboring abruptly snapped. It was sheer stubbornness that made her protest. "You don't know that. We can't even be sure whether the military is searching for us."

"Let's just say I know what I'd do in their place." He reached up, sluiced the water off his beard-roughened jaw. "They've had not one but two security breaches in the last several days. At least I heard that the man they were looking for had fought with a senior cabinet member."

Wariness flickered. "I heard that, too," Ana said.

"I have no idea what the first guy was after, but they can't afford to let you off the island alive."

The chill traveling over her skin owed nothing to the

rain. How much had he put together? "I...you're being overly dramatic."

"Think about it." His expression, his tone, was implacable. "You witnessed a drug transaction and then saw a high-ranking government official conversing with the suspect in his office. I happen to know that Laconos is petitioning the Global Trade Organization for a higher level of participation. If word got out that the government was running drugs here, it would sink the vote in London next week."

Mind whirling, she looked away, afraid of what he might see in her expression. Jones knew a bit more than she'd expected about the Laconos government and their possible motives. Not for the first time she wondered at his background. It had been glaringly apparent for the past twenty-four hours that he was more, much more than he seemed.

And even wondering about that couldn't detract from her worry over his words. He hadn't said anything she hadn't feared already, but hearing the fears spoken out loud made them more real somehow, more threatening. For the first time it hit home that she was in no position to help Sam anymore. It would be all she could do to help herself.

"I didn't mean to scare you." Her gaze flew up to lock with his as he ran a crooked finger along her jawline. "I'm just saying that in their place, I'd do exactly the same thing. We're traveling the length of the jungle, but if they have the manpower, they'll split up and come in from the shore every few miles or so, and cross its width. Crisscrossing that way, they'll have a better likelihood of running into us. So it'd be smartest to stay away from all the areas they'd expect us to stop."

Silently she nodded. He'd obviously far greater expertise in tactical maneuvers than she. And though she'd give a great deal to know where that experience came from, she couldn't afford not to use it…for as long as it took to get them both out of there.

"Look at it this way." His thumb skated across her bottom lip, before dropping away. "You're getting that jungle tour you talked about."

Recognizing his attempt to lighten the mood, she forced an answering smile. "Maybe you could expand your business after this. Deep-sea fishing. Ocean charters. Guided tours of the rain forest. Rescuing damsels in distress."

He looked away, hanging the binoculars around his neck, stuffing the extra lens in his backpack. "I'm no romantic hero. If you're looking for a white knight, you've got the wrong guy."

The distance that suddenly yawned between them had nothing to do with proximity. But it was there all the same, and recognition of the fact had her stomach abruptly hollowing out. "Well, that's okay," she drawled, wiping the rain out of her eyes. "I've never thought of myself as a damsel, either. Too clingy. I'd much prefer slaying the dragon on my own."

He spared her a glance before picking up his machete and slicing through the tangled vines to their right. There was a grudging note of respect in his voice when he spoke again. "If the dragon knew you were coming, I'm betting he'd run like hell."

Jungle rimmed the village like a bowl, with the huts lying well below the ridge in the semi-cleared center. Rocky slopes jutted sharply upward, to the dense green vegetation that would give way to forest. It was around this ridge that Jones led Annie. He didn't want to veer too far out of their way, nor could he afford to stray too close to the outer edge of the vegetation where they would be visible to anyone below.

He glanced over his shoulder to check on Annie's progress. She never protested and, God help him, never whined about the pace he set or about wanting to stop. As a matter of fact, the only time she'd made a sound in the past hour was when she'd paused to relieve herself and had gotten up close and personal with that spider. The corner of his mouth kicked up. Considering that it was the size of a dinner plate and had a leg span of over eight inches, he couldn't really claim she'd been overreacting.

Since then there hadn't been a peep out of her, and that was cause for some alarm. He was getting used to her pointing out the orchids growing wild on the trunk of a host tree, or the pattern of the lacy ferns springing up wild between the trunks. He could only figure sheer exhaustion had set in, and that she was saving her breath for the trek. He checked his watch. They'd been in the jungle for more than twelve hours already. In another two or three hours it would be dusk. Darkness fell early and suddenly in the tropics. He needed to find them a safe place to stop for the night soon.

He reached for the binoculars and checked the village below. It seemed strangely deserted. A fire had been built in the middle of the clearing, but no one had been tending it as long as he'd been observing, and the rain had extinguished it. The male villagers may well be away hunting or gathering food. But that didn't explain why there were no children playing outside, no brightly clothed women drawing water or tending to a meal on the fire. Unease trickled down his spine.

"What's the matter?"

"Something isn't right." He continued to scan the scene, his instincts sharpening. He lowered the glasses and turned to look at her. She'd stopped, was swaying a little on her feet. She looked, he thought grimly, as if one strong wind would knock her flat. Not that they were likely to get one here. The air was so thick and still it was suffocating.

"I'm going to take a closer look. You wait here." It was a measure of her weariness, he thought, that she didn't protest, just inspected the nearby tree trunks for insects or slime mold before selecting one to lean against.

Strangely reluctant to leave her, he had to force himself to turn and make his way through the thicker vegetation. He would only be a few yards away. There was no reason to feel this ill at ease. He'd be able to hear her if she called out for help, or if an animal came close enough to threaten her.

He stopped in his tracks, logic warring with emotion. Uttering a curse, he returned swiftly, slid the pack off his shoulders and dug in it. "Here." He took out her bag, reached into it and handed her gun to her. "Make sure you don't use this unless you have to. The sound of the shot will alert anyone in the area to our location."

He could see the surprise on her face, but she took the gun with undisguised eagerness. With his Beretta shoved into the waistband of his pants, he grabbed the binoculars and machete and strode away.

They'd traveled the ridge until they were directly above and to the right of the village. Jones hacked and sawed at the dense thicket outside the forest until he had a clear view, then squatted on his haunches and reached for the binoculars again.

The structures below were covered with corrugated tin roofs, orange with rust. Rivulets of the earlier rain ran down in steady trickles off the roof to the soggy ground below. The windows were covered only with oil cloth, which were all drawn closed now. The places had to be stifling.

The hair on the back of his neck prickled. There were shadows moving across the cloth, evident in the sunlight.

More than ever he was convinced something was seriously wrong down there. Maybe there was an illness confining the people to their homes. But even then someone would be moving back and forth between the huts tending the sick, wouldn't they?

Utterly still, Jones kept the glasses trained on the scene below. It was another fifteen minutes before his watchfulness was rewarded. Two fatigues-clad men came out of house, squatted on the dilapidated porch and lit cigarettes Both had automatic machine guns strapped to their backs.

Military.

The knowledge sent adrenaline spiking through his veins. He'd told Annie earlier what he'd expected the men to do. He wished by all things holy that he could have been wrong. Edging back into the vegetation again, he swiftly made his way to her. They needed to get as far away from here as possible, and damn fast. If any more of the troops were spread out in the area, they could end up tripping over them.

He checked his watch again. The more distance they could put between them and the village before dusk, the safer they'd be. Moving swiftly, he retraced his steps to where he left Annie.

The place was deserted.

He gave a low whistle, thinking she was hiding somewhere nearby. "Annie? It's Jones. Let's head out." He scanned the surrounding area carefully, but she was nowhere in sight. There was a click behind him and he whirled, reaching for his gun. And found himself looking down the barrel of an AK-47.

"Lancez en bas votre arme."

Jones didn't need to call on his little knowledge of French to understand the command. He let the Beretta dangle from one finger, then tossed it at the soldier's feet.

"Les mains en haute. Tournez-vous lentement."

Making no attempt to interpret or obey, Jones sent one last sweeping glance around. Had the man or one of his friends already gotten to her? Or had she seen the soldier first and hidden?

Panic slicked nastily down his spine. If she was already in their possession, her death certificate was all but signed. He had no doubts that Shala would order her demise without a second thought.

"Et la femme?" When Jones asked about the woman, interest flickered on the man's face.

"Où est-elle?"

Jones breathed a tiny bit easier. If the soldier was asking about Annie's whereabouts, it was a sure bet she hadn't been captured yet. Maybe he could buy them some time.

"Je vous prendrai à elle," Jones said haltingly.

The soldier was silent, as if weighing Jones's offer to take him to Annie. He must have decided that he had nothing to lose, because he indicated for him to move ahead, saying, *"Montrez-moi. Maintenant!"*

Jones preceded the man, heading into the forest. The dim green twilight there would give him a better chance of eluding him. The muzzle of the gun jabbed into his back, an insulting reminder of his position. He kept his pace deliberately slow, waiting for his chance to overpower the soldier.

A burst of static sounded nearby. The soldier stopped, and it took a split instant for Jones to remember he no longer wore the radio. Before he'd set off he'd put it in the pack, which he'd left with Annie. And the soldier hadn't been carrying one. He glanced behind him, saw the soldier scanning the area around them.

With lightning speed he leaped to the left, prepared to take advantage of the distraction. The soldier immediately recognized his mistake, raised his gun, but Jones was already sending a hard right to his jaw. The man dropped, and Jones followed him down, delivering another blow to guarantee unconsciousness.

Reaching down, he slipped the automatic weapon's strap from the man's neck and then looked up, scanning the area.

Annie stepped out from some huge ferns, still clutching the now silent radio in her hand.

He grinned at her. Her diversion had been sheer genius. "Nice job."

"If that hadn't worked I had a pile of rocks to start throwing."

Striding toward her, he said, "The radio was a surer thing than hoping for accuracy."

Amazingly enough, her nose tilted up. "Hope would have nothing to do with it. I'll have you know I took the softball team to state three years straight with this arm." The arm in question, with its puny muscle, was flexed for his admiration.

He stared at her as if he'd never seen her before. Maybe he hadn't. Not really. The rain had turned her hair into a tumble of ringlets that looked baby soft. Her sky-blue eyes were shadowed with fatigue, her features bearing the unmistakable stamp of weariness. But her head was lifted at a cocky angle, matching the bravado in her voice. And for once in his life he obeyed an urge without question.

Crossing to her he cupped her head in one hand and gave her a long, hard kiss. One that didn't take into account the unconscious soldier at their feet. One that forgot for a moment that more troops were nearby.

His mouth ate at hers, drawing some kind of satisfaction from the contact that he would have denied if he'd been thinking. If he hadn't been only feeling, just for a moment. Her lips parted and she softened against him, nipped his bottom lip in the kind of response that had heat pooling in his groin. A dozen erotic scenarios danced through his mind, all of them featuring her naked, slim body under him. Over him.

His tongue glided along hers, and he steeped himself in her flavor. It traced through his senses, making all sorts of promises. Promises that couldn't be fulfilled right here. Right now.

Breathing raggedly, he tore his mouth away, took a step back. As if by establishing that small measure of distance he could deny the temptation she presented.

"He's coming around."

Her voice was thin, but steady enough. He focused on that, rather than on the way her lips had swelled from the pressure of his, the mark his beard had left near her mouth.

Turning back to the man crumpled on the ground, Jones observed distantly that she'd been right. The soldier seemed to be regaining consciousness. Reaching down, Jones hauled him up by his shirt and clipped him smartly on the jaw. Dropping his limp form again, he held out his hand. "Give me your scarf." She unwound it from her throat without question and placed it in his palm. Expertly he wadded the cloth up and jammed it in the soldier's mouth.

Rising, he grabbed the machete from the bag she'd dropped beside her and strode over to free a stout vine. He used it to bind the soldier's arms and legs, and left him trussed up, still unconscious, on the forest floor.

Looking at his watch, he said, "There may be more of them combing the area. We have to figure that there are. We've got less than two hours of daylight left."

She nodded, but he wondered just how much more energy she had before she dropped completely. She'd had no more than short rests in the past thirty-six hours. He had to get her to safety soon. Someplace she could clean up,

eat and get some uninterrupted sleep. Where they could
both refuel before they set off again tomorrow.

"Stay close behind me, understand? And not a sound.
There's no telling where the rest of the troops might be."

He struck far right, heading much farther off course than
they'd originally planned. He set a fast pace, checking back
frequently to make sure she wasn't lagging behind. Once
she slid in the slippery muck beneath their feet, fell to her
hands and knees. He helped her up, and after that kept a
firm hand clasped around hers.

They walked in silence for fifteen minutes before the
vegetation grew denser. That often meant a clearing ahead
and Jones walked faster. They were due a bit of luck.
Maybe the jungle gave way here to the rockier region like
that edging the village.

After several minutes of sawing through the underbrush
he cleared a large enough path for them to pass through.
From here he could see the ridge bordering the village, but
not the village itself. The sun was sinking rapidly below
the horizon. But it wasn't the rapidly fading sunlight that
had him muttering a string of very inventive curses.

It was the cliff straight ahead of them.

He glanced back at Annie.

"Uh-uh." She raised her hands and shook her head furiously. "Don't even think it."

"There are plenty of footholds. Vines to grab. It's not a
sheer drop. Come and see."

"I don't need to see." Despite her exertion in the last
few minutes, her face had gone completely white. "We'll
just go another way."

He reached for reason. "There's a stream down there.
We could clean up and find a place to pitch camp. The
sooner we get started, the sooner you can get off your feet
for several hours."

"My feet are fine." As if to prove it, she stomped one of them, her gaze still avoiding the empty area behind him. "We'll go around. Or back."

Valuable minutes were ticking by. He reached for a patience he rarely bothered with. "To get to an easier path down we'd have to backtrack at least two miles. And we can't go back the way we came, Annie. You know why."

Her head was shaking furiously, and he got the first inkling that he wasn't dealing with a totally rational argument. "I'm staying here. You go down. I'll meet you there tomorrow. That's right. Maybe by then…"

He took four quick steps and grabbed her shoulders. "We're both going down and we're going down now. It'd be suic— It'd be stupid to wait until dark. We can't waste time arguing."

Her eyes were dark and huge in her face. Under normal circumstances she'd send a fast right jab into his gut for the way he was ordering her around, but it didn't take a rocket scientist to figure that these weren't normal circumstances. He peered at her closely. A sheen of sweat had formed on her brow, and the shaking in her limbs wasn't caused solely by exhaustion. "I won't let anything happen to you, I promise. But you're gonna have to trust me."

He didn't think his words even registered. She swallowed hard, stepped back, yanking herself out of his grasp. He could almost see her reach for control, saw the effort it took for her to tuck away the terror. "I'm sorry." Her voice barely trembled. "I'm not trying to be difficult, really I'm not. I just can't…." Her voice cracked on the last word and he knew they were going to be doing this the hard way.

"Okay." His voice soothing, he began making plans. "Just let me figure something out."

He left her to survey the rocky mountain slope again.

Twenty yards away it seemed less steep. That would be the
path they'd take. His decision made, he strode past her to
the entrance of the jungle. Selecting a young supple strangler vine, he cut it away and approached her with it.

Warily she backed away. "What are you going to do?"

"Tether us together so I can do the work. You just keep
your eyes closed and I'll get us both lowered to safety."

"I can't."

He made quick work of the knots binding them together
at the waist. "Here." He shrugged out of the backpack and
helped her slide her arms through it. "I'll do most of the
work. You just grab finger and toeholds where you can."

"No, I can't do it," she said, even as he was leading her
closer to the face of the cliff. He grabbed a vine that grew
between the rocky side and tugged on it. It'd do. Twisting
back to his feet with the vine in one hand, he went to her,
pulled her close.

"I know you're scared." Her heart was hammering like
a locomotive in her chest. He remembered the trouble he
had getting her to climb down the cable at the capitol.
Heights must be the one thing in this world that she feared.

"Please, Jones…" She bit her lip on the whimper that
threatened. "I just…"

"Shh." His lips brushed her hair. "It's going to be all
right."

Her gaze turned to his, tentative. "Really?"

He nodded, got a firmer grasp on the vine. "Absolutely." He waited until he felt her relax against him, a
quick sag of relief. Then with one swift movement, he had
them both swinging off the side of the cliff.

Chapter 11

She was too quiet.

Jones threw Annie a concerned glance. She was sitting obediently on the large flat rock where he'd placed her. The flashlight he'd handed her was dangling loosely from her grasp. At this distance her dark clothes melded with the night, but her face stood out starkly. She hadn't spoken a word since their wild climb down the mountain slope. As a matter of fact, she hadn't spoken a word since he'd nudged her, oh so gently, off the cliff.

An unfamiliar emotion surged through him, felt suspiciously like guilt. There was nothing else he could have done, he reminded himself, as he unfolded the neat square of mosquito netting over the thick layer of ferns he'd cut. Nothing short of knocking her unconscious, which he tended to think she'd have appreciated even less.

But every shuddering breath she'd taken as he'd let go of one vine to grab for another, every fractured sob that had escaped her lips as they scrabbled for footholds to break their slide down the mountain...all of them had torn through his chest like a blade. When they'd reached the bottom she'd been unable to stand without support. He hadn't spent a lot of time searching for the best place to pitch their small tent. His main concern had been her.

He crossed to the small creek and dipped his hands in, washing off the worst of the day's grime. Then he took off his shirt, peeling off the ribbed sleeveless undershirt beneath. He dipped the undershirt in the water, soaking it thoroughly and wringing it out. Then he went to her, knelt down and dabbed her face with it.

She didn't jerk away. She didn't do anything but look at him with that vacant expression that told him she was edging too close to shock. "Annie." He didn't recognize that soft tone to his voice. "Look at me, baby. Look at me." When she did he saw a flicker of awareness return to her eyes. Encouraged, he moved the damp cloth in soothing strokes along her jawline, down her throat.

"We'll just get you cleaned up and then finish off the rest of those sandwiches, okay? Then you'll get some rest, I promise. How do eight hours sound?" He cleaned her hands with that same easy stroke, murmuring a running litany of words that he didn't even think about. His focus was on her.

And when a great shudder seemed to rack her body he gathered her close, ready for the storm of tears that she surely had trapped inside. But the tears never came. After a while she moved back, and he dropped his arms, his gaze searching hers. "Okay?"

She nodded, avoiding his eyes. "I'm hungry enough to eat a slug rat, though."

Given her disgust for the rodentlike fanged creatures they'd come across a time or two, that was saying something. "One slug-rat sandwich, coming up."

She didn't speak much while they ate sparingly from the provisions he'd packed. Or while they sipped at their precious store of water. He helped her down to the creek, so she could clean and dry her feet to protect them from jungle rot. And when he crawled into the small tent with her and zipped up the netting, she was still silent. She didn't appear to notice that there were only inches separating them as they lay on their sides, spoon fashion. She didn't ask about the phosphorus light gleaming, off in the darkness. Or comment on the bats zooming along, eating their fill of mosquitoes and other bugs. She didn't mention the glowing eyes that appeared every now and then in the distance, or the occasional scream as small animals became prey.

She just lay quiet and still, so still he might have thought she was asleep, if he hadn't been so close to her. Her breathing wasn't slow and even. Her muscles weren't relaxed.

"In case it slipped your attention, I'm afraid of heights." Her attempt at an offhand tone failed miserably. He could still hear the panic that was merely layered beneath the surface. "Acrophobia. Who thinks up those names, anyway?"

"How long have you had it?"

His quiet question seemed to take her by surprise. He surprised himself by how much her answer meant to him. He was unused to letting things matter, especially things that were out of his control. But he wanted this, from her, now. Wanted her to trust him to some small degree.

"Since I was three."

The night sounds faded in significance compared to the words he could feel trembling inside her. Waiting to be freed.

"Two weeks after my third birthday I was kidnapped." He jerked against her, he couldn't help it. Her blunt announcement couldn't have been further from what he was expecting.

"What in hell happened?"

She seemed to go limp then, as if the tenseness that had been holding her muscles rigid streamed out of her like air from a deflated balloon. Without a thought his arm went to her waist, exerting the slightest pressure to urge her to lean against him. When she did, the primitive rage welling inside him was eased, just a fraction.

"Like you guessed, my daddy was rich. Someone wanted a piece of that, I guess. Wanted it badly enough to snatch me out of my bed one night, when the house was asleep. I don't remember much about the whole thing, really. Most of it I learned much later. There was a ransom demand." Her voice turned pensive. He wondered if she was even aware that her hand had gone to the arm he had clasped around her waist, stroking it lightly. "I guess they had to wait for the money to be paid. In the meantime I was kept in a wire kennel. Like a dog cage. Lowered over the side of this ravine that drops down to the Atchafalaya River. They had some kind of pulley on a chain rigged up. And when the wind blew the chain would creak, and the kennel would sway…"

His arm tightened. She didn't have to say more. Didn't have to describe the sight of the river, tiny in the distance below, the desolation of the area, the way the wind would carry away any screams for help a terrified little girl might have made. He could imagine it for himself. All of it.

His throat thick he asked, "Did they catch them?"

He felt her shake her head in the darkness. "No. Some boy ditching school happened across me. There was no way anyone on the ground could have seen me. The brush from the cliff face blocked their view. But he was a daredevil, I guess. Walking across a dilapidated railroad trestle to prove something to his friends. It was just at the right height to spot me.''

"God." He was surprised to discover that he was the one shaking now. Shaking with a kind of helpless fury over an event long ago. One he couldn't put right. A sense of helplessness nearly choked him.

"A month later my parents were killed in a car accident." Her voice had tapered off to a whisper. The backdrop of night noises seemed to recede. His senses were totally attuned to her. "And the worst thing is…I don't remember them. Not at all. I have pictures, you know? And stories that my brothers told me, but that's all they are…someone else's memories. That seems such a cheat, somehow. That the fear has been with me all this time, but I don't have one lousy memory of them to call my own."

He wasn't a man used to offering comfort. Had even less need of it himself. But he reached deep inside for some to offer to her now. "The fear…that's in your mind, right? And your parents…you keep them in your heart. That's closer."

"I guess." The words sounded wistful.

"Besides, you control the fear, it doesn't control you. You proved that tonight."

Her laugh was sardonic. "Yeah, I was pretty heroic up there tonight, Jones. I was practically comatose by the time you got me down."

He lowered his face until her hair brushed his lips. "That's what courage is. Doing something in spite of the fear."

"Does that take into consideration that slight shove you gave me?"

Incredibly, he wanted to smile. She was starting to sound a bit like her old self. "Yeah, I guess so."

"In that case…" She gave a yawn and wiggled against

him to get more comfortable. "Anything you're afraid of? Anything I can help you out with? Pitch you headfirst into a pile of slug-infested carcasses? Give you a tiny push into a pool of piranhas? I'm at your disposal."

His lips curved against her hair. "I'll let you know. Right now you need to sleep."

Miraculously she seemed about to do just that. Her body went totally boneless in his arms, and her voice sounded drugged the next time she spoke. "You, too. Big day ahead." Another yawn overtook her. "Another fun-filled day of dodging bad guys and danger. But not to worry." Her words were slurring slightly as she lost the struggle with sleep. "Danger's…my…middle…name."

He brushed his lips lightly over her ear, nuzzled the baby-soft skin there. "Mine's Augustus. If you tell anyone, I'll have to throw you off another cliff."

The first thing Ana noted when she opened her eyes was that Jones was no longer at her side, despite the fact that dawn was just lightening the forest. The second was the enormous spotted snake that was slithering through the ferns next to her, its breakfast still visibly moving down its long scaly length.

"Jones!"

He must have been nearby, because he appeared in time to see the snake disappearing in the grass. "Don't worry. It's not poisonous."

"Tell that to whatever it just swallowed," she muttered, struggling with the zipper on the tent. He approached and released it from the outside, taking her hand and helping her out. "Here." He thrust a fresh pair of socks into her hand. "I washed your other pair. Put these on and check your boots before slipping your feet in them."

She braced one hand against him as she obeyed. "You're pretty domestic for a he-man type."

He cocked a brow. "He-man?"

"You know." She switched feet. "The kind of guy who can go into the wilderness with a box of toothpicks and build a shelter and a watertight raft."

"Are you by any chance the type of woman who can rustle up breakfast in the middle of a jungle?"

"Unless you're referring to the urban jungle with a 7-11 on every corner…no. I can, however, whistle Dixie through a blade of grass and do the YMCA with my legs." She shrugged as her second confession earned her a long stare. "We all have our talents."

"Before you offer to demonstrate yours, I've got a surprise for you."

Following him, she noted he had his Beretta again tucked in his waistband. She knew he'd had it close at hand while they slept. But that wasn't what had provided her with the feeling of safety that had enveloped her as she'd nestled close to him. That feeling had come from being tucked close to his side, his arm holding her tight and secure through the night.

Blowing out a breath, she trailed behind him as he led her along the streambed for several hundred yards and then around a pile of boulders. She stopped in her tracks, delight holding her transfixed. "A waterfall!"

It was closer to a heavy drizzle than to Niagara Falls, but Ana didn't think she'd ever seen such a welcome sight. The rising sun sent rainbows dancing across the cascading water, cast a brilliant sheen across the frothing bubbles.

"River runoff. It feeds the stream down here. I've already checked it out. Nothing more dangerous in the water than some goldfish. You can put your clothes here." He helped her down to the flat rocks that acted as natural stepping stones into the water.

His appearance made sense then. He was bare-chested, drops still clinging to the curling brown patch of hair adorning his torso in a perfect vee. His hair was wet, and he hadn't pulled it back yet. It looked like he'd finger-combed it off his face, leaving it to curl damply behind his ears. Wearing only a two-day growth of beard and the black jeans and boots, he could have stepped out of history two hundred years past, a pirate roaming the tropical seas.

Her pulse stuttered. The rest of the world had never seemed so far away. Dawn was barely tingeing the sky. The only sounds were the gurgling water, and the ever-present backdrop of chittering insects. Farther in the distance the constant noises of the forest could be heard as the night animals found their beds and the birds and monkeys woke. The sounds of nature. Basic and elemental.

It was easy to feel at one with that primitive setting. The blood in her veins had turned molten, pounding out a pagan primal beat.

She didn't look away from him; she couldn't. She watched, transfixed, as awareness flooded his face, followed by evidence of a response that he didn't try to hide. The muscles in his jaw clenched, and his eyes went the color of smoke.

Swaying toward him, she laid her hand gently on his arm, rigid beneath her touch, and kicked out of her unlaced boots. Without releasing his heated gaze, she bent, dragged the socks off her feet. He'd made no effort to move, nor to look away. His face could have been chiseled from the harshest granite, but his eyes…the look there gave her courage.

Wild. Fervent. With a hint of savage hunger that made her shiver as she reached for the bottom of her tunic top.

Dragging it up her torso, she let it drop to the rock beneath her feet. His gaze painted her with liquid fire, lingering on the black lacy bra that fastened between her breasts. Her breathing grew ragged.

She wasn't certain who this woman was. She'd never, in her life, stripped for a man. Never felt this burning in the pit of her stomach that promised a fiery, painful ache if he didn't touch her soon. If he didn't return the passion burning a comet's path through her system.

Her hands were shaking when she released the tie on her drawstring pants. Without any urging, they slid down her legs leaving her clad in nothing but the tiny black panties and matching bra.

The dawn air was warm, comfortable. So it couldn't account for the sheen of moisture on Jones's chest, the streak of dampness above his lip. He hadn't spoken a word. Hadn't moved a muscle. If not for the avid, intent look in his eyes, she'd have melted in a pool of embarrassment at his feet. How many times had he told her already that he didn't want her?

Just as an all-too-familiar uncertainty jittered through her, his hand lifted, as if detached from the rest of him. His fingers traced the line of her bra where it bordered her skin, drawing a path down to the shallow cleavage. His touch trailed fire in its wake, and Ana had difficulty drawing a breath. For a sudden panicky moment she wondered what she'd been thinking, to try and unleash the hunger she'd sensed in Jones. The hunger she'd sampled for herself on more than one occasion. Her meager experience hadn't prepared her for a man like him. The realization was both frightening and tantalizing.

His fingers went to the clasp between her breasts and released it with one deft motion that rivaled her own for ease. He spread his palm on her skin below the clasp, seem-

ing fascinated as the material trembled, then slowly fe
away to bare her breasts.

Her breath strangled in her lungs. The flame of heat i
his eyes was scorching, the one in her belly equally so. Sh
had the sudden, dizzying thought that once he took her int
his arms they'd likely combust from the scalding intensity
If he took her into his arms. Right now he looked like
man on the edge of an agonizing decision.

In an effort to tip the scales a bit, she swayed forwar
her breasts grazing his fingertips where they were sti
placed on her skin. She reached out a hand, explored th
defined ridges of bone and sinew that bisected his ches
The rest of him would be just that hard, she thought, flexin
her fingers testingly. Just that sleekly muscled.

Those muscles jerked now beneath her touch, an invol
untary reaction that spoke more clearly than words of hi
response. The skin on his chest was roughened with hai
but his sides were taut, smooth. She stroked the expanse o
skin there as she raised her gaze to his, half shy, half daring

His eyes were heavy-lidded, full of promise, as h
hooked his index fingers in the straps of her bra and nudge
them down her arms. She let her arms go loose, allowe
the garment to join the puddle of clothes at their feet.

Jones's face was flushed, the dull red of arousal stampin
his cheekbones, his nostrils flared as if the only response
he'd give her were the involuntary ones. But his voice whe
it came was raspy with checked desire. "Be sure, Annie
Be very sure."

He said nothing else. He didn't need to. She knew wha
he was saying and knew what she was promising when sh
answered. "I'm sure." And then watched the storm she'
unleashed.

His eyes flickered for a moment, the only warning sh
had before he reached for her, with a swiftness that woul

have shocked if it wasn't so welcome. She went willingly into his arms, reveling in the press of flesh against flesh.

It was a dizzying, exultant pleasure of the senses. His mouth crushing hers with a pent-up longing only hinted at by his iron-clad control. The clash of teeth, as their lips twisted together, the play of muscles beneath the biceps she clutched, the hard band of his arms around her back.

Somewhere in the distance a large jungle cat roared for its mate, and seconds later an answering howl was returned. Ana could feel that answer beating in her blood, pulsing in her body. The call of the wild reached below surface civility and beckoned to the most primitive response known. The desire to mate with this man owed as much to the emotional as to the sensual, but it was the sensual that ruled now. Basic, elemental and primal.

He reached behind him, pulled the gun from his waistband. Ana's hands were trembling on his zipper, especially when she worked the tab over the hard straining length beneath. She would have liked to go slow, but Jones was setting the pace. Backing a few steps away from her, he swiftly divested himself of his clothes, setting them with the revolver on the rock within easy reach. She wasn't offended at the cool logic of the move. His survival instincts were just as keen as the promise in his touch.

He straightened and she drew a sharp breath. His arousal jutted huge and hard from a patch of dense hair between his thighs. He put his thumbs in the sides of her panties and dragged them down her legs.

"Step out of them."

She obeyed his ragged command a moment before she was swept up in his arms, his eyes glinting down at her. Slowly, deliberately, he stepped down the rocks and into the water. It was deeper than she'd expected. Jones kept moving until he stood directly in front of the cascade, the water lapping at his waist. Dipping his head, he nuzzled a tender, swollen nipple, his beard rasping her skin, before taking the nipple into his mouth and suckling hard.

A kaleidoscope of color burst behind her eyelids. With each strong flex of his mouth he drew another spiral of pleasure from deep in her womb, until she was squirming against him in unspoken demand. He didn't release her, continuing in a deliberate way, almost lazy, his tongue and teeth providing a dual torture that scraped her senses raw.

His hand reached between her legs, and with very little urging parted them enough to allow his fingers to explore her sensitive folds.

Ana raked both hands through his damp hair in an unspoken plea. Unlike the endless, sensual minutes that had spun out between them on the shore, now it was as if they'd been caught in a vortex of passion, spinning her more and more quickly closer to the edge. And she didn't want to topple off that edge alone.

She lowered her hand, reached for him, at the same moment that he entered her with one long smooth stroke of his finger. A broken sob escaped her lips, and he shifted her to allow him more freedom.

Her fingers closed around him in the water, his heavy heat a shocking contrast to the cooler water surrounding him. His hips lunged in her grasp, urging her to explore the length of him, from the blunt velvety tip to the root of his arousal.

He lifted his head, pressed a hard kiss to her mouth. "You're rushing things."

Ana smiled, slow and secretive. "Yes." She stroked him again, before his hand went to hers, forcing it away. He shifted her in his arms so that she was facing him, and she clasped his hips with her knees. Then he took a step backward until the water poured over them both.

She gasped, pressing against him, and he took immediate advantage. Grasping her ankles, he drew them around his waist in a position that left her intensely vulnerable. His mouth went to her neck, slicking along the rivulets that poured down her throat, and his hands smoothed her wet hair back from her face.

The sky was painted with the beginnings of a glorious sunrise, but the beauty was wasted on Ana. She was a mass of crashing, unidentifiable sensations, each one with its own keen edge of pleasure. There was the scrape of Jones's whiskered jaw as he rubbed it against the dampness of hers; the flood of desire as he rolled one of her nipples between his forefinger and thumb; the exquisitely sexy slide of their wet skin as they slipped and rubbed against each other; the feel of his shaft pressed against her softness; a promise for the end of this torment.

She rose above him, dragging her torso up his chest and down again in a rhythmic movement that had him groaning. He reached down, positioned himself at the entrance of her opening, and his hands went to clutch her bottom. He gave a violent lunge upward as her hips came down to meet him, and this time it was she who cried out, a hoarse primal sound that seemed torn from her very depths. He was seated deeply inside her, the length and breadth of him stretching her to a point that bordered on the most delicious kind of pain.

"Jones," she half moaned, half sobbed. He was motionless inside her for a moment, as if giving her time to adjust to his penetration.

Then his forehead dropped to hers, his voice coming just as desperate. "Annie. More."

Even as she wondered at her ability to respond to his sensual demand, her hands were climbing to his shoulders, searching for purchase. She felt his fingers flex tightly on her hips, lifting her slightly to bring her back hard, to meet the slam of his hips.

The pleasure careened and collided inside her. Nothing else existed. There were only his slick muscles beneath her fingers, flexing and releasing with his every movement; his hard chest pressed against hers, his harsh breathing as it mingled with her own; the tight grip he had on her hips and the incredible full sensation of being possessed by him.

With every surge he seemed to seat himself more deeply inside her. Her desire was honed to a rapier edge as she moved with him, felt the bite of his fingers as he set the motion faster, harder, hotter. Her head fell back, too heavy for her neck, and the dazzling passion whirled faster.

His hand went between them and he stroked her where she was open and vulnerable, tapped the sensitive bundle of nerves hidden there. She tensed, something unfamiliar just out of reach. He urged her on, his dark words working their own sensual magic. "Let go, Annie. Let go now."

And then sensation surrounded her as he bent and took her nipple in his mouth, biting down gently. His clever fingers stroked and smoothed her quivering flesh while he kept her locked against him, surging faster and faster into her. And when he bent her back, slammed his hips against hers in a wild shuddering lunge, the sudden implosion of her climax seized her, the release spinning into endless aftershocks of pleasure.

She reached for him, her only anchor in the violent culmination of pleasure, and felt him tense, thrust wildly, and groan her name as the passion took him, too.

She'd never realized that being dressed by a man could take on almost the same intimacy as being undressed by one. Ana would like to believe she could have managed on her own. Okay, her legs were shaky and weak. She throbbed in places she had never, ever throbbed before. There was a delicious afterglow affecting her movements, making them seem slow and lethargic. But she was still certain that donning her bra wasn't beyond her.

"Let me."

She stopped trying to bat his hands away and allowed him to fasten the clasp between her breasts. "It occurs to me that you're a little too familiar with the way these things work."

Something suspiciously close to a smile sounded in his voice. "I like working with my hands."

She refrained from pointing out that he was extremely accomplished in that area. His ego didn't need inflating. "I think I can finish on my own."

Reluctantly he moved away. "If you insist." In the time it had taken her to draw on her panties and slip into her bra, he'd gotten fully dressed again, with the exception of his socks and boots.

There was a slight frown on his face as he regarded her. "I didn't use protection."

She stilled. Not out of fear for the risk they'd taken, but because his words summoned a vivid, erotic memory. Clearing her throat, she assured him, "It's not the right time." It was difficult to maintain eye contact during the intimate conversation. But he merely nodded. She reached for her tunic.

"By the way, Smith, if I forgot to mention it…"

A flash of something close to anxiety flickered to the surface, to fade when met with his wicked grin.

"…you have a truly excellent ass." He seemed to take pleasure in the hot tide of color that surged to her face. "Makes it hard to understand why you wanted to mar perfection with that tiny little penguin you had tattooed to your right cheek."

Her brows shot up, and one hand streaked behind her to cover the cheek in question. Feeling fabric beneath her fingers, she glowered at him. He must have glimpsed it sometime while they…well, sometime recently. And it was a bit disconcerting that he'd noticed every tiny detail about her when she'd been awash in indescribable sensation. "It was a dare," she finally mumbled.

His teeth flashed. "Don't be embarrassed. It's kind of cute."

He was looking entirely too pleased with himself. She stooped to grab her tunic and pulled it over her head. "I was wondering—" her voice was muffled by the garment she was wiggling into "—after what we've shared here…" She let her words trail off suggestively, watched his grin fade into a more familiar mask of wariness. "…do you think I could call you…Gus?"

His expression was pained. "Not unless you want to be tossed down on that cute little penguin of yours."

Pleased with herself, she took her time drawing on her pants as he shoved his feet into his socks and boots.

A few moments later he straightened. "I need to go out ahead, scout around. I found some plantains and nuts. They're up by the tent. Think you can have everything packed up when I get back?"

His return to the jungle survivalist was a bit disconcerting, given the time they'd just spent in each other's arms. She nodded, giving more attention than was necessary to tucking in her top and drawing the baggy trousers tight. Not for a moment was she going to let him know how momentous the act had been for her. She could be as nonchalant as a man. She just needed more practice at it, was all.

She gasped as he drew her against him. She hadn't even seen him move. He tipped her chin up with his hand, gazing down at her with eyes that saw too much. The kiss he pressed on her mouth was bruising. "Next time in a bed. All night. No distractions."

He released her and, grabbing the gun and binoculars, strode away. The whole moment was over in an instant, which was probably fortunate, because Ana wasn't exactly well versed in witty sexual repartee. As it was she could only touch the lips he'd so recently kissed and replay his words in her head. *Next time.* Her mouth curved in a tiny smile. Oh, yes, there was definitely going to be a next time.

She lost no time getting things picked up and packed away. There wasn't much. Only the wet socks to roll up and stow, the mosquito netting and small tent. While she munched on a plantain, she drew her bag out of his backpack and rearranged the remaining items, so they could be replaced inside taking the smallest amount of space possible.

Not for the first time, she marveled at the contents of the bag. Night-vision goggles and high-powered binoculars weren't picked up in the local department stores. Neither were cables like the one he'd used to enter the government building the other night.

With a swift glance around, she noted that Jones was nowhere within sight and began to go through the endless pockets of the bag. In one she found a set of finely wrought tools she could only figure were picks. The kind used on locks that weren't being opened the old-fashioned way. That explained how he'd entered the rooms in the capitol once he'd gained entrance to them.

She also discovered more ammunition for his gun, the one he'd taken with him, and the radio he'd used to contact Pappy. Their water bottles were there, nearly empty. If it rained this afternoon they'd have to try and catch some fresh water.

Poking into the next pocket she heard the telltale crumple of paper, and curiously drew it out. White and standard size, the letterhead was embossed with the stamp for the Laconos government. The body was covered with odd combinations of letters, symbols and numbers that made no sense.

It was encryption of some kind.

Mind whirling, she stared hard at it. Where had it come from? Had Jones stolen it from one of the offices? The questions faded in significance, as one thing became apparent. She needed to decode it.

It wasn't outside the realm of possibility. Despite what she admitted to Jones, she had a few more talents than whistling and dirty dancing. Designing encryption/decryption software was her job. Tremaine Technologies handled some of the United States government's most sensitive orders.

And she couldn't allow an opportunity like this to pass by. It might have something to do with Sam. With his assignment. Or information that would help sink Bunei's bid for more power in the trade organization.

She had a feeling this stolen sheet wasn't something Jones had planned to share with her. The realization brought a sick wash to her stomach. Digging into her bag, she withdrew her notebook. She wasn't being dishonest, not really. Even as she copied the symbols down in her notebook, a part of her was attempting to rationalize away her actions. A couple days ago it wouldn't have occurred to her to even try. But now things were different. And yet so very much the same.

Because despite making love with Jones, despite the closeness she thought was growing between them, in some ways they continued to be as far apart as ever.

Chapter 12

With a sense of déjà vu Jones led the way through the jungle, with Annie close behind him. They had at least five miles to cover today, and if they kept up the pace they'd set yesterday they would have no problem hitting the north shore by dark. They'd veered quite a bit closer to the shore than he'd originally planned, but as long as the jungle provided cover, they weren't risking exposure to anyone at the shoreline or beyond.

The cover of darkness would actually serve them well. He could use the shortwave hand radio to summon Ranachek, and if the old reprobate wasn't stinking drunk by that time, they could get off this island. He didn't have any doubt that Pappy had convinced the man to do as Jones had asked. Ranachek would sell his sainted mother for the right fee.

He wouldn't be unhappy to put most of this experience behind him. Squinting through the dim green gloom of the jungle, he used the machete on the vines strangling their

path, ignoring the luminous green tree constrictor twined
around a trunk near them. Dodging bullets and dabbling in
espionage brought back memories that were still much too
close to the surface, regardless of the efforts he made to
bury them.

There was, however, one part of this experience that he
wasn't in a hurry to see end. He turned his head, checking
on Annie's progress. She sent him a brilliant smile, one
that caught him hard in the chest. You'd think the woman
was on a vacation junket in the Ozarks. That she hadn't
just given herself to a man who'd forfeited his job, his
honor, and nearly his life in return for the simple pleasure
of being left alone.

Of course, she couldn't know what kind of man he was.
Grimly he faced forward again. He did a damn fine job of
hiding, had made it his life's work for the past three years.
There hadn't been a moment's regret in that entire time for
the choices he'd made.

Guilt, an ugly fanged creature, raised its evil head. He
hadn't spent the past few years denying himself any particular comforts, so there should have been no hesitation about
taking what Annie was offering. There *would* have been no
hesitation if he'd been able to convince himself it was just
sex. Just about the moment. But of all the lies he'd told in
his life, when dishonesty had been a tool of his job, he'd
never once lied to himself. With Annie, sex was all of it.
And none of it.

He reached back to help her through the opening he'd
cleared and dropped her hand again as soon as she'd moved
through it. He hadn't wanted this—any of it. The resentment welling in him was almost a relief. He'd never again
wanted to feel this violent surge of emotion for anything.
For anybody. Not for a woman. Not for his job. Not for
his country. And he resented fiercely that this tiny woman

with her shock of bright hair and mixture of secrets and innocence should jolt him out of his comfortable pattern.

"Oh, did you see that!"

He stopped to follow the direction of her pointed finger, watching the small lizard fold its skin back against its sides after it safely changed branches. "It's a flying dragon."

Her expression was disbelieving. "It looks like a lizard to me."

"It is a lizard. At least it's in that family. And it doesn't really fly, either. It uses that extra skin to help it glide from one branch to another."

"I know what I saw, ace. And it was definitely flying."

His lips twitched. "Okay, it was flying."

His easy agreement seemed to please her. "I knew you'd see things my way." They walked on in silence for a few more minutes. "Do you think the military is searching for us again?"

"Probably. If the team in the village is able to communicate to others, they'll get reinforcements to cover that whole area. But they don't know we detoured down that ravine. We're a good two miles west of the direction we were heading before."

Something in her silence alerted him. He glanced back to see the comprehension on her face. If there were other reinforcements in the area, two miles wasn't much of a safety net. But instead of giving voice to the thought, she said, "Whatever comes…we won't regret what happened between us, Jones."

It was half promise, half plea. And it called to an answering elemental instinct. "No." As much as he'd like to deny the truth he couldn't now with this woman. Couldn't deny it to himself. "We won't regret it."

They made fairly good time the rest of the day, despite a late-morning rainstorm that slowed their progress and made them both miserable. It gave them an opportunity to replenish their water supply, however, which had gotten dangerously low.

The soggy ground grew stickier and slippery in the afternoon heat. Once they happened upon another ridge much like the one that had rimmed the village, but not nearly as steep. When they'd attempted to scrabble down it, Annie had lost her footing and slid, rolling several yards before he'd grabbed ahold of her shirt, stopping her descent. His rescue hadn't come in time to save her from contact with several large rocks along the way.

The abrasions she'd suffered had needed immediate care. Left unattended, injuries could rapidly develop infection in this environment. Despite a game effort on her part, they made slow progress the last couple of miles. It was late afternoon before the jungle began to grow rockier, hinting at an upcoming change of terrain.

Jones stopped, sliding his arms out of the backpack to withdraw a directional navigator.

Annie stopped, too, breathing heavily as she watched him punch in their approximate longitude and latitude. "How do you know the right coordinates?"

"After three years, I know the waters around these islands pretty well."

"Three years? That's how long you've been running a charter service? What did you do before that?"

There was nothing in her tone but honest curiosity. It shouldn't be responsible for this vise squeezing his chest. His answer, when it came, was purposefully vague. "I was in…research."

"Research?" She wiped her face on the edge of her tunic while he kept his gaze trained intently on the navigator. "Like science? Marketing?"

"Not exactly." He slipped the instrument back in his

pack. "I'm going to go up ahead. I think the forest comes to an end close by up here, and using the glasses, I ought to be able to see if our ride is here."

"Then I'm coming with you," she said determinedly. "I don't want to stay in this damn jungle one single instant longer than I have to."

If she expected an argument, he wasn't about to give her one. At least she'd dropped her earlier line of questioning. But a half hour later, after they hacked their way out of the dense growth around the jungle's perimeter and he used the glasses to look out to sea, her earlier questions paled in significance.

Jaw clenched, he studied the horizon and silently swore a blue streak.

"Well, is he out there? Has he come yet?" When she would have tugged the binoculars from his hand, he refused to relinquish his grasp on them. "I'm calling first dibs on the shower when we get onboard. Of course, being the sweet-natured person that I am, I'm willing to share."

When her offer failed to elicit a response, her voice became more cautious. "Jones? Isn't Ranachek there yet?"

"He's there," he said flatly. He took the strap off his neck and handed her the binoculars. "Unfortunately, he's got company."

He gave her time to look for herself, to see Ranachek's red-and-white ship anchored peacefully at sea in the distance.

With two Laconos government cutters cruising nearby.

She swallowed hard as she lowered the glasses. "Maybe you could radio him…tell him to move to another site…"

Jones shook his head. "The government will be covering the frequency just waiting for any kind of communication to make their move. Ranachek can't convince him he's fishing or dolphin watching forever. By tomorrow he'll have to head back to Bontilla. They'll be covering any ship or plane that could get us off the island.''

"Then we'll find another way." Her tone had determination layering over the bleakness. She handed him back the glasses, and he raised them again. Something else caught his eye, and an idea began to form.

"Maybe there's another way, after all," he said slowly. When she looked up at him quizzically, he lowered the glasses to look at her. "How do you feel about another hike?"

"You stink, Jones. No, I mean it. You really stink." She ducked when he would have come closer. "And what's worse, *I* stink. You don't have enough hot water on your ship to get rid of this smell. I think it's in my pores." Ana strode as quickly as she could to where the *Nefarious* was rocking at the Bontilla dock, breathing through her mouth. It was safer that way.

"You know, I expected a little more gratitude," he said mildly. "I did get you safely back to Bontilla, away from the Laconos government, at no little risk to myself. Most women would thank me for that."

She stopped in her tracks. "Do I seem ungrateful? Well, let me just write you a little thank-you note right now." She pulled the notebook from her bag, found a pen and scribbled furiously. Ripping out the sheet she handed it to him with a flourish, fire in her eye.

He looked at it, then at her. "There's no *F* in *thank*," he pointed out.

"Read between the lines." She turned and marched to the ship, dodging his help when he would have given it and nearly falling over the side of the ship in the process.

"Be reasonable, Annie. The circumstances called for

desperate measures." He jumped nimbly aboard ship and followed her down the companionway.

"A garbage scow? That's pretty desperate, Jones. As a matter of fact, as rescues go, that's about the bottom of the barrel."

"It got us back to Bontilla, didn't it?"

"It did." She nodded grimly. "And in only eighteen hours, spent inhaling the putrefying stench of a country's accumulated garbage."

"Better than the alternative," he said bluntly.

The fact that he was right didn't improve her mood. Events of the past several days would put a sizable dent in anyone's disposition. "Remember my offer to share the shower? Well, you're uninvited."

"Honey, the way you smell, you're not hurting my feelings."

His remark had her slamming open her cabin door, in search of her toiletries. She planned on using every drop of the hot water. Every last drop. And she hoped that Jones froze in the water she left for him. If she decided to leave any at all.

He was still in the hallway, struggling with the lock on his stateroom. She paused to sneer at him. "You stopped to lock up your valuables before deciding to burgle the capitol?"

"No, Pappy must have locked it, but for the life of me, I can't figure out why he would…" He finally got the lock released and pushed the door open, only to stop in midsentence. Giving him a curious look, she peeked inside to see what had him suddenly speechless.

And stared, jaw agape.

"Sam!"

The bearded, gaunt figure lying in Jones's bed froze in

the middle of a grin he was greeting Jones with. "Ana-liese?"

"Sam!" Pushing beneath Jones's arm she leaped across the room and threw her arms around her brother. The same brother she'd sometimes feared she'd never see again. "My God, how did you get off the island? I knew you were hurt…oh!" She drew back suddenly, searching his form with anxious eyes. "Where are you injured? Do you need medical attention?"

Two hard hands held her away from him as he surveyed her. "What in God's name are you doing here?"

She opened her mouth to answer, looked at the man still watching them silently in the doorway, then snapped it shut again.

Short on patience, Sam Tremaine followed the direction of her gaze. "Jones? What the hell is my sister doing with you?"

"Your sister?"

When two incredulous narrowed male gazes swung to her, Ana detected a surge in testosterone in the room. The kind that boded ill for the lone female focus of their regard.

For some reason it was Jones's gaze she chose to meet. His eyes were flinty. "You're Tremaine's *sister?*"

"Well, technically…" she hedged.

"What do you mean, technically?" Sam roared. "Dammit, Analiese, will you tell me what's going on here?"

"Analiese? Tremaine?"

Jones could have been spitting the words like bullets. Ana nodded miserably. "I came to find Sam. I knew you were his way to Laconos, and I thought if I could retrace his steps, I'd stand a better chance of figuring out where he was."

"You'd better start at the beginning, Ana. How'd you

know where I went on…vacation? And why in hell would you take it into your head to follow me?''

Sam's imperious tone was a little too familiar to be tolerated. ''You weren't on vacation, you were on assignment,'' she snapped. ''If you want me to tell you the whole story, at least do me the courtesy of saving the fairy tales. In case you haven't noticed, I'm a little cranky at the moment.''

''I can attest to that,'' muttered Jones.

She didn't spare him a glance. She was too busy glaring at her brother. ''I don't know what agency you're working for. Given the level of encryption in your files, I figure CIA, but it doesn't matter. I've kept quiet about it for this long and will in the future. But don't try patting me on the head and feeding me a line of bull while you castigate *me* for the chances I take. I'm a little old for that kind of behavior, in case you haven't noticed.''

Both men were looking at her wide-eyed, caution blooming on their faces. ''Ana, you've always been too dramatic.'' The soothing note in her older brother's voice had her clenching her fists. If he hadn't already been injured, she'd have lunged for him. ''You've blown this whole thing up into something clandestine when there's a rational explanation…''

''She's not going to buy it.'' Jones's tone was flat, his gaze hard as it rested on Ana. ''She set this whole thing up, set *me* up precisely because she's too damn smart for her own good.'' He waited until Ana's gaze met his before going on, in that same expressionless voice that made something inside her cringe. ''I knew all along that something about you didn't add up. So this doesn't come as a total shock. What'd you think you were going to accomplish with this charade?''

"When I found out that Sterling had no idea where Sam was, I was desperate—"

"Sterling!" Sam's voice was panicked. He straightened up in bed, wincing at the effort it took, and stared hard at his sister.

"I've been doing courier work for him for two years," she said simply. It would have been impossible to miss the two men's reaction. But somehow it was the vile curse that Jones muttered that sliced the deepest. "I didn't think you'd want me unleashing Cade and James on you, so I thought I'd trace your steps, see if I could discover something about your whereabouts."

"You haven't told them any of this, have you?" When she shook her head, Sam relaxed a fraction. "Thank God for small favors. And Sterling?" Something in his voice alerted her. She searched his face carefully. "How much does he know?"

"I haven't been able to reach Sterling since the first night I hit Bontilla. There's no answer, and I only have the one number for him."

"Christ." Sam rubbed both hands over his face. "This is like a bad dream. Honey, I think Sterling is the one who set me up."

"What?" Jones's and Ana's words came simultaneously.

Sam dropped his hands, looked at them. "I came on a…fact-finding mission. But I didn't get very far, because someone tipped off the Laconos government."

"Icanno Shala claimed you'd breached the security at the capitol," she said.

"Shala." His voice was hoarse, his expression dazed as he swung his gaze to Jones. In a few succinct sentences Jones relayed Ana's involvement with the man, beginning with the drug deal she'd witnessed and ending with their escape from the building.

"I never accomplished my mission," Sam said grimly. "Because they were waiting for me as soon as I'd gotten inside the capitol. That's when I was wounded, when one of the men knifed me."

"How many did you take out?"

Ana sent Jones a disparaging glance. What difference did that make now?

Sam brightened. "Six were down at last count, but there were at least twenty others. I didn't like my odds, so I took off."

They actually shared an amused grin. Ana wanted to brain them both. Were they stupid enough to find that brush with death something to revel in? Their attitude took male idiocy to new heights.

"Let's dust off our testosterone chargers for the moment and focus, gentlemen," she said dryly. "Sam, what makes you think Sterling would set you up? What's in it for him?"

"Money. The right price can buy betrayal and treachery regardless of position." It was Jones who answered, and somehow Ana knew that he was speaking from personal experience. But her mind refused to leave the matter alone.

"Then why wouldn't he answer his phone once he knew I intended to follow Sam to Laconos? It would have been a perfect opportunity for him to keep track of me."

Sam shrugged, obviously bothered by the question. "I don't know. But he was the only one who knew of my mission, unless this goes a lot higher than him. That's why I stuck around and waited for you to get back here. I'm not real sure who else I can trust right now."

"The joys of living in the shadows," Jones said sardonically. "Never knowing who you can trust or where the bullet's going to come from. You should have gotten out when I did."

Suddenly everything clicked into place for Ana. She

turned to face Jones, accusing. "Research? You were in the Agency, too."

"You weren't exactly forthcoming yourself, so you can drop the recriminations. And the fact that I was in the life once means that I know exactly how dangerous it was for you to even dabble in it. What the hell were you thinking letting Sterling talk you into doing courier work for him?"

"It's not exactly rocket science," she said acerbically. "Getting an envelope or a briefcase from point A to point B doesn't usually involve much glamour or intrigue." She thought it prudent not to mention the one time the assignment had nearly gone awry. She doubted either man was in the mood to deal with that news rationally.

Sam was pinching his brow. "I don't even want to think about what James would have to say about this."

"I'll make you a deal, bro. You don't tell him what I do on my 'minivacations' and I don't tell him that being an international lawyer is only a front for you."

He dropped his hand to glare at her. "You're not in the position to be cutting deals, Annie. Don't push it."

"Yes," she said quietly, "I am. Look at me, Sam. I'm all grown up. I'm not a little girl anymore, and I don't need around-the-clock protection."

"We had reason to protect you."

"Yes." She hated the defensiveness in her brother's tone. Hated herself for putting it there. "But there came a time when I could choose either to smother under all that protection or go my own way and live life. Which would you have chosen?" When he remained silent, stubbornly so, she sighed, a wave of weariness overtaking her. The damned Tremaine code of honor was so ingrained in her brothers that she doubted it would allow them to see anything outside their perception of events. And while she returned their love, she wouldn't allow them to use those feelings as a mantle to suffocate her. Not anymore.

"How did you get off Laconos? Try as I might, I couldn't figure out how I was going to let you know I was there and could help you."

Sam said, "I had someone helping me. She was watching the pier and letting me know which ships were docked, and their ports of origin. I thought I was dreaming when I heard the *Nefarious* was back in port."

Suddenly something else clicked. Ana looked at her brother. "And you sent a message to Jones the last night, letting him know you were there." If she had to guess, the message said more than that. Enough to encourage him to break into the capitol and finish whatever assignment Sam hadn't completed. Neither man answered, but they didn't need to. She was certain she was correct.

She saw the way Sam's hand went to rub his thigh, and concern took precedence over curiosity. "Have you seen a doctor since you got back?"

He nodded. "My leg will be fine. There's not much muscle damage. I'll still be able to beat you in a race, even hopping one-footed."

A powerful surge of gratitude welled up inside her. Things had turned out much better than they'd had any right to expect. Leaning forward, she kissed him on the forehead. "It's time you learned that I only let you win those races because you're such a poor loser."

"Just keep telling yourself that, honey." He caught her hand in his, gave it a squeeze. "You've never lacked heart, Annie. I can be thankful for what you tried to do, while still wanting to paddle your butt for doing it."

"You could try, anyway. And just remember…" She pulled away, deeming it best to remove herself from his side in case he was tempted to try. "If it hadn't been for me, the *Nefarious* wouldn't have been in port. Think about that while I shower."

On her way out the door she risked a glance at Jones. His stoic mask had her heart dropping to the vicinity of her shoes. From all appearances he was taking her revelations with even less grace than her brother. And for some reason that fact wounded far more deeply.

"Hell." Sam's voice was weary after Ana closed the door behind her. "Her involvement is the last thing I figured. If I hadn't been slowed down by this damn leg, I'd have gotten off the island sooner, and maybe prevented Ana from jumping into this mess."

"You could have tried, anyway," Jones replied. "She doesn't take orders very well."

Sam gave a short laugh. "Figured that out already, have you? Never took direction worth a damn, to tell the truth. 'Bout wore us out trying to keep her in line. Maybe she's right, we might have tended to be a little overprotective, but we had plenty of reason."

"Yeah, she told me about the kidnapping." Jones paced to the porthole, peered out sightlessly. He didn't want to think about the vulnerability that had nearly shredded her control the night she'd told him that story. Didn't want to feel the surge of emotion again that the news had elicited. It was far more comfortable living with a lid on all emotions. Easier not to feel at all.

Certainly he wouldn't be feeling this bubbling fury at her deception, fury that was slightly irrational. Annie, *Ana*, he corrected himself bitterly, hadn't kept any more from him than he'd kept from her. Hadn't trusted him any less. Or more. It was that fact that burned the most.

The feeling was familiar. It wouldn't be the first time he'd lowered his guard with a woman only to find out she was completely different from what he'd thought. The first experience had nearly cost him his life. He wasn't going to pay any type of price this time. He made himself that vow, and meant to keep it.

Shaking off that line of thought, he turned back to Sam. "You said you had help. Who was she?"

Amazingly, the man went red. "After I was ambushed, I was bleeding like a pig. I wrapped a tourniquet around my leg, but I knew I was going to bleed to death if I didn't get help quick. Broke into a house close to the edge of town. A widow was living there alone. I scared her to death, but she patched me up. Was actually more help than I expected."

Something in the man's tone alerted Jones. "Don't tell me the Tremaine charm worked its magic again?"

Sam grinned, but looked a little uncomfortable. "I could never match your reputation with the ladies, Jones. But she, uh, seems she had a beef with the government. When she guessed who her houseguest was, she was more than cooperative."

"What kind of beef?"

"Her cousin was part of the royal family that was murdered six months ago by Osawa Bunei. When the new government took over, apparently the surviving family members were given short shrift. She's not the only one who has an ax to grind with them."

"And once she'd nursed you back to health you sent her strolling the docks."

Sam nodded. "I was going to smuggle myself aboard one with a homeport closest to the U.S. When she mentioned yours, I couldn't believe my luck." He grimaced. "Of course that was before knowing you'd brought my sister to the island."

His sister. Jones neatly sidestepped the flicker of guilt

that threatened. Somehow he thought Sam would be even less understanding if he knew just what had transpired between him and Annie. To distract them both, he told Sam about their run from Shala and the militia, resulting in their trek through the jungle. "You traveled back in a bit more comfort than we did, though."

Sam gave an exaggerated sniff. "Yeah, I was too polite to mention it before, but...you reek, buddy. Big-time. When my sister finishes, you could use a shower."

"It's all yours." Ana strolled in the room, toweling her hair. She was wrapped in a terry-cloth robe that wasn't the least bit revealing. So there was no explanation for the sudden clenching in Jones's gut when he looked at her. Except that her skin was dewy and faintly moist, her hair wet and tousled, reminding him all too clearly of the last time he'd seen her damp. When he'd held her wet, writhing body against his and filled her, over and over again.

With an effort he tore his gaze away from her, only to find Sam eyeing him narrowly. To divert the man he said hastily, "Well, you might have come back with nothing to show for your assignment, but I covered your ass for you." He dug in the backpack he'd dropped on the floor, and retrieved the sheet he'd stolen from the capitol. "I sprang a safe in Shala's office. Maybe this will give us an idea of what he's up to."

Sam studied the sheet for a moment. "What I wouldn't give for my computer."

"I may be able to help," Ana said. She disappeared for a moment, came back with that infernal notebook of hers.

"Have another grievance to write down?"

She frowned at him. "Keep cruisin', Jones." Flipping through some pages, she stopped when she found the one she'd been looking for. "I think I've figured out a little. It's not much, but maybe you can make sense of it." She handed the notebook to Sam, before seeming to notice that both men were staring at her again.

"You went through my bag?" Jones's tone was low and lethal, the dangerous rage trapped inside. "Mind telling me when this was?" She didn't, he noted savagely, directly answer the question.

"Considering the fact that you pawed through my things on several occasions, it's a little hypocritical to be crying foul, don't you think?"

"Where'd you..." Sam flipped through the notations she'd made. "These can't be right. This isn't junior decoders, Ana, it's top secret encryption. You can't expect to just sit down with a pencil and figure it out."

"Have you forgotten what I do for a living?" she snapped.

Pieces clicked together in Jones's mind. *I work for a software company.* Tremaine Technologies. His mouth flattened. Analiese Tremaine, aka Ann Smith, was just full of surprises. He knew from his long friendship with Sam the nature of some of the company's more confidential jobs.

Her words had Sam looking intently at her work. He stopped, peered closer at some of the notations she'd made, and looked back at the sheet Jones had handed him. When he didn't respond for a long time, Jones said, "Well? Does any of it make sense?"

"Maybe." Sam's tone was cautious. "If this is right, there are dates of deliveries noted here. Quantities. Points of origin and of delivery." Slowly he raised his gaze to theirs.

"We've already discovered that Shala and probably Bunei are involved in drug smuggling," Ana said. "I suspect I was taken to the capitol only to be interrogated again by the king. I think I convinced them I was harmless until I spotted Shala with the drug dealer who threatened me."

Her words had fire leaping to Sam's eyes again, so Jones skirted the upcoming argument by saying, "We know Laconos is petitioning the Global Trade Organization for an increased role in the international marketplace. I think they're supplementing their income by running drugs, possibly from South America, cutting and repackaging the cocaine before shipping it elsewhere."

He succeeded in distracting Sam for the moment. "We suspected the same. I was trying to gather information on it, and about whether the Osawa Bunei multiple murder suicide was staged to bring about a shift in power."

"So they got rid of the royal family and the old cabinet to cover up what they were going to be doing," Ana surmised. "I wonder who the visiting dignitary was and if he had anything to do with their plans."

"What dignitary?" Jones asked.

"They were having some sort of reception for the man at the capitol the night I went there with Shala. I didn't get an introduction. But I heard him speak, and he sounded like he had a German accent."

"Describe him," Sam ordered.

"Tall, over six foot with a stocky build, running to fat. Bald, except for a fringe of brown hair, with gold wire-rimmed glasses. He had a gold tooth, not a cap, but a backing on one of his upper top teeth."

Sam had an arrested look on his face, but Jones was already way ahead of him. "Was he wearing any jewelry?"

"He had this gold insignia ring," she answered. "Kind of a crest, with a dragon twisted on the gold, with rubies for eyes. Creepy looking."

"Oppenheimer," muttered Sam. "Dammit!"

"He'd have the money to bribe Sterling," Jones said grimly.

"And the money to buy his own empire on a faraway island."

"Who is this guy?" Ana asked, clearly impatient at being left out of the loop. "And how do you know him?"

Jones let Sam answer. After all, that wasn't his world anymore. He'd made his choices years before and never looked back. You couldn't get much further away from espionage and cloak-and-dagger intrigue than running a charter service in the tropics.

"He's an international crook posing as a businessman. He's been involved in just about every criminal activity you can name. But right now he's trying to shift world trade agreements to his advantage."

"Which explains his interest in Laconos," Jones couldn't help putting in.

Sam nodded grimly. "Exactly. But I need to verify this information and get it in the right hands. That vote is the day after tomorrow in London."

"You're not going anywhere but home," Ana told her brother bluntly. "That wound needs to heal, and then you'll probably need physical therapy. Besides, don't you need to be debriefed or something?"

Jones and Sam looked at her and then at each other. "She watches way too much TV," Sam said.

"Apparently. But she's right about one thing. You have to get out of here, and I need to get this ship away for a while, too. I'd hate to have someone trace us here from Laconos and plant a nasty little explosive aboard it."

Sam looked torn. "If I go, would you step in for me?"

Jones froze, his gaze battling his friend's. "You know better than to ask. I left that long ago." His idealistic goal of serving his country had been shattered forever by that bullet in the back. He knew that if he could be fooled that easily by a woman, he damn well shouldn't be in a position where lives depended on his judgment.

"I don't know who to trust," Sam said, not letting him off the hook easily. "There's no way to tell for sure how badly the Agency's been corrupted. I can't go to my superiors until I find out. Right now I have to track down Sterling. At this point, every agent he supervised is in danger. We don't have a lot of time to waste."

His palms were damp. Jones resisted the urge to wipe them down the front of his filthy pants. "You've got contacts in the field. You can get this information into the right hands."

"Neither of you have to do it," Ana said calmly. "Because I'm going to."

Her words nearly brought Sam off the bed. "No way in hell! You're getting your butt back to Louisiana where you belong."

"Use your head," she said evenly. She was too logical, Jones thought. His stomach twisted sickly at her offer, equal only to the sensation he experienced at the thought of entering that life again. Even briefly.

"It's not like I haven't done this before. I'm just escorting a piece of paper from one point to another, transferring it to the right person and coming home. How hard can it be?" She misconstrued their stunned silence for agreement. "I'll make some phone calls. See when the flights are."

"If you think I'm letting you go to London, you've lost your mind," Jones said flatly. He didn't register the look Sam threw at him. Not then. His attention was on Ana. She'd fisted her hands on her hips and jutted out her jaw, just itching for a good clip on the chin. "I'll hog-tie you and deliver you home myself before I allow you anywhere near the GTO."

"You'd try," she said, her voice a taunt. "But you'd be lying in the hospital beside Sam when I got done with you."

He almost laughed at her fierce statement. Would have if he hadn't been certain she meant it. "You're not going, Ana." She went through the door, and he started after her. "Ana!"

"Jones." Something in Sam's voice stopped him. He gave an impatient glance back at the other man, who was struggling to get off the bed. As he went to help him, something in his friend's expression alerted him. Here was danger of another sort. Jamming his hands in his pockets he raised a brow.

"Yeah?"

Sam was standing now, if swaying a bit on his feet. "Mind telling me just what kind of relationship you have with my sister?"

Jones opened his mouth, closed it again. What the hell was he supposed to say? "Yeah," he replied finally. "I do mind."

It's not that he didn't see the fist coming. Sam's right jab had his head snapping back, and for a moment he saw stars. Wiggling his jaw back and forth a couple of times, he ignored the savage throbbing and narrowed his gaze. "I deserve that one, but you only get the one shot."

"You sonofabitch." There was more than fury in Sam's tone. There was a baffled kind of betrayal. Jones was familiar enough with the feeling to identify it. "You're one of my best friends, but you're the last guy I want involved with my sister. What the hell are you intending?"

"I'm intending to keep her far away from London."

Sam's expression turned calculating. "You said yourself, there's no stopping her. Looks like you'll have to accompany her."

Jones tossed the man a fierce look. "You just got done saying I'm the last man you'd want involved with your sister."

"And it's true. But you're the first man I'd want protecting her."

Chapter 13

Ana looked up to watch Jones prowl their London motel room, tension riding every movement. He'd been like this since they'd boarded the plane, and the entire trip across the ocean. Dangerously contained. Lethally controlled. It was like waiting for an explosive to detonate.

"Are you going to pace until we meet that guy at three? Because I have to tell you, it's starting to wear on my nerves."

He glanced over to where she was curled up in the center of one of the double beds, meticulously painting her toenails a shocking shade of pink. "Yeah, you look pretty stressed."

She blew across the wet polish before answering. "You let off steam one way, I'll do it my own way. If you're interested, I've got a bottle of Raspberry Rhapsody that I could use on you."

A snort was his only reply. He went to the window, pushed the shade aside to peer out, dropped it again. The man reminded her of the big cats at the zoo, striding back and forth across the cage, barely leashed danger in a seductively ferocious package. The description, she noted silently, fitted Jones to a tee. There was no mistaking the air of latent menace emanating from the man.

"You said yourself it's doubtful anyone from Laconos could have tracked us after the pains you took to disguise our trail. Relax. All we're going to do is hand the sheet and the notes I made over to the contact Sam arranged for us, and come back here to wait to hear about the decision."

"Nothing's ever that simple."

"Some things are exactly that simple." Her dispute was more an effort to distract him than a desire for an argument. Lord knew, he needed the diversion. Without it, he was likely to combust. Something was definitely eating at the man, something other than the task at hand.

"Complications arise when you least expect them. It's better to walk into a situation understanding that, and be prepared."

Something in his tone warned her. Tucking the nail polish brush back into the jar, she surveyed him carefully. "Is that what happened on your last assignment? You weren't prepared?"

"No amount of training prepares you for taking a bullet in the back from someone you trust." It was the total lack of inflection in his voice that was the most alarming.

"Why did he do it?"

Jones turned to look at her, frowned. "Who?"

"Your partner. Why'd he shoot you? What was he after?"

He gave a twisted smile. "It wasn't a he. Tessa Gardner was working the assignment with me. And she probably did it for the same reason most people betray another. For greed. Money.'' His shrug was negligible, as if it didn't matter. But Ana knew that it did. Terribly.

Her stomach did a slow roll as another thought formed, one even more awful. ''Were you…did you…love her?''

His laugh was sardonic. ''Why do women always assume sex means love? The answer is no. But I cared enough for her to lower my guard. It nearly got me killed.''

His answer, brief as it was, answered so many things. And it shouldn't be allowed to wound. *Wouldn't* be allowed to. He couldn't have stated any plainer that what they'd shared at the stream hadn't meant anything to him. Despite her brothers' efforts, she wasn't totally naive. She knew well that sex didn't equate love. It hadn't in her limited experiences. But making love with Jones hadn't been similar in any way to those experiences. At least, it hadn't seemed to be.

Pushing aside the hurt that threatened to bloom, she asked, ''Was she ever brought to justice?''

He jammed his hands in his pockets, crossed to the window again. ''Not in the way you're probably thinking of. I killed her before she could finish the job on me.''

She swallowed hard. He'd had to have been half-dead himself. It was a wonder he hadn't been paralyzed. She'd seen for herself how close the bullet had come to his spine. And his words, brief as they were, explained so much.

She'd known from the first he wasn't a man who let himself become involved. Not emotionally. She'd never met an individual more in control of his feelings. There'd been several occasions when she would have sworn he didn't own any. But then she had only to remember being held through the night after their grueling descent down the cliff; the stamp of arousal on his face when his control had finally snapped and he'd reached for her, beginning their spiral into passion; and the concern mingled with frustration when he'd tried over and over to thwart her plans when she was trying to discover information on Sam.

"Did they ever find out who she was working for?"

"I never asked. I was in the hospital for six weeks and two surgeries. Then I had three more months of rehab after that. The day I was given a medical release was the day I walked away from the Agency for good." He removed his hands from his pockets, and then, as if unsure of what to do with them, folded his arms. "I had a lot of time to think in the hospital. And I figured out that nothing was worth the kind of price I almost gave. Not my country, and certainly not a woman. Since then I've made it my business not to get involved."

Her eyes widened. He actually looked like he meant it. And he certainly didn't seem in the mood for her to point out the contrast between his words and his actions. Not now.

With exaggerated care she looked away and unscrewed the cap on the polish again. "Okay." She'd meant to keep her tone noncommittal. So there was no reason for that snap to enter his tone.

"Okay? What's that supposed to mean?"

With one stroke she spread the polish smoothly across her nail. "It means…okay. You believe that. Maybe you need to. And that's all right."

"What the hell are you talking about?"

With a sense of déjà vu she was reminded of a conversation they'd had on his ship when she'd tried to convince him, with a notable lack of success, of her scores of lovers. "It means…we all have some illusions about ourselves. To some extent we have to. Maybe it protects us from stuff we're not ready to deal with, I don't know. But eventually it catches up with us, too. Like yours is catching up with you now."

"You've been sniffing the fumes from the polish for too long," he said flatly. "You're babbling."

"Am I?" She did look up then, and caught his gaze with hers. It'd be easier to let it go. Easier to lick her wounds in private. But she'd never sought the easy way in life, not even when it had been presented to her on a silver platter. "Then ask yourself this, Jones. Why are you here? Why would a self-professed loner, one who doesn't care about anything or anybody, fly halfway across the world to deliver a piece of paper? Why would he care so much?" She used the hand holding the brush to gesture. "It's not like any of this affects you personally."

When he merely clenched his jaw and looked away, she pressed further. "Seems to me a man like that would say the hell with it. All I care about is myself and my ship. The rest of the world can sort itself out. But you didn't do that, did you?"

His countenance was thunderous, his voice hard. "I may have left the life behind, but Sam's still my friend."

Pointing the brush at him, she said, "Exactly. And a man who goes to these lengths for friendship isn't quite as cut off as he'd like to believe."

"Think you have it all figured out, don't you?" If she'd thought he'd been dangerous before, he was positively radiating challenge now. "Maybe I felt like I owed him something, did you ever think of that?"

A river of ice shot down her spine. She licked her lips, which had gone suddenly dry. When he looked away from her, something inside her registered his meaning. "You mean because of me. Because of what happened between us." The deceptively calm voice was due to numbness, she knew. Once that emotion wore off, the pain would dart in, like angry little arrows. "Well, that's some warped code you have, Jones. Cut yourself off from feeling a thing, but sleep with a guy's sister and he can ask anything of you.''

She returned her attention to the nail polish, grateful to have a center for her focus. She observed distantly that her hand held the slightest tremble. "A word of advice—guilt is a lousy motivator. And adding guilt to sex sounds like an excellent way to end up in therapy.''

She studied the polish she'd completed on her big toe, deemed it satisfactory. "Now me, I think sex is best without emotion at all. Emotions lead to expectations, and we know how messy they can be.'' Ana would not, in this lifetime, hint at the turbulent emotions careening inside her from his confession. She couldn't even identify them at this point herself. Although the ache in her heart was pretty self-explanatory.

"You don't believe that.''

She froze, refusing to look up, afraid he'd read the truth on her face. "Oh, but I do. As a matter of fact, I think we'd all be better off to be a bit more clear-headed about the act altogether. You take my first time. I chose Billy Ray McIntire only because he had, I thought, a certain reputation. I mean, with a nickname like One-Shot Billy, one would assume, right?''

It was hard to discern if the strangled sound he made was agreement or negation. "My approach couldn't be faulted, but my research was faulty. Had I done more inquiries prior to our...ah...time together, I would have found out that the name was derived from his prowess on the golf course.'' Although come to think of it, it had ended up describing the boy's sexual technique, or lack thereof, pretty well, too.

Stroking the polish over her last nail, she lifted her head, examined her foot critically. She screwed the cap back on the bottle of polish, reached for the box of Kleenex. "Men just assume women want more from them than sex. Probably an ego thing. But I'm here to tell you, that's just not true. Sometimes it's just a spur-of-the-moment thing. A...release." Pleased with the word, she risked a glance up. He was watching her from beneath hooded lids. There was no guessing at his thoughts. "So you can tuck your guilt away. It's nobody's business but our own if we decide to mate like minks while we're here before going our separate ways. Who would we be hurting?"

"An intriguing proposition." Was that a note of sarcasm in his voice? "But I think we need to focus on the matter at hand."

She finished separating her toes with little rolls of Kleenex, then bent forward and blew lightly on the fresh polish. When he didn't continue, she looked up, caught his gaze on her pursed lips. A crazy little pinwheel whirled in her stomach, only to be doused when he glanced away and continued.

"It'd be best if you stayed here and I made the drop-off."

A sliver of amusement struck her. "Like that's an option." He glared at her. She glared back. "Do you want to waste your time with an argument you're going to lose, or do we discuss our plan of action?"

He drew a deep breath, probably to keep from strangling her. She didn't care. Regardless of what else he felt for her, or, more correctly, what he *didn't* feel for her, he wasn't going to shove her out of the action. Not at this point. She may not be a woman destined to fire any kind of lasting desire in a man, but she could take care of herself. She thought she'd earned the right to do so.

"If you're coming with me, there are going to be a few conditions."

She managed, barely, to avoid rolling her eyes. "I'll bet."

"You do exactly as I say. Stay close beside me, and don't open your mouth unless I tell you to. If something looks like it's going down wrong, you run like hell. We'll set a place to meet if we get split up."

Wiggling her newly polished toes, she said airily, "Relax, Jones. Nothing is going to go wrong." At least not with the assignment. Things had taken a decided turn for the worse the moment they'd started this conversation. And she had no idea how to set it right again.

After Jones's dire warnings, waiting for the drop-off seemed more than a little anticlimactic. Through the contacts Sam had set up, before he'd been dispatched off to a hospital in New Orleans for a consultation on his leg, they'd arranged to have the assistant to the chairman of GTO pick up the information Jones had taken from Shala's safe.

The steps of St. Paul's Cathedral had been chosen as the meeting point. Ana thought the constant stream of tourists toward the attraction, not to mention the nearby bustle of the city's financial district, should make even Jones feel a bit safer about the transaction. But he didn't appear ready to lower his defenses just yet. His gaze assessing, he constantly scanned the area. He'd insisted on arriving early. Although he hadn't explained himself, Ana figured it was another security precaution. One that threatened to freeze her. Although April, the wind was chilly, heavy with dampness. It bit into the bones and permeated the muscles. It didn't seem possible that only hours ago they'd been sweating on a tropical island.

Huddled in her light jacket, Ana promised herself that

they'd stop in a pub to warm up after this. Regardless of what Jones intended.

The traffic in the area made New Orleans seem tame by comparison. Taxis jammed the streets, along with buses, limos and cars. The result was a cacophony of horns and shouts from irritated drivers. It wasn't until one of the limos slid to a stop, and the back door opened, that she straightened, glanced at Jones. His narrowed gray gaze was fixed on the man emerging from the vehicle.

"Show time," he muttered under his breath. With a hand under her elbow, he steered her casually in the direction of the person approaching the steps.

"Mr. Mashuki."

The man turned, carefully looked them over. "Do you have something for me?"

"As soon as we see some ID."

The man reached inside his coat to the breast pocket of his suit. Ana could feel Jones tense beside her. But Mashuki withdrew nothing more formidable than a slim leather case, which he flipped open to reveal his picture and position in the GTO.

After inspecting the ID, Jones took an envelope from his pocket, passed it to the other man. "You'll need to have it decrypted. It's only partially done. But tell chairman Shimbun to be sure and have it completed before the vote comes up for expanded trade advantages for the isle of Laconos."

"I will do so. If this contains the information I have been led to believe, you have done the world a great favor."

Jones didn't seem in the least impressed by that fact, Ana noted. He just seemed anxious to get away. "I'd like a phone call when this is over. Let me know how it plays out. My number is on the envelope."

The man bobbed his head. "It shall be done." He turned to go, and Jones reached for Ana's arm again. Mashuki strode back toward the limo. Jones began to steer her in the opposite direction. It was on the tip of Ana's tongue to suggest the pub idea. Surely the man had to feel the cold. He *lived* in the tropics. She'd only spent a few days there.

The window on a car in the street beside her shattered. Confused, Ana looked at it, then at Jones. But before she could open her mouth, he was dragging her past the car and into the street. "Run!"

There was the ping of metal creasing metal, a pepper of sound as they dodged cars and trucks veering toward them. In some numbed, distant part of her mind, she understood that whoever was shooting at them was using a silencer.

Brakes were screeching as they ran through the snarled traffic, drivers shouting. Ana's breath sliced through her lungs with every stride she took. She would have stumbled over the curb on the opposite side, if Jones hadn't been pulling her along so fast her feet barely grazed the pavement.

They raced down the sidewalk and around the corner. The streets were teeming with people. By elbowing into their midst they were either putting them all at risk or hiding in the most effective fashion possible. There was no debating the issue with Jones. Using his superior strength, he pushed his way, and hers, through the throng, letting it swallow them up. Only when they came to a line of taxis lined up at the curb waiting for fares, did he break away from the crowd, opening the door on one and all but shoving her inside it. Ana heard that telltale ping again as a bullet skimmed the door, even as the driver pulled away from the curb and headed in the opposite direction.

"And could I interest the two of you in a tour of London proper today?"

The driver looked in the rearview mirror to catch their

reaction, but his smile faded when he saw Jones's expression and heard the tone of his voice.

"Just drive."

Their new quarters lacked the opulence of their former hotel room, but only a fool would head back there. Instead, Jones had found a touristy bed-and-breakfast, one that touted the intimacy and home-cooked meals of home.

The room was certainly private. The bubbly elderly woman who had taken their money and shown them to the upper floor of the Victorian home had chattered nonstop about it. They had the entire floor to themselves, she'd assured them. The former attic had been remodeled to a deluxe suite, complete with a hot tub for two tucked in the corner of the loo. But although Ana had obediently trailed the woman, looking at the amenities, Jone's gaze had been fixed on the bed.

One bed, and a double at that. If he hadn't been so tired he'd have sworn, vividly and imaginatively. The couch in front of the TV was short enough to promise a night of intense discomfort. But it would be better than the guilt he'd deal with if he slept with Ana again, knowing there was no future for them.

Prowling the room, he looked out the window. The neighborhood street below was quiet. A stranger would stand out here. It wasn't the type of place where residents turned a blind eye to anything suspicious. At least he was counting on that.

Without his conscious volition, his gaze traveled to the bed again. An ancient four-poster, it was draped fussily with lace. But beneath the feminine coverings it'd be soft. Inviting. The kind of bed he'd promised her for their next time together. Back when he'd planned on there being a next time.

Crossing to the small desk in the corner, he dropped the paper bag of supplies he'd stopped for before finding this place. He heard the woman tell Ana, "I'm afraid you've missed dinner. But if you'd care for a spot of tea and scones, I could fix up a tray for you."

He took out his wallet, handed the woman a bill, saw her eyes widen when she looked at it. "We'd like a real meal. It doesn't matter whether you cook it, or order it from a restaurant and have it delivered."

"I don't...well...that is..." Her fist closed around the bill and she shoved it deep in the pocket of her housedress. "I'll take care of that for you, sir."

He nodded, waited for her to let herself out of the room, then locked it behind her.

"Do you think Mashuki got away safely?" Ana strolled to the bed, sat on its edge, bouncing a little, testing it.

"I'm pretty sure he wasn't hit. I saw him dive for the limo, and then it pulled away." Whoever the shooter was, he'd arrived minutes too late. Any earlier and the transaction wouldn't have been completed. "We'll have to wait for the call before we know anything for sure."

She stood and kicked off her shoes, shed her coat. Pulling at the covers, she folded them back neatly before sprawling backward on the bed. A knot in his gut clenched at the sight.

"What do you think happened?" She didn't open her eyes as she phrased the question. "Could we have been tracked from Laconos?"

"Maybe, but I doubt it. They certainly wouldn't have waited this long if they were following us from the start. And I think we covered our trail pretty well."

Her eyes popped open, their brilliant blue color startling against her pale face. "So they had to figure where we'd be taking that information."

He laid out the materials he'd picked up at the hardware store and began to fashion crude but effective booby traps should an intruder try to enter through the door or window. "I think it was probably simpler than that. If Oppenheimer is involved in this, he's going to have contacts within the GTO. He has to, to wield the kind of power he's been accumulating in the last decade. He must have been tipped off about the call we made today. Maybe he's got the phone lines tapped. Who the hell knows? But it's a sure bet that once he found out that we were prepared to share this information with Shimbun, he was going to send someone to stop that from happening."

"A few minutes earlier, and they would have succeeded," she murmured. "If you hadn't gotten us there early, and Mashuki hadn't come a bit early, as well…"

"No use considering that," Jones said shortly. He certainly didn't want to. Remembering just how close those bullets had come to Ana had his chest tightening. He gave a vicious twist to the pieces of metal he was bolting together. She didn't belong here, and she sure as hell didn't deserve to be a part of this. Only another twenty-four hours and she wouldn't be.

There was no reason for the shaft of desolation that plunged through him at the thought. She'd return to what sounded like a laid-back life in Tangipohoa Parish, and he'd be looking for a new port to call home. Bontilla was a little too close to Laconos for comfort. Come to think of it, he'd have to change the name and number of his ship, too. He didn't want anyone able to trace him through it.

But try as he might to distract himself from thoughts of Ana, they crept into his mind like insistent little ants. The two of them had said all they had to say earlier, before the meeting with Mashuki. At least he had. What she'd said didn't really bear thinking about.

It's nobody's business but our own if we decide to mate like minks while we're here before going our separate ways. Who would we be hurting?

She couldn't have been serious. He risked a glance her way and immediately wished that he hadn't. She'd shed her blouse to reveal a formfitting undershirt beneath, and nothing else. His mouth immediately went dry. The garment left little to the imagination, and his memory supplied him with erotic images of what she looked like beneath it.

Guiltily he shifted his gaze away. She'd been feeding him a line earlier; she had to have been. If there was any woman in the world who shouted strings and commitment, it was the one lying on the bed. Maybe she didn't even realize it, but she was about as far from a good-time girl as it was possible to be.

The trouble was, it was getting harder and harder to remember that. And even more difficult to care.

Thirty minutes later he finished with the crude mechanisms and carefully put them into place. He turned to find her lying on her side. Elbow propped, her head in her hand, she was surveying him intently.

Being the focus of that intense regard made heat pool beneath his fly. "What?"

"You don't look much like an Augustus. What's your first name?"

When he just gave her a look, her tone went wheedling. "C'mon. If you tell me I'll tell you one of my secrets."

"You have no secrets," he said bluntly, recalling the story she'd told about her first time. The story he definitely hadn't wanted to hear. He had no desire to think about a man touching her. Kissing her. Making love to her. He released a breath. No other man, that is, but him.

The walls of the room seemed to shrink then, compressing the available oxygen. The hours before them suddenly seemed to stretch endlessly. There was no telling how long before the phone call would come. There was no place to go…he couldn't jeopardize her safety. And he couldn't leave her alone for the same reason.

He hauled in a deep gulp of air. He'd learned patience with the CIA. All the tedious details of putting an investigation together took time, the months of planning sometimes punctuated with short, vicious bouts of action. But somehow that training didn't seem helpful in this instance. He'd never had to endure interminable hours of torture, but he had a feeling he was in for exactly that tonight.

"Do you remember what I said earlier tonight?"

Did he remember? He wished like hell he could carve it out of his mind.

It's nobody's business but our own…. Who would we be hurting?

"You said a lot of things." He walked to the bathroom, washed his hands with more thoroughness than the act called for. But there came a time when he had to walk back into the bedroom. A time when he had to look at her and find her watching him with a hint of sadness in her eyes.

The look was out of place on her. Her face was made for expression, those quick blinding smiles, the sulky pouts, the exaggerated brows. But sorrow didn't belong there. And knowing he was responsible for it made him feel like driving a stake through his heart.

The time for dissembling was over. "There's no use doing anything else we'll be sorry for later, Annie."

Her voice was soft and sure. "I thought we'd agreed not to regret this."

A stronger man, a better one, would have turned away. Perhaps two weeks ago he could have. Before some of that emotion he'd so carefully tucked away had been allowed to leak, an insidious path that couldn't be undone.

"You made me a promise last time." There was the slightest tremble in her voice. He looked carefully, but her eyes were clear. "A bed, you told me. All night. No distractions. Are you a man of your word, Jones?"

It was all he could do not to lunge for her then. Desire flooded through him in a demanding tide, like a river of fiery little demons pounding him from the inside with wicked scorching fists. If he gave in to it, he knew he'd never forgive himself. And if he didn't, the same would be true.

She held out a hand, inviting him. Tempting him. "No expectations, remember?"

But there were, despite her words. Expectations and regrets and a million reasons why this was a bad idea. The worst. After tomorrow or the next day they'd never see each other again. There'd be nothing between them but miles and memories.

And in the end it was those same reasons that compelled him to move.

He crossed to her, slowly took her hand in his. Turning it palm up, he pressed it to his lips, watched her eyes turn misty. If memories were all they were going to have, he vowed, they were going to have a store of them to draw from. Magical images that would warm the nights that would forever seem cold without her.

He knelt in front of the bed as she sat up, faced him. When she released his hand her fingers skated along his face, her soft skin feeling like velvet against his rough jaw. He tugged at her waistband and she rose, the vee of her thighs close to his face. Jones reached up, unsnapped the jeans, and with both hands tugged them down her legs.

Tossing them aside, he stood, stroking his hands from her calves to her thighs. Her lips opened under his, a hint of desperation in her taste. It called to an answering wildness in him, one he savagely tamped down. The hours that so recently had stretched interminably now held a measure of promise. He was going to make them last.

He kissed her deep, hard and thoroughly, enjoying the way her flavor traced through his senses, firing nerve endings along the way. Her tongue glided along his, and need clawed through him, hot and urgent. This wasn't the kind of hunger that could be satisfied easily or quickly. Perhaps it couldn't be satisfied at all. But he was going to try his damnedest.

Her hands were busy, tugging the shirt from his waistband, shoving it up to skim her hands over his chest. He could feel his muscles quiver, as if conditioned to her touch. The reaction was both tempting and troubling. How had she gotten under his skin so fast?

The thought barely registered as he scraped her full bottom lip with his teeth. She gave a little gasp and swayed closer against him, and he broke away to yank his shirt over his head and threw it aside. Then he put his hands on the narrow expanse of her waist, lifted her and tossed her lightly back onto the bed, following her down.

He stretched out above her, enjoying the freedom the position gave him. Her nipples stabbed against the thin cotton of her undershirt, taut peaks that tempted. Leaning forward, he took one between his teeth, teased it lightly.

Her hips jerked off the bed, coming into contact with his. He settled himself more intimately against her, wanting that pressure without any barriers, knowing the folly of ridding himself of his jeans. Not now. Not yet. There was too much to be savored to rush.

Reluctantly, he lifted his head, surveyed her. Her shirt was wet from his mouth, her nipple turgid beneath the damp cloth. He took great pleasure in driving himself a little crazy, peeling the cloth up her torso a little at a time, ducking his head to press wet openmouthed kisses against each inch he bared.

Her skin was like rich, smooth cream. He was hardly aware that her hands had gone to his hair, released the thong he used to keep it tied back. He was steeped in the taste of her, greedy for more. He shoved her shirt up a fraction higher, leaned down to run his tongue along the underside of her breast. There was a bolt of lust tightening in his loins, making it difficult to move slow. He stroked the shirt over her head, baring her breasts. Her curves were delicate, her nipples pink and impudent, begging for his lips. He bent his head to suckle from her, took savage pleasure from the bite of her nails on his shoulders as she clutched him closer.

Sweeping his hand up her thigh he placed his palm over her mound, stroking and rubbing the heated flesh beneath the silk until the cloth was damp and slippery under his fingers.

There were alarms shrilling in his mind, distantly sounding, with what might have been logical excuses for turning away from this exquisite torment. But reason was impossible to summon. There was only Annie, twisting beneath him, chanting his name in a broken voice; her hands fumbling with the release to his jeans; her knuckles pressing against his engorged manhood.

He lifted his head, hissed in a breath. His intention of taking it slow was thwarted by the sight of her nipples glistening from his tongue; the soft skin of her breasts bearing the mark of his mouth. Logic receded when she lay beneath him, clad in nothing more than a tiny piece of thin flaming-red silk.

A boulder-size knot formed in his throat at the sight. It was difficult to swallow. Difficult to remember to breathe. She didn't make matters easier when she slipped her hands in the front of his jeans, squeezed him gently. Giving a heartfelt groan, he levered himself away from her, stripping off his jeans and underwear then returning to her.

He pressed moist kisses on her breasts, finding the hollow of her throat, the soft area behind her ear. His hand returned again and again to that moist flesh that was still hidden from him. His fingers slid beneath the elastic of her panties and found her slick dampness.

A broken cry came from her lips, unleashing something raw and wild inside him. This was how he wanted her. Had always wanted her. Naked, twisting beneath him, hands skating over his flesh, sobbing his name as he brought her to pleasure. This was the image that would torment him long after this was over, the image that would refuse to remain tucked safely away.

He parted her and slid a finger deep inside, grinding his mouth against hers as she bucked beneath him. The tight heat of inner muscles worked against him, even as he rubbed rhythmically at her in the way guaranteed to bring her climax. And when she cried out he swallowed the sound with his mouth, redoubled his efforts, letting her release slide over his fingers and make her even more slippery to touch.

Only when the shudders seemed to be subsiding did he move away, reaching for his jeans and taking out a foil packet. He wasn't going to take a chance with her again, wasn't going to give her reason for worry. She surprised him by sitting up, batting his hands out of the way and rolling the latex over his shaft. He was close enough to the edge that even that touch was enough to have his vision hazing.

But not yet. Not just yet. He peeled her panties down her legs, leaned over to press a kiss to her still quivering flesh. Then he fitted them together, side to side, with her facing away from him. He was pressed against her curvy bottom, and the sensation was both heaven and hell. Ducking his head, he nipped at her shoulder, then laved the sting away with his tongue. He stroked his hand down her thigh, enjoying the whisper of muscle beneath the smooth skin. Urging her knee up, he opened her to him, and used the position to slide between her hot slick folds.

A strangled groan came from him as moved into her. Her earlier release had moistened his way, and she surrounded him like wet hot velvet. Gripping her hips, he surged closer, enjoying the twin pleasures of pressing against her tight round bottom, even as he lodged himself more deeply in her softness. One of his hands went up to toy with her breast, but already a red mist was swimming across his eyes. There was only sensation, one slapping into another. Need was slashing through him like a savage vicious blade, and he lunged harder, wanting more. Wanting all.

"Annie." His mouth was at her throat, his hips pistoning against hers. Each hard thrust took him closer to the edge, drew another cry from her lips. Sensation after sensation flashed inside him. The contrast of tight curves and heated flesh. The urge to move inside her harder, deeper, faster.

She pressed her hips against him, and he surged inside her, his climax gripping him in a sudden savage grasp. And as his hips slammed against hers, his breath sawing through his lungs, he knew that this would never be enough.

He'd never been one to linger in bed with a woman beside him once the need had been filled. But there was an odd sort of pleasure in having Annie draped over him, her fingers stroking the hair on his chest, one of her legs lodged between his.

"You want to tell me what your name is now, don't

you?'' It was the last thing he'd expected her to say, and a smile tugged at his lips. ''I can feel it.'' Her cheek was pressed against his heart, her fingers tracing lazy patterns on his skin. ''It's that soft mushy side of you, Jones. Makes you inclined to babble after sex.''

''I never babble.''

She tilted her head up to look at him, as if too depleted of energy to lift it. ''If you tell me I'll stop talking.''

''Finally, an offer I can't refuse.'' He winced when she yanked at a hair on his chest. His hand tightened on her bottom. ''It's worse than Augustus.''

''I hate to tell you this, but *nothing* is worse than Augustus.''

He took a deep breath, staring at the ceiling. Amazing that this conversation should have him lazy and contented, unwilling to spoil the mood. ''Not even…Xavier?''

She reared up to look at him. Probably thought he was joking. Fat chance. He didn't have that good a sense of humor.

''Xavier Augustus…Jones?'' Her tone was awed.

''No.'' Her position had put her nipple in intriguing proximity to his fingers, so he reached over to tug the velvety softness. ''Jones was my first cover, and it stuck. My real last name is Wilkey.''

''Xavier Augustus Wilkey.'' She cupped his face in both her hands, her expression mingled amusement and pity. ''I hate to break it to you, Jones. But your parents really, really hated you.''

His arms tightened around her as he started to laugh. Really laugh. Her giggles joined his until they were both shaking with mirth, and he became distracted by the way the movement had her breasts jiggling against him. Then he rolled her over and the pleasure flickered to life again. Kissing her deeply, he let the passion take them again.

* * *

The soft gray light of dawn was spilling through the window and Jones was still awake. The night hadn't been endless after all. He and Annie had made love over and over, stopping only to eat the food, long cold, on the tray outside the door.

He stroked the silky curve of her back, lightly enough to avoid awakening her. Choices made long ago weren't meant to be overturned lightly. He'd made his decisions, and until recently he hadn't questioned them. There had been no reason to. If he was wise, he'd avoid questioning them now.

But it wasn't wisdom he considered as his arms tightened around Annie's sleeping form, pulling her closer. Shutting his eyes against a growing sense of desolation, instead he tried not to think about how empty his arms were going to feel when he put her on that plane tomorrow. Alone.

Chapter 14

Jones flipped his cell phone shut and looked across the room at Ana. "They must have had people working on the paper all night. Mashuki says they've decoded it."

Ana dropped to the edge of the bed. "Were we on the right track?"

"Were *you*, you mean?" His mouth quirked. "Yeah. He was guarded about saying too much, but there's definitely enough there to make the Global Trade Organization delay the Laconos vote. He led me to believe that there would be various organizations taking a closer interest in the new government down there, investigating the Bunei murder-suicide."

"If the Agency shares any of its information, that should speed things along."

"We'll see. Sharing information wasn't exactly part of our job description."

"Well." In a dizzying rush it occurred to her that this was it. There was no reason now to linger. No reason to delay their parting. And because it would hurt, far, far too much to have him say it, she decided to be the one to broach it first. She spread her arms to indicate her nonexistent luggage. "I'm all packed."

"Yeah." He looked away with an odd expression on his face. She refused to let it give her hope. She'd known how this was going to end before they'd wound up in the bed together last night. And despite that, or maybe because of it, she wasn't going to regret it. Not a moment of it.

He cleared his throat. "Mashuki is also going to have someone go to the hotel, get our stuff sent to the airport right away."

She bobbed her head. Without their passport documents, they stood little chance of getting out of the country. "Sounds like you thought of everything."

"Not everything," he murmured, staring intently. "Not nearly everything." After a moment he cleared his throat, looked away. "I have one more call to make, then we'll catch a taxi. Okay?"

It took every ounce of acting ability she had to fashion a smile. "Okay." She rose and headed to the bathroom, intent on leaving him to that last phone call in privacy. She didn't have any experience at morning afters. And even less with final goodbyes. But she had a feeling that she was going to be getting that experience, real soon. She might as well start preparing for it now.

Heathrow Airport was even more busy than it had been the day before. They disembarked at the international gates and headed inside. Jones had mentioned that they'd take the same flight back to the States. He hadn't said more, but he hadn't needed to. Once there they would split up to the separate flights that would divide them forever.

It was funny, Ana thought grimly, how the distance already seemed to yawn between them. She almost wished they could find different flights home. She didn't know which would be more torturous: sitting next to Jones for several more hours, knowing it would be their last time together or a quicker more final division. Either would be equally painful, she decided unhappily. It was just a matter of timing.

She barely noticed the quick, assessing glance Jones sent around the airport before steering her toward the nearest information desk. It was here that Mashuki would have left their things.

"Don't move until I get back."

She nodded, and Jones joined the long line in front of the desk. She leaned against the column where he'd placed her. She hadn't gotten a lot of sleep last night, and exhaustion was seeping into her limbs. It mixed with the ache that was spreading as she contemplated the bleakness of her future.

She'd survive of course. Ana swallowed, blinked rapidly. Jones wasn't the only man in the world. What was it that made him so special? He'd thrown her off a cliff, a fact she hadn't quite forgiven him for, fashioned a rescue in a garbage scow...not exactly the stuff of hero stories. So why was there a hollow place where her heart had been?

Something sharp poked her. "My dear Miss Smith. How delightful to see you again." She froze, the familiarity of the voice, the weapon at her spine, sending glacial splinters of ice through her veins. "No, don't look around. Just turn and come with me, or you and your friend will die right here."

Shala. A shudder of revulsion rippled through her. He was next to her, on the other side of the column, hidden from Jones's sight. She could only see him from her peripheral vision. "My friend? You must be mistaken. I'm alone."

The blade at her back pressed punishingly closer. "I have an associate nearby who has him covered. If you don't cooperate exactly we'll leave him dead on the floor here. A rather fitting end for a thief, don't you think?"

"You're taking a stupid chance." With effort she kept her voice steady, willed Jones to turn and look her way. "Shimbun has the paper, and it's already been decoded. The scheme Laconos came up with to broaden their trade agreements isn't going to come to a vote today. Once they finish their investigation of your country, it will never come to a vote."

"And someone should pay for that, don't you think? So slip around this side of the column, very carefully."

Ana sent a glance to Jones. He was watching her, a frown beginning between his brows. She had a moment to send him one beseeching look before a hand grabbed her, urged her to comply. She was yanked around the other side of the column to face Shala himself.

Ana had a moment to recognize that the days had not been particularly good to the man. Gone was the polished sheen of civility, and all that remained was a common thug who'd found himself divested of the power he'd once held.

Which made him all the more dangerous. A man with nothing to lose, desperate to salvage something from the situation, or bent on revenge—it didn't matter which.

He crowded her against the column pretending a lover's reunion, the blade pricking her back and a mask of malevolence stamped on his face. "You have caused me…" He shuddered in a breath. "Everything I hold dear. Because of your meddling an entire country will suffer. I really think you should atone for that, don't you?"

"You're going to have to run long and far when this is

over, Shala.'' Where was Jones? Did he interpret the look she sent him? Was he on his way? "You'll be a man without a country, have you ever thought of that? One on the run across the world. What kind of life will that be?''

"Bunei doesn't seem to think it will be a problem at all. Of course, he's already dipped into the country's treasury to cushion his new life. Me, I must start much smaller. It's only fair that you will provide some of the financing. You cost me—'' his face grew mottled with rage ''—everything. You'll draw out what you can from that business of yours, and then we'll see if your life is worth anything to your family.''

Ana strained her neck, scanned the area beyond his shoulder for signs of help. The area was crowded with people. Surely if she screamed, made a diversion, she could…

"It would be a shame if you tried something clever,'' he said, moving back and prodding her with the knife he had up his sleeve. To all outward appearances, he was merely keeping a friendly hand around her waist. "Then, of course, it will be your fault when your friend dies.''

He pushed her toward the doors. Ana knew if they reached them, her chance for survival would drop drastically. At the same moment she saw Jones, with a man slightly behind him, heading in the same direction. He was watching her intently, his eyes strangely reassuring.

The expression she saw in them did anything but calm her. He was planning something, she could tell. And it could well end up getting him killed. Terror rippled through her heart. She couldn't let that happen. Wouldn't let it.

She pretended to stumble, and had an instant to watch Jones's eyes widen before the scene split with action. Whirling away from Shala, she evaded the grab he made for her and drove the palm of her hand hard upward beneath his nose. She heard screams, the sound of running feet.

Shala's blood splattered. Like a dummy deprived a support, he dropped to his knees, both hands going to his face. Ana didn't wait to see more. She swung her head in Jones's direction, took a few steps and stopped. He was no longer there.

Frantically she scanned the crowd. There was a hand at her elbow, a murmured, "Ma'am?" Without thinking she drove her elbow into the person's stomach and darted away. And straight into the arms of the man she'd been looking for.

"Annie!"

"Jones!" She struggled in his arms, looking, in vain, for the man she'd seen near him earlier. "We've got to get out of here."

"Settle down." There was mingled amusement and exasperation in his voice. "We can't afford any more collateral damage."

"Huh?" She looked at him then, finally, and he lifted a finger to point. Swinging her head in that direction she saw a bloodied Shala with his hands being cuffed behind him, and the man who had threatened Jones being held up between two others.

"The detective scowling at you is the one you rammed in the gut. When I called the Yard this morning, I forgot to warn them you were dangerous in your own right."

His words made no sense. She wasn't usually dense, but it was hard to concentrate on his words when she was busy looking him over to be sure he hadn't been injured. He didn't, she decided with a sense of relief, look any the worse for wear. Which was more than she could say for the man Shala had set on him. His mouth was smeared with blood and he still seemed to be only semiconscious.

"Detectives?" She studied the men who had the two in custody. "You called the police this morning?"

"Scotland Yard." He hadn't let go of her yet, and Ana decided not to fight the sensation. It felt too good to have this extra time in Jones's arms. Now that the excitement was over, her knees were a little weak. Or maybe that was his effect on her.

In the next moment, though, suspicion bloomed, and she wedged her elbows against his chest to look up at him. "You expected Shala to jump us here?"

"Not necessarily Shala, but I thought there was a possibility that someone would. I didn't see who was shooting at us yesterday, but Mashuki called the Yard after he got in the limo. I called them again today and asked for an escort to the airport. Given the far-reaching nature of this mess, they were happy to comply." His eyes were strangely intent, and he crooked a finger, ran his knuckle over her jawline. "I wasn't taking any chances with you."

The gesture, curiously intimate, had her stomach doing cartwheels. "Hmm…well…" was the best she could do. "I guess I can appreciate a guy who plans for all contingencies."

His expression remained serious. "Can you? Because I've been thinking…"

"Mr….Jones, is it?" One of the detectives came forward and interrupted them. "We need to get these guys booked. We're going to ask you both to come in to answer some questions."

"Give us a few minutes, will you?"

Ana's brows raised at the long look the two men exchanged, before the detective backed off, looking as though he were preparing to wait. The other three were already bustling Shala and his associate toward the entrance.

Her gaze ping-ponged back to Jones. She hadn't seen him look this uncomfortable since…well, since the time he'd told her, without much finesse, that he wasn't interested in sharing her bed. And although he'd done just that, only a few hours ago, she could only imagine that he was preparing that goodbye she'd tried, without much particular luck, to steel herself for.

"Look, I know what you're going to say, but there's no reason to belabor it, is there?"

"There's not?"

"We said it all last night." It took effort to speak around the concrete block that had settled in her chest. "It was fun while it lasted, but it's time to move on. That's all right. Really."

"No, dammit, it's not all right." He bit the words out tersely, and she glanced warily at him. That muscle in his jaw was tight again. What had she said to cause that?

"If you'll let me get a word in edgewise…" He threw another look over his shoulder at the detective, who pointedly consulted his watch. Jones shifted his back toward the man, blocking Ana from his view. "Listen, I was doing a lot of thinking last night. I didn't get much sleep."

There was a funny jittering in her pulse. She wished she could fast-forward through this scene and get it over with. She felt as if she was going to hyperventilate. Or throw up. Or something. "I know, you spent the night planning. Good for you. I mean, calling the Yard was a great idea. Of course, you could have shared that idea with me this morning, so I didn't get the fright of my life thinking someone was going to kill you, but…" She gave a magnanimous shrug. "I guess you can't think of everything."

He looked on the verge of explosion. "Christ alive, Annie, would you stop talking!"

Affronted, she pulled away from him. "Fine." Couldn't he see that she was just trying to make it easier on him? Let him off the hook? She crossed her arms over her chest. He was determined to do this the hard way. Every word he uttered was going to stab that knife just a little deeper into her heart, but it appeared he wasn't going to be deterred from doing things his way.

She only hoped she survived it without disgracing herself.

He jammed his hand in his hair, which he hadn't tied back that morning. Actually he couldn't tie it back because she'd been unable to find the thong she'd pulled from his hair the night before. She hadn't really looked that hard. With his hair brushing his shoulders, his jaw unshaven, he looked a little untamed, a little savage. And she decided the look suited him completely.

"I thought about what you said last night, about why I accompanied you here. It's true I'd do almost anything for Sam. But I wouldn't have done this if it weren't for you."

Like a roller coaster, her emotions took a dizzying upward lurch. "You wouldn't?"

"Sam has lots of contacts in the field he could have called. I know that. I could have walked away with a clear conscience. But not if you were going to continue to involve yourself in this. I couldn't let you do that alone. Or with anyone else."

Her emotions plummeted again, an arrow falling from the sky. "Because I'm Sam's sister."

He looked impatient. "No, not because your Sam's anything. Because you're mine." The words seemed to startle them both. At least, she assumed her face was as shocked as his was. He hauled in a breath. "Because you're mine." He said it again, and it seemed to come a little easier. Hope was doing an enthusiastic tap dance in her heart. "I never saw it coming." He frowned then, looked a little accusing. "That's quite an impact you have. Dazzle a guy with chatter while you're winding your way into his heart."

Dazzle? Heart? She grinned; she couldn't help it. The

joy welling up so fast and forcefully inside her needed some kind of release. "Some technique, huh?"

He reached out, hauled her back into his arms. "I never knew what hit me," he assured her. "I still don't." He did, she noted, look a little dazed. "It's been a long time since I cared about anything. Even longer since I cared about anybody. I knew from the minute I saw you that you weren't a 'no-strings' woman. I never guessed I'd end up wanting those strings attached to me."

"You make me sound like a puppet master," she murmured. "I don't want to control you, Jones. I spent too much of my life struggling against that myself. I just want..." She drew in a deep shuddering breath. Now wasn't the time to talk about what she wanted. But maybe what she'd settle for. "I just want to be with you. It doesn't have to be more complicated than that."

His kiss was brief and bruising. "It's going to be more complicated than that. We're in this for the long term, Annie. Sam's not going to be too happy about this, but I guess he'll have to get over it. When love sideswipes me, even I know enough to grab for the brass ring. And then put it on the lady's finger." He rubbed his thumb over her lips, still swollen from his. "I love you." He looked bewildered by the emotion. "Maybe it's not fair to rush you into anything. I have some decisions to make here. I can't very well ask you to live on a ship subsisting on a charter ship captain's income. Not after what you're used to as a Tremaine."

"Yes," she assured him, "you can. I don't eat much. Really. And I have no vices, so I'll be cheap to keep around." She watched, pleased with herself, when a smile tugged at his well-formed mouth. "You do have some things to figure out, but we'll do it together. It doesn't matter how my brothers feel, because I love you, too. I'm not sure when it happened." She pretended to think back.

"Somewhere between dodging bullets and cliff diving. I do have some conditions you'll need to meet, though."

His expression went serious. Too serious. "Okay, that's only fair. Let's hear them."

She spread her palm over his heart, felt the steady beat. "You can't throw me off any more cliffs."

Although he didn't smile, his expression lightened a fraction. "I'll avoid the temptation."

"You can't get all overprotective when I'm going to do something."

He seemed to hedge his words. "We'll...approach that on a case-by-case basis."

"And you have to...this is a deal breaker, here, Jones...you are going to have to change your name." His rumble of laughter mingled with hers.

He rested his forehead against hers, uncaring that the detective had come closer and was coughing discreetly. "You got it. What do you prefer—Smith-Jones or Jones-Smith?"

She linked her arms around his neck and smiled brilliantly. "Jones will be fine. Just Jones."

* * * * *

THE TREMAINE TRADITION
continues with

ENTRAPMENT

*in May 2003 when Sam joins forces
with an international thief to bring down
Oppenheimer once and for all!*

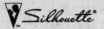
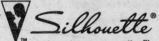

USA TODAY Bestselling author

CHRISTIANE HEGGAN

Abbie DiAngelo has the life she's always wanted. Then her stepbrother arrives.

Straight out of prison, Ian McGregor claims to have proof that implicates Abbie's mother in a twenty-five-year-old murder. Proof that Ian will keep to himself...for a price. But when Abbie arrives to pay Ian off, she finds his murdered body.

Homicide detective John Ryan quickly realizes that there's more to the murder than he originally thought and no one—especially Abbie—is telling the truth. But when Abbie's son is kidnapped, she has no choice but to trust him. Because someone is acting with deadly intent....

DEADLY INTENT

"...provocative subject matter, likeable characters and swift pacing..."
—*Publishers Weekly* on *Moment of Truth*

Available the first week of January 2003 wherever paperbacks are sold!

INTIMATE MOMENTS™

is proud to present a thrilling new miniseries
by award-winning author

INGRID WEAVER

Elite warriors who live—and love—
by their own code of honor.

Be swept into a world of romance, danger
and international intrigue as elite Delta Force
commandos risk their lives and their hearts
in the name of justice—and true love!

Available in February 2003:

EYE OF THE BEHOLDER (IM #1204)

After putting his life on the line to rescue beautiful
Glenna Hastings from the clutches of
an evil drug lord and landing in a hidden jungle prison,
can Master Sergeant Rafe Marek protect Glenna—from himself?

Continuing in April 2003:

SEVEN DAYS TO FOREVER (IM #1216)

Available at your favorite retail outlet.

If you enjoyed what you just read,
then we've got an offer you can't resist!

Take 2 bestselling love stories FREE!

Plus get a FREE surprise gift!

Clip this page and mail it to Silhouette Reader Service™

IN U.S.A.	**IN CANADA**
3010 Walden Ave.	P.O. Box 609
P.O. Box 1867	Fort Erie, Ontario
Buffalo, N.Y. 14240-1867	L2A 5X3

YES! Please send me 2 free Silhouette Intimate Moments® novels and my free surprise gift. After receiving them, if I don't wish to receive anymore, I can return the shipping statement marked cancel. If I don't cancel, I will receive 6 brand-new novels every month, before they're available in stores! In the U.S.A., bill me at the bargain price of $3.99 plus 25¢ shipping and handling per book and applicable sales tax, if any*. In Canada, bill me at the bargain price of $4.74 plus 25¢ shipping and handling per book and applicable taxes**. That's the complete price and a savings of at least 10% off the cover prices—what a great deal! I understand that accepting the 2 free books and gift places me under no obligation ever to buy any books. I can always return a shipment and cancel at any time. Even if I never buy another book from Silhouette, the 2 free books and gift are mine to keep forever.

245 SDN DNUV
345 SDN DNUW

Name	(PLEASE PRINT)	
Address	Apt.#	
City	State/Prov.	Zip/Postal Code

* Terms and prices subject to change without notice. Sales tax applicable in N.Y.
** Canadian residents will be charged applicable provincial taxes and GST.
 All orders subject to approval. Offer limited to one per household and not valid to
 current Silhouette Intimate Moments® subscribers.
 ® are registered trademarks of Harlequin Books S.A., used under license.

INMOM02   ©1998 Harlequin Enterprises Limited

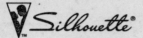

COMING NEXT MONTH